The Tongue Is Sharp

An Anthology of Feminine Rage

Rowan Redfield, Jinapher J. Hoffman, Maggie Burns

Copyright © 2025 by Rowan Redfield, Jinapher J. Hoffman, Maggie Burns. Copyright of individual works is maintained by the respective writers.

All rights reserved.

No portion of this book may be reproduced in any form without written permission from the publisher or author, except as permitted by U.S. copyright law.

Organizers: Rowan Redfield, Jinapher J. Hoffman, Maggie Burns

Cover Design: Jinapher J. Hoffman

Chief Editor: Maggie Burns, maggieburnsbooks.com

Assisting Editors:
River Ari, betterthansexediting.com
Heather Doig, pnpbooks.com
Wren L. Helgren, helgrenediting.com
Leigh Teetzel, leighteetzel.com

Artwork: Mithlista, Rue Ellewood

Formatting: Julia Greenshaw

Contents

1. American Hex — 3
2. Eve/Lilith — 5
3. give me back my girlhood — 7
4. Grief on Crack — 9
5. Hail Mary — 10
6. I am just a woman — 12
7. Invocation to the Mother of Rage — 14
8. I WILL NOT — 16
9. "Not all men" — 17
10. Wolf Song — 18
11. Words have power — 20
12. Bitter Threads — 22
13. Blood in the Water: A Siren Revenge Tail — 35
14. Bloody the Love — 46
15. Cursed is the Man Who Dies — 61
16. Five Rules for the Dutiful Housewife — 66
17. Humility and Gratitude (will pave your way in this company) — 78

18.	I Think We're Alone Now	87
19.	Of a Heart	104
20.	Pretty Little Bird	117
21.	Secrets of the Moon	133
25.	10 Minutes: A Tale of Violence, Justice, and Healing	151
26.	These Lunar Bonds	164
27.	The Blossoms of Twilight	180
30.	The Infinite Ethereal	197
31.	The Sins of the Flame	214
38.	This Foul Heart	239
39.	Vanessa	251

For all the rage-filled women out there, may our voices never be silenced.

American Hex

Danielle Salerno

CW: violence, abortion, death

America, keep me away from fire
Lest I burn you to the ground and light a cigarette from your embers
Breathing in poison and exhaling toxic fumes.

America, keep me away from water
Lest I drown you in the floods released from surges of the storm raging inside of me
Watching dispassionately as the bubbles slowly disappear.

America, keep me away from air
Lest I scorch the very sky and burn all of the oxygen
Looming as you gasp for breath that no longer fills your lungs.

America, keep me away from earth
Lest my retreating footprints turn to sinkholes swallowing you whole
Leaving nothing but fault lines in my wake.

America, keep me away from your God
Lest I invoke the Mother of Rage that birthed Him
To come bring Her righteous destruction to bear.

Unless She already has. Is that what this is?

America is dead.
Long Live America.

Eve/Lilith

Serena Tartaglia

Because the first sin
   was woman, eating.

   And the second that
   she sought knowledge
    from the new, strange, wild world
   around her:

   How does it feel, Eve,
   to know that you are
    more than Adam's Rib,
   that you are a wildfire and
   that no mere man
    can bow to your will?

   Eve, God gave you a
   brain, a heart,
    a stomach and lungs for a reason.
   They belong to you alone:
   to think, to feel,
    to eat, to breathe,
    to make your own way.

   Eve, how does it feel to know that
   men don't rule over you anymore?

Eve, your daughters will
 bite the scarlet fruit that tempted you
  out of rage, out of spite,
out of revenge.
The crunch like a thunderclap;
 the juice dripping down their chins
  like spilt blood?

Eve, how does it feel that
 your daughters crave more than
  servitude?
Eve, be careful.

Adam's sons will burn your daughters' flesh,
 call them witches.
The apple is stuck in Adam's throat, and
 she's still holding the core.

give me back my girlhood

Valeria Eden

CW: implied assault, violence

i am a girl.
because of this, i am not afraid of blood.
    but i am of the men who would make me bleed.

i was only seven
the first time a boy hurt me and laughed about it.

eleven when i got my first period,
became aware of my body,
of how to hide it,

          and why.

eighteen when the boy i loved stole my choice from me,
    and twenty-four when politicians did the same.

when we moved away to college, my brothers got video games,
    gift cards,

                    freedom.

i got a pink taser, a switchblade,
    my mother's terror
           masqueraded as a lecture.

don't walk alone, don't wear that, don't get too drunk, don't be a victim.

                        real girlhood begins when rage does.

when we are old enough to realize that we only have one
natural predator,
        and its not a thing with claws,
                but a smile, a name, a family, a job.

that our bodies, soft and sweet and sacred,
are like calling cards for men with wandering eyes
and hungry hands, who only know how to take.

real girlhood
is glitter and heartache and bad movies and belly-aching joy
and love and love and love and love and
the truth that not one corner of this world is safe for us.

i am a girl.
because of this,
some days, i am still too scared to leave my apartment.
some days, i leave my apartment and hope a man
        sinks into the other end of my knife.

Grief on Crack

Megan Phillips

CW: infertility, grief, religious terminology

My soul is being ripped from my body,
The skin and the muscle from the bone.
I am being stripped away,
Everything is never getting better.
This is who I am now,
A shell of something.

I don't want to–?
>have my particles realigned to be a God.
I don't want to–?
>be naked and blue and glowing.
I don't want to–?
>create my own world.
The world that doesn't want me,
Which leaves nothing to be desired.

This is grief on crack,
An exorcism is happening in my body.
The old me is gone now.
The new me is not yet formed.
I am floating along in between
Straddling the line of what is real and what is not.

Hail Mary

Megan Phillips

CW: infertility, grief, religious terminology

Hail Mary

Full of grace,
   The lord is with thee.
It sure as shit ain't with me.

Blessed art thou among women;
I'm blessed to nothing and no one.
Blessed is the fruit of thy womb;
DON'T GET ME STARTED ON BROKEN WOMBS.

Jesus, Holy Mary, Mother of God;
Fix my fucked up life.
Either I'm the worst person in the world,
Or I did everything I thought I COULD.

There is no Megan Universe™
Megan World™
It's the movie projector starting up and
sputtering.

My movie film is almost out.

Maybe I end it sooner . . .
What's the point of hanging around?

Jesus=crucified.
Mary=watched her son die.
Mother of God;
Megan=eh this name didn't exist that long ago.

I'm the problem;
It's me-high-I'm the problem, it's me.

I am just a woman

Lee VanBeek

> CW: mentions of slavery, misogyny

As soon as I crack, I'm the "villain."
As soon as I yell, I'm "impatient."
As soon as I react, it's "funny."
But when he reacts, I deserve it . . .

My heart is beating like waves on the sand during the violent attacks.
There is a fiery dragon in my chest,
'Uncontrollable' their voices ring my ears.
Yet a tsunami of sadness crashes through my body.

All my choices are being made for me;
My body, my mind, my soul, is now theirs,
But instead of choosing in my best interest,
They choose theirs . . .

My rights are being taken away
Because of the body I live in but don't resonate with.
Soon my body will be a slave to man again;
Only good for cooking, cleaning, children bearing, and being 'irrational.'

"Women are always irrational."

I AM JUST A WOMAN

"Women don't have minds."
"Women are dramatic."
"Women are only good for sex."

Women have thoughts that deserve to be shared.
Women have beautiful souls that deserve to be seen.
Women are more than just 'good sex.'
Women are humans just like the rest of mankind.

But my words won't be heard
Because I'm just a woman . . .

Invocation to the Mother of Rage

Danielle Salerno

CW: violence, sexual violence, abortion, death

Mother of Rage, hear my prayer!
One plaintive wail in a sea of millions
Echoing across time and space
To bloody the ears of those deaf to our cries for Justice.

Let the keening grief spilling from our fractured hearts
Descend like a tidal wave of vengeance
Upon the heads of the ones who stand idly by
As women slowly die.
Sacrificial lambs upon the altar of a False Idol
Held down by hypocrites with one fist around their pricks
And the other wrapped around our throats.
Frantically squeezing the life out.
Suppressing what they cannot control.
Discarding what they cannot profit from.
Forsaking the wombs from which they were birthed.

Bring Your Holy Destruction upon them!
So every little girl grows sharp fangs

INVOCATION TO THE MOTHER OF RAGE

To gnaw her way through the bars
Of their gilded cage of purity.
Give her the strength to snatch back the treasure of
Her own body, her own desires, her own future.

Wage war against those who wage war against women
Banning our voices and our faces and our songs
Bruising and violating our bodies and our minds
Denying our personhood and stealing our freedom
Forcing us to labor in homes and in hospital rooms.
Let our chains be broken, our shackles unbolted!

And to those so warped by their avarice
That they are content to escort womankind
To the Grim Reaper to advance their own power?
Swallow them up in Your breath of fire.
Wear garlands of their severed heads
And dance upon their bones
As we chant songs of gratitude to You
For stemming the tide of tragedies
They willingly inflict to further their own agenda.

Let our bleeding hearts be cauterized
By our burning fury
So we may rise up as one
To lay waste to the systems of oppression
They have so carefully constructed
And stand upon the wreckage
Shouting in one singular voice,
"Let nothing more be built here
Unless it is Ours."
This I pray.
May it be so.

I WILL NOT

Megan Phillips

CW: infertility, grief, religious terminology

I will not be silent because the realities of the world hurt you.
I will not be quiet because my pain makes you flinch.
I will not stop talking about the shame that hides in corners
From people you have never met.

I will not look away, eyes down, because it scares you.
To think that someone's pain is so deep,
That there is a well that will always be dry . . .
Although it was made for heavy water to flow.

I am not broken,
I am one of many.
I am not alone,
I am strong because I faced the storm.

I did not run away from my reality,
That everyday I am reminded of.
When I want nothing more than to have what you have,
For the children I rent for 40 hours a week,
JUST one of them to be *mine*.

"Not all men"

Lee VanBeek

CW: discussion of men's power over women's bodies

"Not all men are bad," they say—
Prove me otherwise.
They all want something in common:
Money and power.

That "need" grows like the world's problems;
That "need" grows like mold on damp trees.
That "need" always stays the same;
That "need" is in all men.

They want money and power;
Power over women's bodies and who they touch,
Power over women's bodies and who or when they talk.

Power over women's bodies and what they wear,
because women shouldn't feel confident in their bodies . . .
For it is too distracting for men.

"Not all men," they say—
Prove me otherwise.

Wolf Song

Lyra Martin

CW: mention of attempted date-rape, violence

we move in packs, we lope along
howling the same wild wolf song
dressed in short skirts and tops to match
oh, wouldn't we be quite the catch?
but alas, we're too good for your sad little self
too pretty to sit on your cold collection shelf
so listen to our NOs, don't hear them as YESes
don't wait there imagining what hides under our dresses
don't stand pleading with cold eyes that never blink
and don't you fucking dare go near my drink
if you do? (really don't, i wouldn't be so stupid)
you better start praying to hades, not cupid
only he can save you when we drop to our knees
start yipping and growling, pouncing through trees
it's a race, it's a chase, and we're preying on you
sniffed out the mark, as all predators do
now you're trapped in the middle of a circle of jaws
no such thing as not guilty in our wild wolf laws
rapist, assaulter, you small feeble man
now so scared of women you're weaker than
an execution, it's decided, the death penalty for you
now just to choose a quivering limb to bite through....

WOLF SONG

your arm, your leg, or past your skull to your brain?
where could we incite the most screams of pain?
but wait—we are many, and can take a piece each
so let us bite into every bit we can reach
tear you to shreds, held down by our claws
crimson lipstick coats our muzzles and maws
your last shrieks fade away into the night
and justice is served under red bloodmoon light.

Words have power

Lee VanBeek

CW: sexual harassment

I feel your hot breath down my neck;
I feel your neglecting words in my mind.
Your words make me a wreck.
Your words have power.
Everyone's words have power—except mine.

I feel your eyes scanning my body;
I feel shivers run down my back.
Your eyes make me uncomfortable . . .
Their power is uncontrollable;
Everyone has power—except for me.

I feel your comments about my body;
I feel the pit in my stomach grow.
Your words make me want to commit something bloody.
Your words have power without you knowing.
Everyone's words have power—except mine.

I feel your demanding expectations in my shoulders;
I feel the anxiety grow in my chest.
Your expectations kill people . . .

You kill people;
Because your words have more power than any woman.

Bitter Threads

H.T. Doig

CW: kidnapping, imprisonment, animal harm/injury, grief

The little cottage stood one hundred meters off the forest path framed by sleeping skeletal trees. Weathered stone walls were covered with alternating moss, lichen, and snow. A lone figure sat in the window, a shawl draped over her shoulders, clutching a steaming mug.

She was waiting; her gaze piercing the sharp winter air.

A blue blur zipped by and slowed just in time to land on the windowsill. The full moon hung low and bright in the sky. She smiled, illuminated by the graying twilight.

She opened the window, pulling her shawl close against the icy wind, her fingers worn and aching from too many nights spent working under dim light. "Hurry in, silly thing," she chided. "It's too cold to stand here waiting!"

The jay hopped through the window, flitting to her shoulder and nestling against her neck, pulling a few strands of salt-strewn brown hair around it.

Twyla sighed. Bramble was home, safe and sound. She could breathe again. Turning from the window, she pulled the faded drapes closed. The single-room cottage was dark; the only light coming from the smoldering hearth. Twyla threw another log on, pursing her lips and worrying her index finger against her thumb. The pile of firewood was painfully low, and, being only January, there would still be several deathly cold days before everything thawed.

Exhaustion laid like a heavy blanket over her shoulders. She placed the kettle over the fire. Sinking into the wooden chair near the hearth, she warmed her stiff bones while she waited for the water to boil. Work could wait a few more minutes.

She might not have much, or even enough, but she was here. Suitors dwindled and disappeared since her body gained the soft edges and weathered lines that came with age. She was one of the lucky ones able to escape the burden of another loveless marriage. Instead, she, at least, was doing what she loved.

Even if it meant she went a bit hungry.

Bramble beaked her ear, breaking her from her reverie. The kettle sent wisps of steam into the room. She picked it up and poured warm water over the used tea leaves.

She ambled over to her loom, running her hands along the worn wooden frame. The fabric was even, fine, delicate—but would sell for pennies. "It'll be good enough," she whispered, though the words were hollow. "If only I could do more than just survive." But that wasn't her life. It never had been.

It didn't stop her wanting.

If only she could have enough. If only she didn't have to charge half of what a man would for her tapestries.

If only.

If only.

If only.

A wind ripped through her home, extinguishing the burning want in one gust.

Bramble snapped his beak and snuggled deeper against Twyla's neck.

A shimmer caught her eye near her still-closed front door. "What in the . . . Hello?"

Twyla pulled her shawl tighter as a shiver ran up her arms. She jumped at the sight of a figure—person—was standing in the doorway. The edges of their body shifted like mist.

"Hello," they said. "Sorry for the intrusion. May I come in?" Their voice lilted in a haunting melody; one Twyla could lose herself in.

Instead, she stood dumbstruck before shaking the fog out of her head. "Forgive my manners! Yes. Come in. I don't have much of a...fire." She pursed her lips. A fire roared in the hearth. Wasn't the fire mostly embers a few moments ago? Twyla closed her gray-blue eyes, rubbing them. Tired. That's what was going on. She worked too much. Too hard. "Please, come sit."

The being took the few steps needed to cross the room, edges fading in and out of sight. Air warmed with their approach. Smells of springtime—warm and awakening—surrounded them before they stopped in front of the loom. They smiled, bright white teeth reflecting the rich blue hues from the fabric.

"This is lovely work," they hummed, hazel eyes shimmering with moonlight.

"Thank you. It's far from finished." Twyla shifted, unease settling in her stomach. "Who are you?"

They laughed, reminding Twyla of harness bells, as they ran their fingers along the tapestry. "You could summon the echoes of forgotten stars if you wanted."

"What do you mean?" Twyla furrowed her brow.

"You could weave something precious. Rare. Powerful."

Twyla scoffed. "If only. Wouldn't that be grand!"

"You'd like that?"

"Who wouldn't? I'd be daft to not." Twyla stared at her loom. Once, she dreamed of fame, riches, and the freedom that came with it. Now, those dreams were gone like candle smoke. No, she was content in her home, alone, with her beloved loom.

"Then it's yours." They said it so softly, Twyla almost missed it.

"What'd you—" Twyla turned to look at them, but she was alone. "Did you see that, Bramble?"

The ache in her back, stiffness in her joints, and perpetual shivers dissipated as she settled into the gentle routine of weaving at her loom.

She sang her favorite working song while her mind wandered through her dreams and desires: enough flour, a full woodpile, and jam. Raspberry jam. As she sang, threads separated from the moonbeams shining through her window and wove their way through the fabric, liquid silver amongst the wool. Tendrils followed the individual picks throughout the weft, integrating with the fabric until they became part of it, adding a slight shimmer. Twyla worried her thumbnail again. This was . . . She didn't know what it was.

Bramble jeered and flitted to the loom. He pulled at the silver threads, but they fell through his beak like water. Twyla smiled, suppressing a giggle.

Twyla continued, falling back into the easy rhythm of her song and the beat of the loom. Soon enough, she was finished and tying the ends. She held up the cloth, tracing the moonlit threads with her fingertips.

She rubbed her eyes. "I must be too tired. Too hungry. Too . . . something." She pushed the shuttle back and threads of moonlight followed the wool. "At least it's pretty," she mumbled, reaching out to Bramble. He hopped onto her Twyla's and fluttered up to her shoulder. "What'd you think, my friend? Think we're able to finish this up and sell this for a pretty penny?" Bramble snuggled into Twyla's hair, and made soft chirping noises as he fell asleep. "That's what I thought."

Turning away from the loom, she stopped short. The pile of wood by the nearby wall was full. She stole a glance at the hearth. Moonlight spilled through the cracks in the walls with the wind, but warmth seeped into her belly. She was lighter. "I don't know about you, but I've got a good feeling about this cloth."

The sun broke the tree line by the time Twyla left her cottage, huddling as deep as she could in her worn gray jacket.

"Bah!" she grumbled against the sharp wind. If it was up to her, she wouldn't leave her cottage until the first spring thaw. The achy, bitter tang of loneliness hit the back of her throat at the thought of spending four months without seeing another soul. She might have thwarted the affections of a husband, but that didn't mean she enjoyed complete isolation.

She trundled on for the next two hours. The sun hung low in the sky, keeping its warmth to itself. By the time Twyla arrived, her fingers were immobile, and she couldn't tell if her toes were still attached to her feet.

Hopefully she wasn't too late and there was still a table for her at the market. She pushed the big doors open, sighing as the warm air stung her face.

Luck was on her side today. There was one table left far away from the door. She shuffled over, quickly moving and trying to avoid the pitying stares from other vendors. She knew how she looked—threadbare and frozen, but she couldn't help the bitter taste at the back of her throat as their gazes bored into her.

Alone, they'd whisper.

Unmarried.

No children.

This was why she rarely came to town.

With a heavy sigh, she unpacked her bag with the woven cloths. One after another, she unpacked the previously unsold fabric, finishing with the newest addition—finishing with the glimmering novel item. She worried her lip.

"Yes, I have a good feeling about this one," she mumbled. Bramble stirred by the nape of her neck, hidden in her hair, and clicked his beak.

Twyla just had to wait now. People milled around, stopping, touching her fabrics, but eventually moving on. It was the way of things. So, she suffered the patronizing glances and tight-lipped smiles.

"Twy!" A stout woman waved. She picked her skirts up and rushed over before smothering Twyla in a hug.

"Hello, Glyn," Twyla said, muffled by the woman's snow-white hair.

"It's been a minute. I was worried we'd have to send a party out to check on you." Glynnis brushed Twyla's shoulders as if clearing off snow and frost. Twyla flinched, worried her friend would notice her prominent collar bones.

"Weather hasn't been good," Twyla said, looking anywhere but Glynnis. "Didn't have the choice today, though."

"Why don't you spend the winter with us? I don't like you out in that cabin by yourself. You aren't getting younger."

"Bah, and do what? Sit around and add to the town gossip?" She huffed. "I *like* my home, Glyn. I don't like what they—" Twyla gestured toward the bustling market "—think about it."

"They'll say whatever they want anyway. This way you won't be alone."

"Yes but, at home, I don't have to hear it." Twyla took a deep breath. "I know you worry, but I'm fine. Really."

"Fine, but—" Glynnis stopped. A man was hunched over at the table, wearing a dark cloak with the hood up, running his hands over the fabrics. He stopped when his hand touched the shimmering cloth.

"Good day sir!" Twyla chirped, a little louder than necessary. "Can I help you today?"

"You're the weaver?" he muttered, not looking away from the table.

"That I am." Twyla shifted uneasily.

"Beautiful work," he huffed and moved on.

Glynnis came up behind Twyla. "That was odd."

Twyla sighed. "It's how it usually goes, unfortunately."

"Still strange. Your pieces are so lovely." Glynnis moved to the table, gravitating to the glimmering cloth, but under her touch, the cloth looked like it was illuminated by hundreds of candles. Twyla blinked rapidly, hoping no one noticed it was almost glowing. "You know, it's been a hard winter. The growing season wasn't the best, everything keeps getting more expensive, no one has enough money. Things feel kind of bleak. But this"— she gestured to the fabric in her hand— "This *feels* different." She gave Twyla a sidelong glance. "What's going on?"

"Nothing!" Twyla said too quickly as she rubbed the side of her finger. "Nothing's going on."

"Look, I don't know wha—"

Three soldiers appeared in front of the table. "Which one of you made these?"

"I did. Is there a problem, sirs?"

"Come with us, ma'am." They walked around the back of the table, grabbing Twyla by the arms.

"Wait! What's going on?" Twyla cried. Bramble woke with a start and scrambled out of her hair, eventually breaking free from the tangled nest.

"Stop! She didn't do anything!" Glynnis reached for Twyla, missing, and falling to the ground with a heavy thud.

"Glyn!" Twyla thrashed against the men holding her, desperate to get away. Her small, soft body was no match for their battle-hardened frames.

One hand left her arm, leaving a biting cold in its absence. The men were exclaiming and swatting at a blur of blue and black feathers.

"Get away, you silly thing!" she called. Bramble, the ever-faithful creature, was mobbing the soldiers, dodging their swats until one found him, sending him into the wall.

"Bramble!" Twyla screeched as she watched his small body fall to the floor. Hot tears burned her eyes as the fight left her body, leaving her limp and sobbing. The soldiers pulled her along, but she couldn't just leave him here, alone. Her friend. Her companion. She pulled back with all her might until she felt a sharp pain and the world went black.

Twyla shifted, sending pain ricocheting through her head. Groaning, she turned, and forced her heavy eyes open. She was covered in soft, thick blankets. Laying on a plush surface. She pushed herself up, immediately regretting the movement as an ache seared on the back of her head.

The cavernous circular room was covered end-to-end in plush carpets. A fire raged in the hearth, making the stone walls warm to the touch. And in the middle of the room, a massive loom stood ready.

Where was she? What . . .

Bits and pieces wove their way back. Market. Glyn. Soldiers. Bramble.

"Oh gods, *Bramble,*" Twyla cried, dropping her face into her hands. His roost at the nape of her neck burned without him. A scream threatened to tear itself from her throat. It was her fault. She made a ruckus. He did what any good jay would do.

The only door creaked open, and a small, waifish woman squeezed in. She busied herself by the side table, laying a tray on the sideboard without making a sound. Twyla cleared her throat, and the woman jumped, raising a hand to her chest.

"Oh! It's just you!" she sang, breathless. "You're awake. Good. It's beyond time for you to be up. Sun's been up for hours."

"Where am I?" Twyla pushed the covers off her stiff legs and stood. Warm, toasty smells came from the tray, and her mouth watered.

"Lord Tarren's keep, m'lady," the servant said, eyes downcast. Twyla wracked her brain but couldn't remember hearing that name before. "I'll be your handmaid for the time. Please, sit. I'll prepare your breakfast." She gestured to the sitting area.

Twyla nodded and ambled over. A plush couch sat across from the fireplace with a large square table in front. She sat stiffly on the softest couch she'd ever been on. She stifled a pleased groan at the sight of the spread in front of her—fried eggs, fresh toast, gleaming pastries, raspberry jam, and strong, dark tea. She shoveled the food in her mouth. No stale, unsalted bread. No tea made from used tea leaves. She was warm and in the most comfortable room she had ever been in.

"What's your name?"

"My name?" The servant's hazel eyes snapped up, boring into Twyla.

"If you're going to be around, I might as well call you something other than 'servant.' I don't like it."

"Very well. You may call me Moira."

"Will I see this Lord Tarren today?" Twyla asked between sips of tea.

"Oh no m'lady! If you're lucky, you'll never see his Lordship."

Twyla pursed her lips. "What do you mean?"

"His Lordship does not visit his possessions. And a visit from him is not always . . . pleasant."

Twyla stopped mid-chew. *Possession.* That was the catch. A trade of freedom for security that she had no say in. She swallowed hard, choking on any semblance of comfort leaving her body.

"But don't worry!" the servant chirped. "You just do as he asks and all will be well."

"And what is it he asks?" This was infuriating. She was a poor woman past her prime. She had no wealth, no power. What would a *Lord* possibly want from her? She had nothing.

"From the looks of it,"—she gestured to the loom— "he wants you to weave."

Twyla stared at her hands. Once they wove for herself, for her own joy, for her own purpose. Now, they would weave for him.

Twyla stared out the window, giving excuse after excuse for why she couldn't weave. The excuses would run out, she knew she couldn't avoid it forever. Patience would wear thin, and Twyla was ever aware of Moira's warning; she didn't want to meet the Lord any time soon.

But she couldn't bring herself to go to the loom. There was a cold, empty space by the nape of her neck that stretched and consumed her chest, leaving a dark gaping abyss. It should be filled with sleepy coos and soft feathers. The edge of the memory was jagged and sharp, leaving no cut but it bled just the same.

"Madame?"

She startled. "Moira." Twyla relaxed a bit.

"Sorry, miss," Moira muttered, her shoulders slumped.

The maid carried nothing. "What's the matter?"

"The Lord. He says you must weave tonight."

"Why? I said my head still hurts too much. I can't—"

Moira raised her hand, interrupting. "I know. But please, Twyla. He'll come down and then . . ." Her lip quivered.

Twyla's mind knotted, impossible to smooth out. "This doesn't make sense. None of it makes sense! I'm just a weaver. I'm not even the most talented one in the land. I'm just...me."

"You don't weave normal fabrics, do you?" Moira's eyes shimmered.

"I don't understand. What does this Lord that I've never heard of before want from me? None of this makes sense." Her thoughts scattered like frightened birds, impossible to catch. Confusion curled in her chest, thick and choking.

"His Lordship is a collector of sorts. He finds people with gifts and uses them to build his wealth. There's a reason you haven't heard of him before. It takes a great deal of wealth and power to keep a name secret."

Twyla pursed her lips. "Fine," she spat.

She stood and stomped toward the loom. Her hands trembled over the machine, hesitant. Sorrow was a quiet thing—sliding itself between fibers of her soul like a weft thread, only visible under the right light. Swallowing, she threw the shuttle through the warp, pulling glittering silver threads with the silk. Each pass, every moonlit pick thread added to the fabric tightened around her, chaining her to the loom. She thought of this mysterious Lord. People like him desired more. *More. More.* Never-ending hunger that would never be satiated.

The movements were second nature to her. She should feel joy, hot and hopeful, losing herself in the rhythm and song of the loom. But this thing that brought her life meaning was now constricting, heavy, burdensome. He would profit from this. From her. Her song caught in her throat, coming out in harsh, cracking tones. Her craft no longer sang sweet melodies for her. It shrieked for him.

As Twyla tied the last thread, the fabric glimmered, sending shimmers throughout the room. A spell cast. A power she had. A flicker of joy snuffed out. This wasn't hers anymore. Nothing she made would be her own again.

"It's done." She tossed the scarf on the sofa. Moira's relief was palpable.

"I'm going to sleep," Twyla muttered, the hollowness in her chest threatening to swallow her whole.

Moira said something before she left, but Twyla was too far into the abyss to hear. She was alone. She had nothing—her friend, her home, her craft, and her freedom, all gone. It was too much. There was too much loss, and it would break her apart with the enormity of it. What does one do with loss when there isn't a space inside yourself large enough to contain it?

But Twyla wasn't alone. Deep in that empty, carved out space, a bitter thread began to coil.

"What is it this time?" Twyla snapped. The anger coiled, contracting around her ribcage with each heartbeat.

"More fabrics." Moira picked up skeins of thread, helping Twyla set up the night's weaving.

"It's always the same, isn't it?" she asked, rearranging the rough, bland threads. Exhaustion heavy on her shoulders. The nameless coil inside her grew, sending tremors just under the surface.

Moira huffed, giving a half-hearted smile. "You're a quick learner. How's this?" She pointed to the differing shades of beige and gray.

"It'll do—" Twyla stopped. Moira's hair smudged, briefly losing its detail, like it was covered in a thin mist. She blinked, and everything was as it should be—her dark brown hair back to normal.

"Everything okay?" Moira chirped.

"Yes, I must be tired." Twyla worried her lip.

Moira clapped her hands together, dusting them off. "I'll leave you to it." The space next to Twyla was cold. Alone. But the solitude wasn't as comfortable as it used to be. Winter had worked its way into her bones, every movement sharp and thought stiff.

Alone is different when you had a friend. Loss wasn't a stranger, but it never felt this vacant, this empty, before. If it wasn't for her greed, her dissatisfaction, her *wanting*, Bramble would still be here. The full moon casted red-silver light as Twyla set the warp threads and wound the weft into the shuttle. Guilt was heavy and cold, whispering relentless accusations.

If I had done more.
If I had kept to myself.
If I hadn't wanted.

She threw the shuttle across the loom, glowing red threads following the wool. Bramble's vacant roost burned. That coil released, weaving through her veins, molten iron heating her from the inside out. Her throat tightened as a new thought formed, sharp and angry: this wasn't her fault.

If he hadn't wanted more.
If he hadn't taken what wasn't his.
If he. If he. If he.

A new verse in her song.

Why should she feel ashamed for needing firewood or flour or clothing? Why should she be ostracized for wanting to have a different life? Why should she feel guilt for wanting to survive?

Rage hummed in her blood, growing with each frantic heartbeat. Heat rose, pressing against her temples, her mind circling the same cruel truth over and over. This wasn't her fault. She was not to blame for wanting to exist. Bramble's blood was not on her hands.

This *lord* could have his wealth and choke on it. Make it his downfall.

"He wants to use me. Profit from me. His quiet little weaver," she sang. Her song evolved beyond a hum into a venomous battle cry.

The shuttle flew, the liquid silver threads picking up flickers of red, back and forth, side to side. She clenched her teeth, the last effort to contain the rage as it surged forward, wild and frantic.

A final thread, ripped off with her teeth and tied with a scream.

The loom quivered as the moonlit threads snapped into place. Twyla threw the fabric to the ground, the weave turning into a smoldering dust.

Breathless, Twyla stepped backward. The weave became erratic, twisting and lashing out, no longer under her control. Moonlight surged in a blinding heat. An explosion, echoes of forgotten stars ringing in her ears. Her rage unraveled, leaving Twyla with only the sounds of her pulse thrumming. The ground rumbled and shifted. A *crack* reverberated through her bones. Burning light spiderwebbed up the walls. This was her masterpiece—terrible, chaotic, and *hers*.

Soft, familiar feathers nestled into their roost. Dust and debris fell as her moonlight carved jagged lines in the foundation. A sick and vicious smile played along her lips. Twyla wasn't alone anymore. Red-silver threads wove between her fingers. "This is what they forced me to become. Let them reap their rewards."

And she pulled, bringing the walls down around her.

A blue jay called overhead before disappearing into the night. A lone woman stood in the center of a ruin, moonlight flicking salt to her hair.

The air rippled, and a figure appeared in the mist, calling the woman closer. And she followed, stepping into the world between shadow and moonlight.

Blood in the Water: A Siren Revenge Tail

Sarah Zane

CW: mentions of sexual assault, blood, drowning, death

I didn't recall much of my life from before my transformation day. Despite how hard I tried, I couldn't remember anything from before I heard the call of the sea and was claimed by the waves.

My transformation day was all that lingered in my memory. Those final hours were burned into my mind, and into the siren's.

The siren remembered and called for blood—for *their* blood. The siren yearned to attack every ship that passed, to bring it to the bottom of the ocean in case one of the men responsible for my transformation was on board. Every time a ship passed, I had to yank hard on the siren's leash, trying to fight her urges.

I knew the siren and I were one and the same, but it was hard to think of the siren as myself. The siren felt foreign to me, like a state of mind that took over when I couldn't fight my new instincts. I imagined my sisters had all faced the same internal struggle, but they were well enough adjusted now that it was hard to picture.

I was the newest of the pod, my sisters all having surrendered their humanity long ago. Their eyes were wild and their teeth were sharp when they grinned. They were almost animalistic. I knew I must look like that too, but the remaining surface-dweller part of me was scared of them. They weren't cruel to me, though. They cared for me, had saved me, but it was hard to ignore the glee they took in drowning and torturing men. It was hard to digest the glee the siren took in it, that *I* took in it.

With every new ship that passed, the urges grew stronger, and I had to try my best to suppress them. Hard as I tried, I was still learning. The siren screamed for blood and sometimes I couldn't stop her, and sometimes I didn't bother. My sisters understood. They all dealt with the same urges. If my siren attacked, they would follow. No siren was left behind; if one fought, we all fought.

But it was dangerous. The hunters didn't mess around. They had their weapons against us, and sometimes one of us wouldn't make it. Sometimes, they would use nets. We took extra pleasure in killing those who tried to capture us. We all knew the risks, and we all knew we would rather die than be captured.

Word had spread through the ocean about a siren who had been captured and had unspeakable things done to her. By the time I came to the pod, it was common knowledge that death was preferable, so we took precautions. We all wore poisonous seaweed around our necks, harmless to the touch, but toxic when eaten. My pod had lost a few sisters that way when they weren't able to free themselves from the nets.

It was a steep price, so my pod tried to keep to ourselves and out of trouble. I tried to keep a leash on the siren's urges, and the others seemed adept at doing the same. As a result, we usually avoided the hunters, but it seemed like lately there were more ships about, and most carried hunters.

It was nearly impossible to avoid them. As hard as my sisters and I fought our urges, with hunters as close as they were, we were attacking more than was safe.

My siren was growing angrier with each passing day, and harder to control. Even when we attacked the ships, it wasn't enough. The blood didn't sate her for long. I was starting to suspect it wouldn't until the blood belonged to one of the men from my transformation day.

I remembered every moment of the day those men used me for their ritual. I was sure I would recognize the faces of almost every man who had touched me.

I could never forget their rough hands shoving me down as they took turns doing whatever they wanted to me. I was terrified and in pain, screaming, but still they didn't stop. They just shoved a dirty rag into my mouth to stop my screams. They didn't silence me out of fear of discovery, but simply because my screaming annoyed them. They laughed about it and said it was a pity they weren't going to be keeping my pretty mouth available. I thought maybe then they would stop, but they didn't. There were still more that wanted their turn.

My memories of my surface days started and ended with the pain on that ship. I couldn't remember what the ritual they were doing was or why I was there in the first place, but if that's how surface dwellers were, it was better that the waves had claimed me.

Even with the rag in my mouth, I had still screamed my lungs out, but they hadn't cared or stopped. I prayed to anything that was listening that it would stop, but it didn't. Only when I was so badly hurt that I was wishing for death did it stop.

The hands finally let go.

I was thankful, for a moment. I'll never forget how I breathed a quick sigh of relief, as well as I could through the gag. Until the hands were replaced with rough ropes around my arms, binding them behind my back. I was too tired to fight much, but I pushed back against the men with everything I had left. I pulled against the ropes, but it was no use.

I flailed, kicking with my legs, but they were swiftly bound until I couldn't move an inch. The ropes burned against my bare skin. Any of the skin unmarred from their advances had been rubbed raw by my attempting to get out of the ropes.

Two of them hoisted me up, and I prayed whatever happened next would end my life quickly. It wasn't until I felt the fresh air on my skin that I realized what they intended, and I felt the tears come.

Those waters were infested with sharks. I hoped I would drown quickly and just slip away peacefully beneath the waves, but if I didn't, I hoped that sharks would get me before the sirens did. At least the sharks would make it quick. Falling into the hands of the sirens was a far worse fate than being found by sharks. But I would have taken either rather than stay on the ship with those monsters. If given the choice, I would pick the sea every time. There wasn't a fate worse than what had already happened.

The men tied something heavy to my feet, dashing my last slim hope of escape. They were still laughing when they tossed me overboard. The hard slap of the ocean against my legs stung almost as much as the salt water on my wounds. My entire body was on fire as the water closed in around me, silencing the world.

I opened my eyes. The salt stung and all I could see was blue. I tried to push the rag out of my mouth with my tongue, but that only hastened the water entering my mouth, so I stopped. I tried tugging on the rope around my wrists, but it wasn't any use. The weight continued to drag me down as I watched the surface slowly grow farther and farther away. I wasn't going to survive this. I tried to make my peace with the end, until a moment later when I saw the flick of a tail out of the corner of my eye.

I tried to thrash when I felt a fin brush my back, but I was too wrapped up to move my body.

Please be a shark, please be a shark.

A moment later, my worst nightmare floated into view. It wasn't a shark.

The siren had a long grey tail like a shark. She had piercing eyes and white flowing hair, but I knew better than to be taken in by her beauty.

She moved closer, and I flinched.

She grinned at that and her sharp teeth made me scream. Water rushed in through the little space around the rag in my mouth. Panic overtook me, until a thought that felt foreign broke through the haze of terror.

Hush, little one. Death has you in its clutches, but there's another way.

I felt my vision going hazy as I clung to life as hard as I could.

Tell me, little one, do you want to live?

I was either hallucinating the siren or the voice in my head or both, but I still considered it and her with my last remaining moment, and I did. I wanted to live.

The world went black, and when my senses slowly returned, there was something warm pressed against my lips. If this was death, maybe I was wrong about wanting to live.

The warmth pulled back, and I opened my eyes to find I was staring at the grey-tailed siren. She had just had her lips on mine. I gasped and touched my lips with my fingers. This couldn't be real. I quickly realized a few impossible things; I didn't appear to be dead, I wasn't choking on the water, I didn't have the rag in my mouth anymore, and my hands were free.

I don't understand.

A melodic laugh flowed through my mind followed by the thought, *Of course not, little one. It's quite common to be confused on your transformation day.*

I blinked and looked at the siren.

That was your voice!

She nodded. *Ah—a bright one. I do hope that will make this easier for you.*

I didn't know where to begin or what to think or ask.

Why am I not dead?

Would you rather be? the voice of the siren asked in my mind. I could hear the curiosity in her words.

No, I suppose not, I thought automatically. *But what now? And how am I still here?*

Now, we welcome you into the pod. It's been a while since we've added a sister. The others will want to meet you right away.

But...but...I can't join you.

And why not?

Because I'm a surface dweller? Because I should be dead? Because I don't belong here? Because none of this should be possible? A million answers rushed through my mind before I settled on the most obvious one. *I'm not a siren. If you would just unbind my legs, I can make my way back to the surface and won't have to burden you.* I hoped my thoughts were convincing.

She just blinked slowly, looking down at my legs and then meeting my eye.

I'm afraid I can't do that.

I knew this was a trap. I knew it—or I should have known, anyway.

Some of that must have shown on my face, because she shook her head. *You're not understanding, little one, look down.*

I did and couldn't comprehend what I was seeing. Where the brown ropes had been was a mass of violet. I tried to move my legs under it by kicking my feet and screamed in surprise when a tail flicked out where my feet should have been.

*I'm—I'm—*I couldn't even finish the thought. *But that's impossible!*

You wanted to live, and my sisters and I try to save those we can, but you were too far gone to be saved. A choice between living under the waves or dying under them was all I could offer you. I'm sorry that I didn't find you sooner.

I tried to understand, but I was slow taking in the reality of my situation. I had lived above the waves all my life. I was sure of that. I wanted to get back to the surface, wanted to fight for my life above the waves. I was sure there were memories of that life somewhere in my mind, but I couldn't think, couldn't understand what I had been fighting for. All I could remember was the pain those men had put me through. If that was all the surface had to offer, I was better off below the waves.

I let the siren take my hand and lead me into my new life. The grey-tailed siren, Charia, brought me into her pod and the rest of my new sisters were just as welcoming as her.

I wanted to leave the nightmare of my surface life behind, but the memories of my fear and pain were still visceral, and the siren clung to them. I kept wishing the siren inside would forget so that I could, too, but the memories weren't going anywhere.

Every one of my sisters had a story just as gruesome. Rezi, one of my siren sisters, had been found with wounds that took months to heal. When she refused her ship's captain because she preferred the company of women, they had driven nails through the flesh of both of her hands and fastened her to the front of the ship. They said if she loved women so much, she would make good siren bait. They were right. The moment my siren sisters sensed her fear, the men didn't stand a chance. The ship had been brought down swiftly, and Rezi was adopted into the pod. I hadn't yet succumbed to my fate, so I hadn't witnessed the monstrosity, but the still-visible scars on her hands were reminder enough of the dangers of the surface and the men who hunted us.

My only regret was that my sisters hadn't been around when Charia found me, so the ship got away. It wasn't often a ship made it away from our pod unscathed, so they could count themselves lucky. Until I found them again.

I felt the vibrations in the water before I heard or saw any sign of the incoming ship. The ocean itself was vibrating, warning us, whispering, *A ship is coming.*

Here we go again.

I had lost track of time, but several lunar cycles had passed since my transformation, and we had taken down more than a few ships, but I already knew this one would be different.

Even the vibrations of the water felt different this time. The waves themselves seemed to know something big was coming. My siren was already yanking at the tight leash I kept her on. Too soon, too hard. I had thought I was ready to fight her off, but I wasn't ready for her intensity. She knew this felt different, too. I tried to hold her back, but it was useless, so I let go.

She took over. I was only watching through her eyes. I couldn't control a thing. I wanted to close my eyes, to look away. I hated this part. I took no pleasure in the animalistic, bloodthirsty way she took down ships and murdered men, but I had no choice but to watch.

With her enhanced senses, I noticed what I hadn't before; the ship coming toward us looked familiar, but more importantly, she had already heard the pleas, the cries for help. Feminine cries, followed by male laughter. She turned to my sisters and, from the grins on their faces, I knew we were all feeling the same. The ocean was going to run red with their blood.

I sent the thought to my sisters, more of a warning than a request, but they nodded. I was taking the lead on this. They would follow. Ostoma and Rezi would be ready to tend to the women if they were joining us, or to help them to safety if they weren't. The other three followed closely behind my siren.

I swam up to the boat and...

THWACK!

My siren slammed my violet tail against the hull of the ship.

With sharp-toothed grins, my sisters set to work doing the same. The ship was smaller than the hunter's ships we were used to.

THWACK!
THWACK!
THWACK!

My siren's tail and my sisters' tails continued to beat against the hull until we heard male screams. I couldn't see the men, but I could hear their panic and almost taste their fear as we launched the ship sideways.

THWACK!
THWACK!
THWACK!

We kept at it until finally the hull gave way, our tails puncturing holes in the ship where we had been hitting. I grinned at my sisters and signaled. I took the lead with Lucia and Sypher behind and Charia bringing up the rear. In formation, we were fast, precise, and deadly.

We moved away from the ship, weaving as we did in case of counter-attack, but none came. There were only panicked cries of scared men. I reveled in their fear. I was going to put those low-life surface-dwelling scum into a watery grave.

The ship started to sink lower as it filled with water. They rushed to their lifeboats and piled in. When we saw that the distressed women who had caught our attention were being left on the ship, I knew my siren had made the right decision. The despicable hunters weren't even trying to save the women.

Ostoma and Rezi were under the ship now, waiting for their opportunity to rescue the women, leaving the fun part for the rest of us.

We watched from a short distance as the rowboats hit the water. Sometimes my sisters would untie the lifeboats, taking away all hope of escape from the men, but when I was in charge, I always kept them there. Lifeboats or not, they wouldn't escape us, and it was delicious watching their hopes be dashed when they saw us. Delicious knowing they had tasted escape before we tasted their blood.

As the lifeboats started to move, I felt a tug toward the one on the left.

That one is mine, I thought and then flicked over to it, staying under the water, out of sight. There were four other boats, and the others doled them out among themselves. It hardly mattered—this one was mine.

The men all rowed hard, but in the wrong direction. The shore was close by if they turned around, but they kept going the wrong way. I flicked far enough away into the distance and popped my head out of the water, just enough so I could see, and looked around.

The air was thick with fog. The fog was no match for my siren eyesight, but it wasn't hard to imagine that the surface dwellers likely couldn't see the land they were rowing away from. They didn't seem to be able to sense it, either. They were a sorry excuse for seamen. Even if we weren't here, who knows how long they would have survived.

I resubmerged and waited for them to get a little closer. When they were halfway to me, I surfaced again. This time, I pushed my head fully above water, and the siren began her call.

The song was always the same, a lament to lost love, full of sorrow but promise, promise that things could be better if only they would get in the water, if only they would listen and surrender themselves to me, to us. We could make all their problems go away.

My sisters joined in the song, taking up their positions near the other lifeboats.

I crept closer, feeling the waves respond to me, feeling my song calling out to them. I heard the men's hearts quicken a moment when they sensed the danger, sensed me. Then they were enthralled and their hearts slowed. There were only fifty of them, ten in each boat. A smaller crew than normal, but there would be enough to go around. My sisters could have the rest. I only wanted him. This lifeboat had called to me because of him. I remembered enough to know he was one of the men who held me down on my transformation day. He had held me down and shoved the dirty rag in my mouth.

Tonight, I would have my revenge. Tonight, I was the hunter, and he was going to pay.

Before I made it within a hundred feet of his boat, I heard a splash. I almost broke my song to laugh. That must be a new record. Normally, the men held out much longer. Normally, they tried to resist. I felt the water move around the man, felt the vibrations of one of my sisters coming from below. She pulled him under. The moment the water filled his ears, the spell was broken.

I felt his screams vibrate the water and the laugh of my sister as she bit into him. So it was that kind of night. I grinned through my song, ripe with anticipation.

We didn't eat the men. We weren't monsters, we just exacted vengeance. The worse the condition of the women we rescued, the slower the deaths we gave the men. This man had put me through hell, and he was going to die screaming, alone, surrounded, and afraid, like he and his friends had intended for me.

I was within fifty feet now. A few more went overboard and were quickly dragged under. Then there were five. It seemed my prey was one of the stronger-willed. Good. The stronger the will, the more pleasurable it would be to break. I would take my time with him.

The men could see me now, slowly emerging from the fog. The very image of their desires, the answer to their darkest prayers. *Come to me,* I sang just for him, and he did. The others jumped into the water, too, following close behind, but he was the quickest. I watched as he closed the distance between us, letting him come to me. It was sweeter that way, making him chase his own doom.

I signaled with a flick of my tail in his direction, claiming him. I knew my sisters were lurking about. I didn't care about the other men. They would only get in my way, but *he* was mine.

I felt the others get pulled under the water. Perfect timing. He closed the final distance and wrapped his arms around me. I wrapped mine around him. Then, only then, seeing the lust and devotion in his eyes, holding him tightly in my arms, did I stop singing.

I watched his eyes, watched the dawning realization that I wasn't whatever fantasy his mind had come up with. Watched as he took in my face. I brushed up against his leg with the end of my tail. I felt his heart speed up and saw his pupils dilate. His muscles tensed, and I knew he was right where I wanted him.

Right before he tried to pull away, I grinned, letting him see my razor-sharp teeth. He screamed as I pulled him under.

My sisters and I slept well. We always did after such an active night. Well, most of us did. Ostoma and Rezi stayed up tending to the new recruit, whom they had saved just in time. The other women had been alive enough to be brought to shore, but this new one had been unsavable. Even now, in siren form, she was only alive thanks to Ostoma's healing. I knew it would be far from an easy night for her. The first night was always the hardest, but she was in good hands. And more importantly, the other hands that had touched her were food for the sharks now.

I rested easy knowing those particular hunters would never touch anyone else ever again.

Bloody the Love

M. O'Hara

CW: blood, gore, body horror, misogyny, sexism, grief, suicidal ideation

It was in the early hours of the evening that Sylvaine knew she would not live past the night. Despite the few stars that freckled the night sky, the absence of the moon was a proper omen; there was no light left in her life. Darkness enveloped the forest in a stillness that was only broken by the trees swaying to the occasional breeze.

The whetstone glided along the witch's hunting knife with practiced strokes, sending small flakes of rust fluttering to the ground. Her bones seared with pain as she continued. She swallowed down the hurt with the rage and grief boiling at her core. Dark circles colored the pale skin beneath her amber eyes. Long brown and silver strands of hair were neatly pulled back into a braid that reached the middle of her spine. Sylvaine clenched her jaw as another hot flash of pain traveled up her arm. For a moment, the physical pain was almost comparable to the roiling turmoil within her.

For a moment.

The old woman sat back in her chair and scrutinized her handiwork. The dagger glinted dangerously in the dim light from the hearth, looking as it had when the witch had been in her prime: dreadful and frightening. She swallowed down the bitter lump that had formed in her throat at the thought of the carnage this knife had wrought decades before, the bloodshed that bathed her and the sickening euphoria that she would bask in. Despite how hard she had tried to leave that life behind, it dogged after her like a shadow. Now, it had finally showed itself to her once more, when all that surrounded her was the inescapable darkness of grief.

The crone stood with a groan as she sheathed her knife into the scabbard strapped to her thigh. The dying light of the hearth waned as the minutes burned away. She threw another log on the fire and watched as the flames roared back to life. The shadows of dangling herbs and chimes flickered along the walls with renewed energy. Her breath caught in her throat at the sight of the specter lingering in the doorway. Sylvaine felt her heart break all over again as it smiled at her. When she blinked her eyes, it was gone.

Sylvaine shuddered as a shaky breath left her. She cursed herself for allowing herself a moment of weakness. Tears were useless; they wouldn't bring her daughter back. She had failed to protect the one thing that mattered most to her.

Silence had haunted the witch's home since before the dawn when she had awoken to find her Calia still missing from her bed, the furs cold and neatly arranged over the straw mattress; she had not returned from the village the previous night like she was supposed to. Despite calling her name over and over again, Sylvaine had not found her anywhere amongst the trees.

The panic racing through her veins had become pure terror. The old woman had run as fast as her legs would carry her. The burning of her lungs and the stabbing pain in her knees had done little to slow her down. She had pressed on, gasping for air, not caring if she died soon after finding her daughter.

Calia was the only thing she could think of. Her beautiful, innocent daughter, the last remnant of a husband long since dead—the complete opposite of what Sylvaine had been when she was the same age.

Tears leaked from her eyes and trickled down her aged, wrinkled cheeks. The old witch's grief surged within her once more, opening the void that had once been her heart. She still remembered the sound of her own screams of horror that morning at the sight of her daughter, her body bound to a wooden stake, face contorted in agony as though she would let out a blood-curdling shriek, body charred black beyond any hope of recognition.

And yet, somehow she *knew*.

She hadn't known she was screaming until her throat was raw. Her legs had given out beneath her and she had fallen to her knees, barely registering the damp grass soaking through the fabric of her roughspun pants.

Gone.

Her daughter, her last reason to live, had been taken from her.

Tonight, Sylvaine would join her daughter, after avenging her death, be it by her own hand or another's.

The wind told her of the village men approaching her hut long before she heard their voices. Sylvaine felt the weight of their footfalls through the damp earth floor of her hut. She reached out to the mana that swirled around her, that lived within the forest, in every tree, every spirit that dwelled there. It answered her call immediately as though it had *longed* for this moment, for the bloodshed and violence that would undoubtedly unfold within these sacred woods.

Bright, verdant swirls of mana fluttered in the palms of her hands. She watched them for a moment, felt them hum as she held them. It had been what seemed like a lifetime since she had truly summoned her magic. Twenty years of hiding it, suppressing it and the murderous urge that came along with it. It felt like a coiled spring had snapped within her, all of the tension in her muscles and the aches in her bones leaving her body like a sigh. Yet, the old witch despised the relief that washed over her.

Sylvaine wrapped her aged fingers around the medallion that had sat idly around her neck for the past two decades. It pulsed against her skin, the dark magic within it eager to be called upon once more. The last remnant of hesitancy she possessed surged forward. Was she really going to kill again after so long?

She would have suffered for the rest of her life, endured an eternal existence of pain and agony if it had meant Calia could live a pain-free life.

And yet she had failed her daughter in the worst way possible.

The old woman blinked back the tears that threatened to spill down her face. She clenched her hands into fists, tried to ignore the burning of her lungs that felt as though they were filling up with water and she was drowning. Grief mutated into rage as she heard the collective footsteps of the village men coming toward her home. Those monsters had shown no remorse over the way they slaughtered her child. They deserved the suffering she would inflict upon them.

She looked up, amber eyes now a xanthous color as she stared at the door, slowly straightening to stand at her full height. The witch clenched her hands into fists, cracked her neck and rolled her shoulders in preparation for the impending fight. She inhaled deeply, feeling a fire of hatred now burning within her. Its heat coursed through her veins and soaked into every crevasse within her body.

No longer was she a normal woman who lived a peaceful life amongst nature—she was once again a war bringer, a harbinger for death. She would not leave this world until she had her vengeance.

The crone strode toward the door and threw it open.

A mob of thirty village men awaited her a good fifty yards from her home, torches burning brightly and weapons drawn. The witch recognized each and every man that stared back at her; fathers who came to treat their ill children, husbands who wished for a safe delivery of their unborn children, farmers who wished for a prosperous harvest season. Their eyes gleamed with murderous intent, something that the witch had no qualms reciprocating.

She took a few steps toward them, scrutinizing the crowd before her for the smallest inkling of an attack. Any reluctance she had about returning to her murderous ways left her as soon as she gazed upon them.

"She-Witch!" a voice called out from the throng. A man stepped forward, skin pale as snow with a hideous scar on his brow above a foggy right eye. It was Ferro, the right hand to the village leader. He stood before her, armed with only a sword that rested in its sheath on his hip, and wearing a set of leather armor.

Sylvaine hardened her glare at him. It took all of her self-control to not end the man's life there and then.

"We have come for your head, Bride of Death!" the man shouted. "Your reign of terror ends now! You will meet the same fate as your daughter for your practice of the dark arts of witchcraft."

The smell of charred flesh burned at her sinuses, eyes stinging from the black smoke of a dying fire. She saw Calia's corpse tied to the stake embedded in the middle of the pyre, her body contorted as it silently screamed. The blood-tinged morning light illuminated what was left of her daughter and permanently seared the image behind her eyelids.

"My quarrel is not with you!" she yelled in reply. "Bring me the men who killed my daughter, and you can all go about your lives as though nothing has happened." Her eyes landed on the village leader, hiding behind his men like the coward he was.

Ferro scoffed. "We don't negotiate with the likes of *witches*!" he sneered.

Sylvaine inhaled a shaky breath as she stared him down. Her voice sat heavy in her throat like a leaden stone. A growl was the only thing that she could coherently form. The gold of the medallion glinted in the light of the torches; the sanguine gem embedded in the middle housing the monster she had once been. It pulsed against her palm, the sensation crawling up her veins and stealing into her heart like poison. Her eyes flicked between it and the villagers.

The witch drew her hunting knife and impaled the medallion with it. The gem cracked; black wraiths of smoke seeped through the fissures that appeared. As the blood gem disintegrated into pale ash, it spilled into a pile at the old woman's feet, trickling down like sand in an hourglass,— counting down the seconds until Sylvaine had changed completely.

The old woman's legs shook as she fought to remain standing. The black wisps of magic formed a violently swirling vortex around her. Her screams were drowned out by the ferocity of the winds that tore through the forest. The brown and silver locks of her braid were blotted out by an inky darkness spreading from root to tip. A scarlet tinge bled into the xanthous color of her eyes, forming thin rings around her pupils.

Sylvaine gasped for breath as the gale died down around her. Her chest ached as the power she had kept sealed away for so long flooded her heart once more, bending her and corrupting her from the inside out. A wicked smile spread across her lips as she looked up.

She found a sickening sense of amusement in watching them cower away from her, tripping over their feet. "Well," the old witch finally said. "You wanted to see the Bride of Death, did you not?" She began approaching the mob with slow, measured footsteps. "You wanted to be the ones to slay me, yes?" The old witch stopped and raised her arm, hand reaching out to the side. A sanguine cloud of fog appeared from her hand, extending outward as a long, black blade materialized in her grip.

"What are you waiting for?" the Bride of Death asked with a villainous laugh. "I'm right here."

A chilling silence loomed over the forest. The wind carried the panicked whispers of the villagers as they beheld her, frozen with fear. Sylvaine's eyes scanned the crowd as she waited for the mob of pathetic fighters, worms writhing helplessly in the dirt at her indulgence, to advance. Her eyes darted to one of the men along the outskirts of the horde as he notched an arrow.

The old woman's blade sliced through the air in an upward arc as the arrow was loosed. It cut through the flimsy projectile, splintering it into tiny pieces of wood in front of the witch's face. A blistering ache consumed her bones as she moved, her body now a blur. The nearest villager had her blade in his neck before he had the opportunity to scream. Sylvaine ripped her sword out of the dead man's throat. His hot blood sprayed her chilled skin; it splattered the horrified faces of those who stood too close to him. Another was dead before they hit the ground as their head tumbled from their shoulders.

Blood-curdling screams of terror rang in the witch's ears. The coppery tang of blood on her lips twisted her insides. The monster she had once been had risen from its slumber. She found herself enjoying this despite knowing she shouldn't, but the pacifist she had been for over two decades had died with her daughter.

The entirety of the world could stand before her, and she would inflict every agony imaginable upon any fool who dared to get in her way, pile body upon body until the mound reached the heavens and slaughter them all until her vengeance was complete. She would not rest until they knew the absolute misery and despair she did. Every man, woman, and child would beg for the mercy they had failed show her daughter.

They would all know the absolute suffering and horror the Bride of Death was truly capable of.

Sylvaine turned just in time as an old, rusty pitchfork was jabbed at her head. It was a young man, a father whose first son had just been born the previous spring. The old woman snarled when the villager yanked on the weapon, trying to pull it free from her braid. An arm wrapped around her neck as another hand grabbed at the sword she was holding. The witch cursed as the sword tumbled from her grasp. A scream tore from her throat as the boy ripped the pitchfork out of her hair.

"I've got 'er!" the second man yelled in her ear. She felt his breath fan against her face, stale with rot and beer.

A hideous grin spread on the first man's mouth as he readied himself to strike again, this time aiming at the old woman's heart. A black blur appeared behind him an instant before Sylvaine's sword pierced through the man's jaw.

The second villager that had been holding the witch screamed as he stumbled backward. Sylvaine grunted as she fell onto her sword arm. A searing, hot pain traveled up the limb as she collided with the ground.

Blood sputtered out of the first man's mouth as the lower half of his jaw fell to the ground. A grotesque gurgling sound muffled his screams as he clutched his head in torment. The other villagers backed away in horror, leaving a wide space between themselves and the dying man.

Sylvaine laughed quietly as she rose to her feet. The dying man looked up at her from his bloodstained hands, trembling. He lunged at her, his blood gurgling as he tried to scream. She sidestepped him with ease. The man fell as he tripped over the witch's extended foot and was sent tumbling downward.

She watched as the body fell near a large oak tree with long vines of ivy embedded into its wooden trunk. An abandoned torch from one of the mob illuminated the base of the tree and the tendrils of liana that were gathered there. The old woman glanced back at the sword as it continued to slice and cleave its way through the throng of villagers, unbidden. She looked back to the tangle of vines at the foot of the tree. The haze of hatred in her mind faded away for a moment as she recognized the old, abandoned play sword that had been consumed by the ivy's ravenous growth.

The witch stared at the wooden toy, feeling her grief rip out more of her insides the longer she looked at it. Calia had lost that sword over a decade ago, her most prized possession for quite a few seasons until it had gone missing one day at the height of the summer of her thirteenth year. They had spent the entirety of the following morning searching for it, only to come up empty-handed. Calia had been inconsolable for days afterward; it had been the last gift she had received from her late father.

"Mama, look!" A seven-year-old Calia appeared in her mind's eye. The late morning was sunny even as clouds rolled overhead and began to blot out the sun. High above, the birds sang; butterflies fluttered near the hut and sucked on the nectar of the flowers. The child grinned up at her mother as she proudly dangled her prize "I killed a worm!"

"Calia!" the woman snapped as she smacked the young girl's hand. "What did I say about killing things?"

"But it's gross!" the child whined. "Why do we even need worms when all they do is hide underground?" Her honey-colored eyes wavered with tears. Sylvaine sighed as her daughter began to cry.

"How would you feel if someone tried to kill you because they thought you were 'gross'?" Calia's mother asked.

Her daughter looked down, averting her eyes to look at the grass between her boots. "Sorry," she mumbled.

Sylvaine kneeled down so she was at the child's height. "Calia," she said soothingly. "Look at me, please." The girl slowly lifted her head to look at her mother. She wiped at her nose as a sniffle escaped her. "All life is sacred and serves a purpose," the woman continued. "We cannot simply kill what we find grotesque or inconvenient. There are consequences to such careless behavior. That worm you killed would have been food for a bird or its hatchlings, and now they may starve and not survive because of what you have done. In turn, other creatures who rely on the bird to survive may not. Do you understand?"

The girl nodded as she swallowed. She flinched as her mother raised a hand and wiped at the tears on her face. The witch smiled softly; she stood and placed a kiss on top of the girl's head. "Very good. Now, come along. We have much to get done today..."

In the blink of an eye, the witch's daughter disappeared from her sight. Sylvaine turned her head at the sound of a hoarse yell. The blade she commanded floated in the air in front of one of the village men, now in the shape of a large, wooden play sword. The man stumbled over one of the corpses as it approached him, crawling backward along the ground. "Please!" he screamed. "Please don't do this!"

"There are consequences to such careless behavior," a nobler version of her had said time and time again, one that had chosen life, peace, and to live the rest of her days with her daughter in the forest. The nearest village was almost an entire day's worth of travel away and the two of them could live out their lives together in peace.

But Calia was gone, stolen away from her by feeble and weak-willed men. There would be no peace so long as Calia's killers continued to walk amongst the living.

The toy sword morphed back into its original shape and impaled the man through his skull with a sickening crunch. Bits of brain matter and bone flew from his head as the blade wrenched itself free. The witch reached out to her side, summoning the sword back to her. She watched as the sword decapitated another one of the villagers before returning. Sylvaine bit back a cry of pain as it flew into her grasp. She gripped the pommel of the sword, a fiendish grin spreading wide across her face.

There were eighteen of them left. Twelve corpses lay on the forest floor, blood soaking into the ground. The Bride of Death's eyes trailed over the remaining villagers as they trembled before her. Her breathing grew harder as the adrenaline faded from her veins.

The old witch swallowed a curse from the pain. She chuckled when none of the cowards dared to approach her. Her gaze fell on the leader of the horde, standing on the outer fringes of what remained of the mob. A twisted glee took hold of her and warmed her insides, hastened the beating of her heart for a moment. "Afraid, are you?" she asked, voice slightly strained.

A strong wind blew through the trees, sighing as it passed through the branches overhead. She felt the tie she had to the land persist despite the weakness she felt as her body betrayed her. "Well?" she called again in a louder voice. "Are you afraid of an old hag skinning you alive? Feeding you to the flames the way you did my daughter?"

The village leader pushed his way through the crowd and snatched a bow out of one of the men's hands. He fumbled as he grabbed an arrow and lit the tip of it from another man's torch. He notched it with a slight tremble as he aimed it at Sylvaine.

The old woman darted for the ground, rolling out of the way as the arrow shot through the air. Her lungs singed as she struggled to regain her breath. She turned to look over her shoulder where the arrow had embedded itself. The witch's anger subsided momentarily as she watched the fire quickly spread from the doorway of her hut to its walls, eating away at the wood as though it were a ravenous beast.

The home she had shared with her daughter for two decades was now lost. All of her daughter's things, the strands of hair that had been caught in her brush, her favorite clothes, the scent of her, everything she had ever touched; the one place that had been a sanctuary for the both of them—gone. Stolen away from her.

All the rage, every ounce of fury and grief that she possessed roared to life in a monstrous inferno within her. More of the red tint in her irises crept over the original xanthous coloring. The witch growled out a shuddering breath.

There would be no mercy.

Sylvaine raised an old, withered hand in front of herself. Thorny vines shot out from amongst the trees and wrapped around one of the villagers. The man screamed as the bindings violently pulled him backward and pinned him to the trunk of a tree. More of the briar wound itself around his body, burrowing its way into his eyes. Another yell was cut off as a thicker barbed tendril climbed down his throat. More vines darted out from the darkness of the forest. Two more of the men were caught in their snares and met the same fate.

Large tree roots shot up from behind the mob and pierced through the bodies of five of the remaining villagers. Their panicked cries for help abruptly ended as the roots dragged them beneath the forest floor, the ground consuming them. More vines descended from the treetops and seized three of them by their throats. Their necks audibly snapped as the lianas strung them up from the boughs above.

The witch turned her glare toward several of the remaining villagers as they threw their weapons and turned to escape. Scarlet devoured the remaining amber of the witch's eyes. She raised her arm in their direction. Her hand closed into a fist as she yanked her arm back toward her chest. More briars erupted from amongst the trees, racing along the ground.

The thorny vines twisted around their legs and abdomens, the bramble tearing through cloth and flesh as they quickly pulled backward, dragging the fleeing men deeper into the woods. Howling cries of torment and anguish echoed into the night as their bodies were ripped apart by the tendrils.

The Bride of Death's body pulsed as waves of pain constricted her bones and tore at her muscles. The glow of the flickering flames devouring her house behind her cast long shadows along the ground and deep into the thicket surrounding her. She felt the tongues of heat against her back. Her vision blurred as vertigo washed over her. Smoke drifted on the wind and burned the inside of her lungs. Sylvaine's chest racked as a coughing fit overtook her.

Despite the persisting rage within her, the witch's strength seeped from her body as the seconds ticked by, stretching out into days, months, years. Her heart pulsed in her head. Blood rushed in her ears. Smog filled her veins with its poison.

Sylvaine cursed her traitorous body. There were only four of them left. She should have killed them all by now, yet the sword in her hand steadily grew heavier, her grip on the pommel grew slack. She would have succumbed to her fatigue long ago were it not for her roiling fury.

Her ears twitched at the muffled sound of hurried footfalls. She looked up to see one of the remaining villagers charging toward her, sword raised in the air, poised to strike. She darted out of the way, slower now. The blade struck the earth where she had been standing a moment before. Another strike quickly followed as the sword arced through the air. The woman dodged again, out of breath. The edge of the sword grazed her cheek and left a cut in its wake.

The witch was ready this time when the man lunged at her a third time with a stabbing motion. She sidestepped him with ease and grabbed the man's face. He froze. His face gave way to horror as the Bride of Death's hand began to grow hot.

A ball of flame consumed the man's head and ate away at his flesh. Sylvaine released her grip on him as he panicked and flailed, desperate to put the fire out. His movements slowed as he toppled to the ground and died.

Another one of the men charged toward her flank with a scythe raised. He swung downward, prepared to take the Bride of Death's head off in one clean strike. She blocked the attack with her blade and shifted out of the way. Her attacker stumbled over his feet, giving her the perfect opening. The old woman raised her blade over her head and swung down with all her strength, severing the man's torso from the rest of his body.

Fatigue swept through her body once more, this time more powerfully. The crone's vision swam as white stars blinked in and left iridescent exposures behind. She bit the inside of her cheek as she forced herself to remain focused. The coppery taste of blood in her mouth helped sober her mind; it grounded her again.

Her eyes flicked up to the two remaining men from the village—Ferro and a taller man standing beside him with a strong build and a beard. He wore a set of leather armor similar to Ferro's with his shoulder-length hair tied back.

Hanniel, the village leader.

The one who had ordered her daughter to be killed.

Her throat burned as another breath left her. Several trees had now been claimed by the blaze, which continued to grow closer.

She felt the rage and suffering of the land roil within her, merging with her own. Her fury had scratched beneath her skin, shrieked ferociously in her head for more death. Images of Calia playing amongst the woods throughout the years as she grew flashed before her. Sylvaine could hear Calia's laughter, see the way the sunlight shimmered in her daughter's golden eyes, and feel their hands grasped together as they walked hand in hand back to their home.

Hot tears trickled out of the witch's eyes as she glowered at them. She straightened her stance, readied herself. Her legs buckled beneath her as she took a step. The witch fell onto her knees, wheezing.

"I'll handle this," Ferro spoke with a grunt. He walked toward the old woman at a leisurely pace. The man stopped in front of her, the corner of his mouth twisting up into a smirk as he raised his blade overhead, preparing to strike.

The old witch was on her feet in the next instant. Her sword parried the strike as Ferro brought his broadsword down. His eyes went wide as her blade bore through his throat. Blood trickled out of his mouth and dribbled down his chin. The woman tore her weapon out forcefully. He clutched at his neck as he fell to the ground, dying.

She coughed as more smoke seeped into her lungs and constricted her throat. The smog wafted through the air, the breeze spreading the fire around her. Hanniel blurred in and out of existence as the blaze raged on.

A crossbow bolt whistled through the air as it flew directly toward her. Her arm felt sluggish and heavy as she deflected it with the front of her blade. A strained breath left her from the exertion. The witch bit back a cry of pain as a second crossbow bolt pierced her waist, one that she hadn't seen coming until it was too late. She stumbled backward, fighting to stay standing as the pain made tears prick at her eyes.

Sylvaine planted her sword into the ground and braced her weight against it. Hot, red blood leaked from the wound in her side and between her fingers as she tried to staunch the bleeding. Her entire body was throbbing with anguish. The witch looked up to see Hanniel standing there, grinning like a mad dog. He lowered the crossbow.

"I'm going to take great pleasure in putting you down, She-Witch!" he yelled, grabbing a bolt from the satchel at his side and loading it into the flight groove.

The crone leered at him. She fought with the last ounces of remaining strength she possessed to take one step forward, and then another. The grin from the village leader's face fell as she slowly drew closer. "What are you doing?" he asked, now frightened.

Sylvaine raised her free hand and stretched it out in front of her as she staggered toward him. Thorny vines slithered out of the undergrowth and wrapped around Hanniel's arms, legs and neck. As she lowered her arm, they brought the man down to his knees. The crossbow fell to the ground beside him.

The witch reached down and picked the weapon up, inspecting it for a moment before she looked back at the village leader. "Please!" the man began to beg. "Please! I'll give you anything you want! I'll make sure no one ever bothers you again. Just—just let me go!"

The crone aimed the crossbow at Hanniel's crotch. He glanced down for a moment, another plea on his tongue when she pulled the trigger and fired the bolt. The man screamed at the top of his lungs. Blood gushed from where the dart had struck.

"PLEASE!" he cried out desperately. "I have children, a wife! Let me go, I beg of you!"

Her face contorted in disgust. A pathetic whimper left him as he moaned in insufferable pain. She forced herself to keep moving, to let her anger keep her alive and conscious despite the vertigo that threatened to force her back on the ground. She ripped out the quarrel and staggered for a moment before stabbing him in the gut with it.

He screamed again, louder this time.

"You dare grovel before me, begging me to spare you for the sake of your children?" the Bride of Death inquired with a hoarse voice. "You *dare* beg me to show you mercy after all you've done?"

Hanniel whimpered, now sobbing. "Please, Sylvaine! I'll give you anything you want! Just let me go..."

She bent to look at him, her sanguine eyes meeting his hazel-green. Sylvaine rightened herself and stared at him for a long, silent moment. The taste of burning wood and foliage sat heavy on her tongue. The heat from the flames surrounding them drew closer. Her head swam from the warmth seeping into her weakening body.

The witch grabbed Hanniel's head and yanked it back. A choked sound escaped him as the thorns constricted his throat and tightened around his limbs. "I want to watch you beg for your life as I take it away from you like you did to my daughter, you piece of shit."

The Bride of Death grabbed his face abruptly and forced a blood-red ball of light into his mouth. When she pulled her hand away, Hanniel's mouth had disappeared entirely. His face moved as though he were trying to speak, but no words left him. The red light pulsed beneath his flesh as it swelled in size. His body moved in a frenzy as he tried to free himself from the lianas, screams muffled behind his sealed mouth.

The witch closed her eyes as Hanniel's head violently detonated, leaving a crater where his skull and neck had once been. The vines retracted and the body fell over silently, blood squirting from the corpse. She stared at the dead man for a moment before she looked down at her wound.

A gasp of pain left her as she tore the bolt out of her side. It slipped from her weakening grasp. Pain overrode her senses, clouded her mind.

She was dying.

Sylvaine tumbled to her knees as she clutched at the wound with bloody and battered hands. She felt the life slowly draining from her body with each passing second, each drop of blood that slipped between her fingers. The searing pain burned her from within as the chill of the morning breeze passed by her. She looked around the dying forest at the bodies that lay on the ground. Smoke and embers burned at her lungs, made tears swell in her eyes.

Dawn crested the treetops as its golden light rose from its slumber. Her eyes stung from its brilliance. She shot out an arm to brace herself from falling to the ground. She cried out as another shockwave of pain vibrated through her bones from the impact.

The blood-colored tinge in her eyes withered away; the jet ink that had colored her hair gave way to the brown and silver locks that had been there before. Sylvaine gasped for more air, only for more smoke to force its way down her throat, and into her chest, strangling her heart from lack of breath.

She was really going to die, she finally realized. The thought startled her, made her want to cling to what little life was left in her and hold it with her trembling hands.

The old woman blinked, unable to make the blur in her vision go away. A familiar shape stepped into view in front of her. Its footfalls were soft as it approached her. A blurry hand extended out toward her.

"Calia," the name fell from her lips before she could stop herself. Tears raced down her cheeks when she blinked. Perhaps the blood loss was making her see things, perhaps what stood before her was simply the imagining of a dying old woman. Sylvaine couldn't bring herself to care either way; her daughter's beautiful face smiled back at her—that was enough to ease the aching in her bones and the agony in her heart.

The old witch's eyes fluttered as her consciousness at last began to fade. Far away, the songs of birds rose as the morning sun climbed higher into the sky. Her dying breath left her like a sigh as she finally let herself fall to the ground. A sobering moment of clarity returned to her vision. The last thing she saw before her eyes glazed over was her daughter smiling down at her, mouthing the words "thank you."

Cursed is the Man Who Dies

T.M. Ledvina

CW: kidnapping, imprisonment

Her heart beat in time to each of his steps as he stalked between buildings, hands fisted in his pockets. This was her element. To her, there was nothing better than the hunt; the gleeful flutter in her belly was impossible to replicate any other way.

She would meet him face to face soon; a clash of hunter versus hunter. His messages on the dating app told her enough about how he saw her—a plaything, nothing more—but she would prove him wrong before the end of the night.

The black satin dress fell gracefully down her legs as she stepped from her car. She shook her hair free and checked her lipstick one more time in a compact. The silver chain around her neck glittered in the streetlight where it fell below the neckline of her dress. Her lips spread into a thin smile.

Two hours later, she lured him back to her house with promises of things that all men love. He was easy to manipulate, as most men were when they saw her. She knew her appearance was her greatest weapon. She only had to gloss her lips and curl her hair for men to eat from her palm.

It was effortless. As easy as they believed her to be.

She knew what darkness lurked in his heart; it was why she'd chosen him as her next quarry. She'd watched the stories about his work on the news. The reports of the women he'd dumped unceremoniously in the fields outside of town. Women treated with no respect, and violated in ways that made her blood boil.

Her vengeance burned white-hot. He would pay for the things he'd done; she would enjoy his screams.

He put a hand on her thigh as they drove to her house. The satin of her dress was slippery against her leg, and the heat of his hand sent a chill up her spine. Anticipation was a flutter in her belly; it had very little to do with his touch.

"Would you be willing," she started, a sultry timbre to her voice, "to do something a little...different tonight?"

His hand tightened on her leg. A good sign. "Anything you want." His voice matched hers, that calculated sensuality she had perfected over her many years of hunting. His was as sophisticated as hers.

And when they arrived, he pulled her into an embrace the moment the door shut behind them. She allowed it; it was all part of the hunt, after all. He was practiced and efficient, a trick she was sure he'd honed to perfection. It was a tool, just as beauty was hers.

She entranced him, that much she could tell. So, when it was time to tug him by the collar and lead him to her basement, he followed easily.

He obeyed her every command. He closed the door behind them, sat in the chair, and let her handcuff him. His eyes followed her around the room as she prepared. She was like a spider weaving her web; he was caught in her trap.

She smiled, her teeth bared—she was ready.

She rolled her head, her neck popping with the movement.

He tracked her with his eyes, following the curve of her neck, the slope of her shoulders, the cut of her dress as it hugged her figure. The skin beneath was flush, dotted with freckles from long days spent in the sun. She knew what men like him wanted; a visual feast is what she'd serve.

Her smile was poisonous as she watched him watch her. "You're being awfully quiet, you know."

He shuddered . . . unwilling to answer, unable to run.

"Oh, come now,"—she pouted, walking towards him with a sultry swish of her hips—"you liked me plenty before this. Why so quiet?"

She approached him then, her dress flowing around her legs as she stopped. She crouched before him and grasped his face in her hand, her long, bloodred nails digging into his cheeks. He wouldn't get away with his silence.

"Am I no longer beautiful?"

He stared into her eyes, his jaw tight. A strand of flaxen hair fell in her face as she stared back, waiting.

He seemed compelled to answer her—finally. "Why?"

She huffed, releasing his face to stand once more. "A taste of your own medicine, perhaps? You're no longer the hunter."

"I'm nothing to you."

She laughed, bitterly. "Oh, how wrong you are. The moment you laid your hands on a woman, you were mine."

She ran her fingers through his hair, scratching against his scalp, then she gripped his hair and yanked his head backward. His eyes gleamed with a cool consideration of her face as she hovered above him. How dare he look so unconcerned while she was holding him hostage.

His throat bobbed. "You believe yourself more righteous than me, then?"

Ice encrusted her veins. She didn't *think* herself better—she *was* better. She wasn't the one who tore innocent women from their families, tortured them, did unspeakable things to them. She wasn't like him. She was a hero. She was the savior of all his future victims; the virtuous revenge for all the girls of his past.

He was nothing but scum.

He didn't deserve her rage in words. He deserved to feel the pain so many women had felt at his hands. She would oblige the universe asking for retribution.

She turned away from him, flipping her hair over her shoulder and pausing with her back turned. Let him think he had a moment without her gaze upon him. Let him relax. He didn't know what she'd done; if he did, he'd be terrified. Just like the others had when she'd let them in on her little secret, her favorite method of destruction.

She sauntered to the other side of the room and draped herself over a plush armchair that faced the center of the room. The slit of her dress fell open high on her thigh, a calculated move. Get his blood pumping.

He watched her, confusion leaching into his gaze. He was waiting for her to make her move. Little did he know she already had.

She hummed under her breath, a tune she'd heard long ago and always sang to herself in moments like this; ones of unbridled joy, of unfettered happiness. She breathed heavily, the rise and fall of her chest forcing the already misplaced strap of her dress to fall further. When she finally turned her head to look at him, she could see the poison was already beginning its work.

He was paler, beads of sweat forming on his forehead. "What," he began, panting, "have you done to me?"

She shook out her curls. Let him sweat a little longer. "Your body is reacting to me."

Her hair nearly reached the floor as she stretched back over the arm of her chair. Her dress was dangerously low on her chest. He could barely focus on the movement, but he tried. *Disgusting*.

"That's not what this is," he said. His voice was breathy. "What have you done?"

She smiled sweetly at him and reached into the bosom of her dress to reveal a small bottle attached to the silver chain around her neck. It was empty now, but it hadn't been earlier that night. "You couldn't have known; after all, you've never tasted the poison you give the girls you hunt, have you?"

His eyes widened. "But—"

She cut him off with a scoff. "'It's not lethal,'" she replied in a mocking tone. "In the dose you give, sure. In the dose I gave you?" She laughed.

He struggled, then. Pulling against the cuffs she'd locked around his wrists and attached with zip ties to the chair. She didn't move—she knew he couldn't get out of this, not with the poison in his veins weakening him with every passing beat of his heart.

She chuckled again. "Too late, I'm afraid." She tossed her dress back over her legs and replaced the strap with a cold detachment. His blood had raced enough this evening; he didn't deserve to see her like this in his last moments.

Standing from her throne, she tossed him a cheeky wave over her shoulder. He would die alone, just like every girl he'd killed. He'd die alone, in the dark, with fear boiling in his gut and fire running through his veins. He'd die choking, scrambling for a breath that would burn his throat.

The heavy metal door did not creak when she unlocked it and opened it slowly. She flipped the light switch, plunging the room into deep, unyielding darkness. And just before the door closed, she could hear him utter one pathetic scream.

Five Rules for the Dutiful Housewife

N. M. Lambert

CW: mentions of marital rape, mentions of slavery, sexual assault, spousal abuse, misogyny

"Congratulations on your wedding!" The strange woman stood just inches from Anna Wadelton's face. Spittle flew from her red-tinted lips as she over-enunciated each word, the droplets fanning out to land on Anna's rosy pink cheeks. A huge smile was plastered on as she extended her arm forward, a single gold-encrusted envelope clutched in her perfect French-manicured nails. "May you have many happy years with your new husband."

Anna's gaze strayed to the strange envelope the woman was holding as she reached to wipe the spittle away with the back of her hand. A strange energy pulsed from it, and she shuddered. *Who is this woman?*

She didn't know. She didn't recognize her, not even from her husband's side of the family, but her mere presence was starting to make Anna uncomfortable. *A friend perhaps?*

"Um, thanks." She gulped, the woman's uncanny gaze practically boring a hole through her soul. "If you don't mind, I'd like to find my husband before—"

"Oh, but you can't!" The woman cut in front of her, preventing her escape. "Not until you receive my gift!" She waved the envelope in front of Anna's face as if she were presenting some grand prize.

Hesitantly, Anna reached out, and the woman placed the envelope into the palm of her hand. The energy practically seared itself into Anna's flesh, and she fought the urge to fling it onto the ground below.

"Read that as soon as possible. Its contents are super important!" the woman instructed, her eyes softening as something akin to pity replaced her otherwise flamboyant expression. "Best of luck in your marriage." And with that, she turned on her heels and vanished into the night.

Anna never saw the woman again after that day, but in the days that followed, she thought about her a lot. The rest of the wedding had carried on as normal, and after it was over, her new husband, Darryl, took her home and worshipped her in all the ways she could imagine. And on their honeymoon to Hawaii, he showered her with affection and lavished her some more.

She forgot all about the strange woman and the pulsating envelope.

Until they had returned to Darryl's place and she laid eyes on it for the first time in over a week, where it had collected dust in her nightstand, and curiosity finally got the best of her. Darryl was in the living room watching some football game, and she was in the bedroom with the envelope in her lap, a single fingernail poised at the seam. The thrill of what could be contained inside sent a chill down her spine, and without further hesitation, she tore into the seam, ripping the thin paper to shreds to reach the contents within.

But suddenly, something in the air shifted. The temperature plummeted around her. A sense of dread and foreboding surrounded her, nearly stealing her breath. Her eyebrows furrowed in confusion when the rest of the envelope fell away, leaving behind a folded piece of paper with a single title etched in gold:

FIVE RULES FOR THE DUTIFUL HOUSEWIFE.

Anna wanted to throw up right then and there. She could feel the click in her mind as some sort of presence latched onto her, and she unfolded the note, suddenly wishing she had burned the envelope and never opened it to begin with. *What kind of hell have I gotten myself into?* Because as the unnatural presence grew in strength, it became apparent she was now a slave to it, a slave to her husband, forced to obey the rules she held in front of her for all eternity.

No longer human.

Now an emotionless robot.

RULE #1: MAKE YOURSELF PRESENTABLE.

Take a moment to rest before your husband arrives. Touch up your makeup, and make sure your hair is flawless and your clothes are wrinkle-free. Your husband has just spent the day with a bunch of tired-looking people at work, and the least you can do is make sure you bring the energy he needs to get through the rest of his day.

RULE #2: DO NOT COMPLAIN TO YOUR HUSBAND.

Remember, your husband is the man of the house. He has had a long and tiring day, and anything you are going through is minor compared to what he has gone through. He can come and go as he pleases. If he is late, that is his right. If he doesn't come home at all, that is also his right. He works hard to make sure you have a roof over your head and food on the table, so be grateful for all he gives you.

RULE #3: MAKE SURE THE HOUSE IS CLEAN.

Make one last trip through the house to make sure it is tidy, orderly, and presentable. Make sure everything is in its correct place and that everything is clean and dust-free. Your husband has just been at work all day and deserves to come home to a house that is free of germs and debris. Doing this shows that you care about him and respect and honor him.

RULE #4: MAKE SURE YOUR HUSBAND IS COMFORTABLE.

Remember, he has been working hard all day, and this is his time to relax and unwind. Allow him to lean back in a comfortable chair or lie down for a few minutes in the bedroom. Offer to take off his shoes or perhaps give him a massage. Anything he asks for, you should provide for him without question.

RULE #5: HAVE DINNER READY.

Make sure you have a hot, delicious meal ready on time. This is perhaps the most important rule. Your husband will be hungry when he comes home, and this will show you are attentive to his needs and even consider them a high priority.

Anna's heart was in her throat with each rule she read, that now-familiar sense of dread growing with each word. *Is this a joke?* She shook her head, disbelieving. *This has to be a joke, right? No way this is real...*

But Anna knew she was fooling herself. Because as she glanced up from the letter, she noticed her new husband standing in the doorway to her bedroom. His lips pulled back in a sinister smile as he regarded her, causing a chill to skirt down her spine. Then, wordlessly, he turned his back to her and returned to his game as the temperature continued to drop around her.

And that was when she knew. The rules were not a sick joke. They were real, and she would be forced to obey them for the entire duration of her marriage.

Anna learned the best way to abide by *Rule #1* was through natural tones. Pink blushes, neutral eyeshadows, eyeliners, mascaras, and more natural-looking lipsticks. She always made sure to curl her strawberry-blonde hair and put it up in a neat bun, since that was the style her husband liked best. And slowly, her wardrobe transformed into nothing but pretty dresses, as if she were a doll because her husband willed it so.

Anna also smiled constantly, making sure her teeth were always on display, because pretty girls were always supposed to smile. Darryl made sure to let her know of this constantly whenever he caught another expression on her face. And each time she did so, a part of her died inside as she slowly became a shell of her former self. She was nothing but a mere vessel, existing purely for his amusement.

Anna had never once tried to break *Rule #2*. Darryl had never felt like a safe person to vent to, so she always kept her mouth shut whenever she stubbed a toe trying to vacuum or when she accidentally ripped one of very expensive dresses Darryl had bought for her, nearly causing her to spiral into a panic attack of not being presentable enough. It was always about Darryl's problems and Darryl's complaints about his job, and she listened attentively as he spilled what had been going on at work. Because it was always supposed to be about him and never about her.

Just like how the rules said.

As the days blended into the next, Anna cleaned like there was no tomorrow. She made sure everything had a place, and every time there was a speck of dust, she would tirelessly clean the area until she was satisfied it had been eliminated. She learned *Rule #3* early on when she'd forgotten to dust a particularly favored bookcase in the big bedroom, and her husband lost it. Any sort of uncleanliness would not be tolerated.

"What are you, stupid?" he demanded as he loomed over her, undoing his belt for the first time.

"No, please!" she pleaded. "It was an accident! I cleaned everything else! I just forgot! I—" But he wasn't listening.

Because he didn't care.

In his mind, she had screwed up and deserved to be punished.

And punished, she had been. She blacked out. He beat her so badly that blood had crusted over her wounds by the time the morning came and she had an extremely hard time completing all her tasks. Not that that mattered to him because he still expected her to do everything.

She never got a chance to rest.

Rule #4 was Anna's least favorite rule, in part because it required so much effort. She always offered to take off her husband's coat and shoes before he ate so he would be more comfortable, and after dinner was over and the dishes were cleared away and clean, he would go to his favorite chair and sit in front of the TV for the rest of the night. Sometimes, he would require her to give him a foot massage, and other times, it would be a shoulder massage. Those were the easier times because though uncomfortable, they meant she could still keep some semblance of her dignity.

But sometimes, he would pull down his pants and boxers and request—"request"—a hand job or a blow job because of how stressful work had been and he needed sexual relief.

And sometimes, he would pester her for sex even if she wasn't feeling up to it because, again, that was a part of his relaxation. And rarely did she feel up to sex anymore, not since that fateful day a few years ago when she'd read through the rules for the first time. Like *Rule*

#4 stated, it was all about his needs, not hers. And she needed to be able to deliver to be the most perfect housewife, even if she had to fake her orgasms so he could get his much-needed ego boost.

Anna had gotten particularly good at *Rule #5* over the years, preparing each meal with ease. And Darryl nodded his approval, making little moaning sounds with each bite as he savored the flavors of a well-prepared dinner. She had learned very quickly what he liked and what he didn't because whenever she cooked something that wasn't to his liking, he would unleash hell on her until she was left a broken and battered mess. Until she apologized and promised she would do better, that she didn't mean to displease him, that she was just trying to be a good wife.

She could still feel the phantom burns on her skin from when he upended the first meal she had ever cooked for him, a typical spaghetti dinner. Some of the noodles were undercooked, which sent him into a flying rage as he launched the piping-hot meal at her head. And she remembered screaming in pain as the noodles and sauce coated her, leaving behind red, angry marks as her skin blistered from the heat. She had many burns—since Darryl's default had always been to scar her with what he deemed imperfect food—which she had gotten very good at covering up with makeup.

Anna had learned to play the dutiful wife so, *so* well. She had perfected the rules and did everything her husband asked. But there was only so much abuse and suffering a human being could take, and after almost five years of this, Anna was tired of keeping up appearances all the time, of being trapped in a loveless marriage where she was made to feel less than human.

But more than that, she was tired of Darryl, constantly wearing her down until she had become a shell of her former self.

Anna was tired, so damn *tired*, of attending to her husband's needs while her own took a backseat. And she knew the rules were to blame for it. Not a day had gone by where she hadn't felt the weight of them in her mind, on her body, and in the judgment of Darryl's gaze. That strange woman with the strange envelope and the even stranger presence had trapped her in this life, and with her husband as well, to twist him into the monster he had become.

It didn't matter anyway.

Because there was no escape.
Unless...

When her husband was at work one day, Anna went online. Bought the arsenic powder on a card she knew her husband didn't check regularly. Then, she waited the five or so business days until delivery, placing the powder next to the ingredients she would be using for dinner on a day that just so happened to be their wedding anniversary. Not that it mattered anyway, because Darryl never did anything for it, didn't even acknowledge it. But Anna kept tabs on it because that was the only way she was able to gauge how much time had passed since she had lost her freedom.

The container Anna had bought contained way more than the lethal dose required to kill Darryl, but she didn't care. She planned to use every ounce of poison as she prepared his pot roast. It was what he deserved after the hell he put her through. Thinking about what she had in store brought a smile to her lips, an almost childlike reverie that she hadn't felt in years.

It had been so long since she smiled, genuinely smiled, that she forgot what it felt like. Her smiles before had all been fake, devoid of any real feeling. An act. They had all been a part of keeping up appearances, to make sure her husband was happy all the damn time. But now, she no longer had to pretend. For the first time in years, true happiness and excitement flooded her veins, mixing with the rage that burned in her soul.

Anna got to work chopping up the vegetables, boiling the potatoes, and cooking the beef to a perfect medium-rare—just the way Darryl liked. As she worked, she softly hummed a tune her mother used to sing to her to help her fall asleep. It was a soothing melody that used to comfort her whenever she heard it, but now? It symbolized something else. A new beginning, as if she were finally waking up after years of hibernation.

And once she was done, Anna plated two heaping portions of pot roast, adding the final ingredient to Darryl's portion before disposing of the bottle in the nearest trash can. Then, she brought both plates over to the table and set them down just as her husband marched through the door, looking completely haggard with fresh bags under his eyes. Normally, Anna would be worried because a bad mood from him often resulted in a split lip for her. But today, she couldn't care less. Because she knew he wouldn't be able to hurt her.

Never again would she live in fear from one of his shit moods.

Anna greeted him, plastering that fake smile he loved on her lips. "Hello, my wonderful husband. It's so nice to see you! How was work?"

Darryl barely spared her a glance as he made his way over to the table. "Stressful. Vincent is riding my ass again. Reports are due by the end of the month, and if we don't get them in, he'll have all our hides."

Anna forced her smile to falter to keep up appearances as the worried, overworked wife. Darryl had talked about his boss a few times, and each time, it was something negative. "I'm sorry to hear that. Here, let me take off your coat and get that chair for you. Is there anything else you need? Can I take off your shoes so you're more comfortable while you eat?" She was perhaps overdoing it, but if Darryl suspected something was amiss, he didn't show it.

Darryl grunted, wordlessly extending his arms out so she could make good on her promises. Anna moved to do just that, first removing his coat, then pulling his chair out so he could sit. Then, she slowly pulled off each shoe and set them by the front door before returning for the coat and placing it on the same damn coat rack she utilized every day. But not anymore. All she had to do was make it through dinner, and she would never have to use that coat rack again.

Darryl turned to his meal and inhaled deeply. Picked up his fork so he could take a small bite, his shoulders dropping as a moan traveled up his throat.

Anna took her seat across from him. Picked up her own fork and took a huge bite. The flavor of the pot roast practically exploded on her tongue, and she moaned in pleasure. Darryl continued to eat, his face practically melting as the flavors assailed his tongue as well.

Anna, you've really outdone yourself this time.

Of course, it didn't take long until the poison started flaring up. It started with a slight tick in Darryl's jaw. Immediately, she feigned concern. "What's wrong? Is the meal not to your liking?"

Darryl shook his head. "Nothing. It tastes like it's supposed to...I just feel kind of—urgh!" Clutching his stomach, his face contorted in pain as sweat began pouring off him in waves. His lips pulled back as his muscles spasmed, and soon, he fell from his chair in a grand display, curling in on himself as saliva foamed at his mouth. The table shook with each spasm his body elicited, and Anna immediately jumped back, rushing to his side.

"Darryl!" she cried, but internally, she was gleeful. Darkness was slowly consuming her soul as she watched her husband writhe with pain.

She'd caused it. It was his own damn fault.

If only he hadn't been such an abusive dick to her, if only he had been more attentive to her and her own needs, it wouldn't have come to this—she wouldn't have snapped, and she wouldn't be internally laughing at his pain and feeling like a psychopath.

If only she hadn't opened that goddamn envelope, perhaps she would've been free sooner.

Darryl couldn't speak, too consumed with his own pain, but his gaze still strayed to her own, and his eyes widened with horror at what he saw. Because no longer was she trying to hide her delight, nor did she care that he knew she was the cause of his demise. She crouched down beside him and traced a single finger along his cheek, wet with his own saliva. "Arsenic," she said without a hint of remorse. "But you never suspected a thing, did you? Because I was always the perfect wife, the *dutiful* wife. I followed the rules to a T, even if they cost me my own sanity. But you wouldn't know a thing about that, would you, *husband*? Because in the end, I won. I don't have to abide by them anymore."

Darryl's eyes narrowed, and he spat out the excess saliva. "Y-you...poisoned me...my own wife..." he ground out. "How could you?"

Anna shrugged. "Everyone has their breaking point. It just so happens I found mine."

"B-but you can't do this!" he stammered. "The spell says—"

FIVE RULES FOR THE DUTIFUL HOUSEWIFE 75

Anna went cold all over. Red pulsed at the edge of her vision in tune to her rage at those words. "What spell?" she demanded calmly, a bit *too* calmly. She could feel herself succumbing to the anger, could feel herself slipping away and becoming lost forever.

Because those words?

Darryl had *planned* all this.

The strange woman and her envelope didn't matter anymore, not when faced with the reality that it'd only happened because of *him*. The pulsating energy, the wrongness of the entire situation, the click in her mind as whatever unnatural presence saturated the list had invaded her very being—it was *all* because of him. Because he hadn't wanted a partner. He'd wanted a submissive wife, a slave, someone who only existed for his sick pleasure fantasies. And he'd recruited someone who could make his dreams a reality.

"What spell?" she repeated, louder this time, but Darryl could no longer provide the answers she so desperately needed. His eyes went glassy, and his chest shuddered in one last, desperate breath before he finally fell silent.

He couldn't harm her anymore.

As if someone flicked a switch, that unnatural presence finally lifted, and Anna could breathe for the first time in five years. She was finally free, at least from that sick spell Darryl had subjected her to.

But she wasn't yet done.

Anna turned her back on her husband for the last time. Grabbed the biggest knife from the kitchen she could find. Left her dead husband in a pool of his own saliva and sins. Crossed the threshold and left the house.

Where the witch was already waiting for her, a genuinely warm smile plastered on her thin lips. There was a certain etherealness in her presence, something Anna had missed before, but now that she knew what the woman was, it was hard to miss.

White split her knuckles as her grip tightened on the knife.

The witch closed the gap between them, seemingly oblivious to Anna's evident rage. "You did it!" she said. "I knew you could!"

"What did you do to me?" Anna needed to hear it from the witch's lips. She needed a confession.

The witch's smile faltered. "I think you already know." She paused, looking worried. "I didn't have a choice, Anna. I've been employed by Darryl's family for generations, and the thing about witches is, we cannot go against a direct order. It has devastating consequences for us. I didn't want to do it, but I had no choice."

The witch's words all sounded like excuses. And Anna was tired, so damn *tired*, of excuses and lies. She shifted the position of the knife so its tip was aimed at the witch's gut.

She wondered if witches bled red like humans. *Time to find out.*

"But you did it! You killed him! You're finally free!" the woman gushed, still oblivious to the danger she was in. "I knew you could! I—"

Anna plunged the knife into the woman's gut, and any words the witch was about to say instantly died on her lips. Black pooled around the wound, spreading out from the entry point as the woman's eyes went wide, her mouth forming a capital *O*.

Black. Of course the witch's blood was black. It suited her, even matched the color of her soul. *Do witches even have souls?*

Anna punctured the woman's chest, her stomach, even parts of her neck as anger consumed her. And the woman, dazed and confused, did nothing to stop her. Anna doubted she could concentrate enough to cast a spell even if she wanted to. Pain did that to a person, made it nearly impossible to focus on anything else.

Anna had learned that the hard way.

And when Anna finally slashed an arc across the woman's neck, more black blood spewed from the wound as the woman fell to her knees. Sticky, black residue dripped down Anna's face and arms, splattering her clothes and completely drenching her hair. She watched as the witch died in front of her, feeling not an ounce of remorse for the second life she'd taken that day. They deserved it, both Darryl and this witch. Their lives seemed like such a small price to pay for the time Anna had lost.

And now, they would no longer be the chains imprisoning her.

Anna dropped the knife. Turned and walked away from her perpetual nightmare, leaving it to stew in its own sins. She never returned to that house again, never even once spared it a second thought. Even as her life continued—she changed her name and assumed a different identity so her old self could disappear forever—Anna refused to give that house any more of her time and energy. It wasn't her anymore. Darryl and that witch's rules weren't *her* anymore.

They'd never be able to hurt her or anyone else again.

The mere thought of that made Anna smile. Because despite everything, she had won. She had defeated the impossible and taken her life back.

She had killed. Blood now forever stained her hands.

But she didn't feel guilt or remorse. And she wouldn't feel guilt or remorse if someone else tried to force her hand. Because her life, her freedom, meant something to her, and no one would take that away from her again.

Consequences be damned.

Humility and Gratitude (will pave your way in this company)

Emily Bellman

CW: toxic masculinity, adult language, mild violence

If you (for some reason) are the kind of person who needs a Daily Dose of Bullshit, you only have to switch on the news. Be it from the Annoying Orange over in the U.S. or the government of my country, which has abandoned their voters' reality to live in one of their own making.

But every now and then, you're gifted a *personal* piece of Bullshit. One that is so mind-bogglingly ludicrous, you briefly entertain the idea of having it framed and hung above the toilet.

Mine went like this: "Humility and gratitude will pave your way in this company."

Spoken with grave conviction by a business coach hired by the above-mentioned company. The fact that the coach was a woman makes it all the sadder.

But before we continue, let me introduce you to the three people who will presently enter the stage:

First: myself. Hi. You can call me Amy. I'm an introverted, boomer-raised corporate millennial, who's discovered that dry sarcasm and hiding inside Netflix series is the only way to survive this shitshow. I'm a marketing manager and (watch out, twist!)—I *love* my job. I really do. I'm fiercely protective of my profession and I'm fucking good at it. I work at a software company together with some seventy other people, most of whom are developers. Those are the ones who keep me sane.

Person number two is Christopher. Christopher is my so-called Team Leader. OK, it's his *actual* title, printed on his little business card and right there in his little email signature. Christopher knows as much about leading a team as a fish knows about quantum physics. Christopher's other title is Head of Marketing. Now, I'm trying to come up with a comparison that trumps "fish and quantum physics." Suffice it to say, Christopher does not know the difference between KPI and USP. If you don't work in marketing, you don't need to know what a Key Performance Indicator and a Unique Selling Point are or how they differ. But if your fucking business card says Head of Marketing, it's your fucking *job* to know the difference.

But let's be honest: promoting people on the basis of *competence*? Yeah, hahaha, I just had a good laugh, too. You see, Christopher's greatest asset is this: he has the whole Humility and Gratitude thing figured out. His head is so far up his superiors' asses that he's sporting a fashionable brown stain around his neck. Which is quite enough to be endowed with Team Leader and Head of Marketing. Humility and gratitude will pave your way in this company, indeed.

Person number three, who we will call Lester, is best described with the following anecdote: A couple of months ago, our company celebrated its twentieth anniversary. We had a big party with business partners, friends, families. Since our logo is green, the idea was that people should wear a green accessory. Like a bowtie or a necklace or a handbag. Lester, who is one of the CEOs and Christopher's superior, brought along his wife—who wore a brilliantly beautiful green dress.

You can see it coming like a car crash, can't you?

The worst part is that it was *she* who said it. "Lester said I'm his green accessory!" Giggling, clinging to her grinning husband's arm.

No one listening thought how gut-wrenchingly wrong it was, not even the wife.

Lester recently discovered LinkedIn. And, oh boy, does he *love* to post about himself. Lester's posts are what parts of my generation, and probably all of Gen Z, would describe as a perfect parody of your stick-in-the-arse, self-adulating LinkedIn BS. But Lester means every word he copies and pastes from what ChatGPT barfs out for him.

And so, here we are: Amy, who is last in the food chain; Amy's (so-called) Team Leader and Head of Marketing, Christopher; and Lester, who is a CEO and Christopher's superior.

Most of what you just read and will read is true. You get to decide which parts.

"Hey Christopher, I need some info on that feature we recently developed for that major customer. Do you know where I can find the documentation? I want to turn it into a blog post," I said, peering at my (so-called) Head of Marketing above my computer screen.

"Hold on, I made a presentation for them that should contain what you need. I'll send you the link."

Ping went the chat and I opened the PowerPoint. I scrolled quickly past the company introduction slides and the agenda, stopping on the first page with content. The header, sprawling across half the slide (Futura, bold, font size 100) read: *This is the hart of our product.* I was briefly distracted by the vision of a majestic stag galloping through the office, tossing his antlers with gusto.

"Um," I said. "You already held this presentation?"

Christopher beamed at me across the monitor barrier. "Yep! Just last week. The customer's branch manager was there, and the regional manager, too. Even their head of marketing popped in."

I smiled back at him and nodded, the muscles in my face locking up painfully.

Now, one more thing about Christopher: he's dyslexic. Having spelling and reading difficulties isn't an ineptitude, not in my books. You're just born with it, like other people are born cross-eyed or lisping.

What *is* a staggering incompetence, however, is knowing full well that you can't get a straight sentence down if your life depended on it, but you're too much of a white, entitled, cis male to have a colleague check your spelling before announcing *The hart of our product* in front of a room of decision-makers for our most important customer.

I sighed inwardly, closing the presentation. Why do I even care? It's not *my* fuck-up; I didn't even know about the meeting in the first place. When I touched the keyboard, a small electric shock jumped from the letter E to my finger. I snatched back my hand instinctively, but curiously, it didn't sting.

Deciding that tomorrow was early enough to start working on that blog post, I instead opened the backend of our website. Some two months ago, I got permission to helm a product launch campaign. I'd started making a timeline, determined marketing channels and KPIs, and designed five key visuals. All this had, of course, happened in coordination with Christopher.

I tweaked the site's layout a little and completed a text, then saved it. "I'm sending you a link to the landing page," I tossed over the screens. "Can you approve it please, so I can publish it by the end of the week?"

"Absolutely!" Christopher fluted.

Christopher *loves* approving stuff. It means somebody else gave it ample thought, made a concept, and did the work. His job is just to praise the output profusely, then suggest minor adjustments. This is how it works most of the time, anyway.

"Amy? Do you have a minute?"

I closed my eyes, suppressing a groan. I knew that tone. I put on an expression of mild interest, then lifted my head above the screen barrier. "Sure. What's up?"

"That landing page... I've got a few questions."

It always starts like this. *I've got a few questions* translates to: *I don't approve what you did there, because I don't understand it.*

"Okay," I replied. I kept my expression gentle.

"Those five key visuals. They're very colorful."

"Uh, yes? I showed them to you for approval two weeks ago, remember? The colors are the central aspect of my campaign, as I'll use them across channels for consistency and recognition of the five key USPs."

"They're not really on brand, though. We don't usually use vector art with bold colors."

"Yes, I know. But it's a contained campaign for a new product and a new target group. I thought we went over this."

"Mhm. Yes. Well, I don't think the CEOs will approve of this."

I tightened the grip around my pen. There it was again, that odd spark jumping from the tip of my finger. I felt a tingle racing up my arm. I dropped the pen, clenching my hand into a fist. Tiny blue lightning flickered around my wrist, briefer than the blink of an eye.

"I can't change the visuals at this point," I said, not bothering to hide my exasperation. "Go-live for the campaign is in three days."

"Mhm, I still think we should schedule a meeting with Lester before we publish."

I stared at him. "You said this was *my* project. I gave you every image, every text, every idea for approval. And you *did* approve them!" I was aware that I was raising my voice.

"I see that this makes you emotional," Christopher commented, entirely unperturbed. "But I'm Head of Marketing and I'm responsible for everything my team produces."

"Then give the responsibility to me!" I snapped. "If I fuck up, let it be *my* fuck-up! I can deal with it."

He grinned apologetically. "Yeah, that's not how it works. How's your calendar look tomorrow? Lester's free in the afternoon. Oh, and he should be in, too."

Ping went the email with the meeting invite. I confirmed it, punching the mouse button hard enough to crack the plastic. I had my head ducked low behind the screen barrier, seething with anger.

"Lunch?" Christopher suggested, smiling sunnily, as if nothing had happened.

Blue lightning played around my fingers, snaking up my arm. I flicked my wrist and it was gone. "Sure. Let's eat," I pressed out between clenched teeth.

The next day, Christopher and I set up the meeting room for our appointment with Lester. One more thing about Lester: it doesn't matter *who* scheduled a meeting—Lester is always the first to talk. Even if he doesn't have the faintest idea what the topic is, he still has a *lot* to say about it. In that regard, Christopher and Lester are much the same.

HUMILITY AND GRATITUDE (WILL PAVE YOUR... 83

Lester—five to ten minutes late, of course—closed the door and flopped down in a chair. Coiffed hair combed back, crisp white shirt over chinos and white sneakers, an easy smile on his (I grind my teeth admitting it) handsome face. People like Lester get promoted for three reasons: One, he has a dick between his legs. Two, he's good-looking. And Three, he just talks *so. Damn. Fucking. Much.*

We started the meeting about my marketing campaign with Lester recounting *his* meeting with the Head of So-and-So, using "cool" language which regularly degraded people to "that bimbo" and "this dude" and the "hot shit" they did.

I had my hands folded in my lap to keep from picking at my nail beds. With a start I realized that they'd begun to glow faintly blue again. I rubbed my palms against my thighs, praying that none of the men saw the odd shimmer.

When Lester was finished with his story (a story nobody had asked for, a story that cost us twenty minutes out of the scheduled hour and had nothing to do with the topic of the meeting), it was, obviously, Christopher's turn.

"So, Amy has done a *tremendous* job developing the campaign for our new product. She intends to highlight the five key KPIs"—*USPs, you idiot. But sure, go on, mansplain my job for me*—"with visuals and corresponding blog posts—"

This was as far as Christopher (or anyone in a meeting with Lester) got, for by then, Lester had studied the presentation on the screen and he now knew *everything*.

"Okay, yeah," he interrupted Christopher's eulogy with a wave of his hand. "We need a flyer for our sales documents. Focus on the use of AI and that the product can be adapted out of the box."

"Actually," I began, trying to keep my voice even. *Objective arguments, Amy. Don't get emotional. It's not going to help you.* "I wanted to run the basics of the campaign by you. A sales flyer is part of it; you'll get it before the launch."

"Christopher filled me in about the campaign during our last jour fixe. If he wants you to change anything, I trust his judgement."

The lightning was now up to my elbow, a thin, blue barbed wire crackling softly—and the men finally saw it.

Christopher pushed back his chair, away from me and the table. "What is that?!" he screeched.

Lester rose, looking confused. "What the fuck are you doing?"

I slowly got up. I lifted my arms, holding my hands out to the side. My fingers were glowing bright blue, as if I had dipped them in a bioluminescent liquid. Lightning was twining around my arms, from the tips of my fingers all the way up to my shoulders.

"I would like," I said, smiling sweetly, "to explain my marketing campaign to you. And I want you to listen to what I have to say." I flicked my fingers and the lightning shot out from their tips, leaping to Christopher's notebook. It gave a sad sizzle, then died. Christopher yelped and scrambled into a corner.

"But I am!" Lester yelled. "I always listen! Everyone knows that they can come to me when they need someone to talk to!" He seemed more angry than scared. "Cut this shit out, Amy. It's not funny!"

I grimaced. "No, it's really not. And you are so full of shit. *You*, listening to people? What a joke. To men, maybe. Men who are like you, who you can understand with your shallow, limited little mind." Then I darted out one arm and the lightning-wire wrapped around Lester's body.

"*Hey!*" he cried, and now, finally, there was genuine fear in his voice.

The lightning immobilized him. I didn't really know what I was doing, what my magic could do, only that I was chock-full of rage. I felt it fueling my powers, felt the anger and frustration of years and *years* feed into the pulsating blue.

"Your fucking job is to lead people." I advanced on Lester, a ragged blue line running from my hand to his chest. "That means you enable them to be amazing. Imagine what we could do if we *actually* believed our CEOs gave a shit about us, or our work."

"What, do you want me to heap praise on you every day? Kiss your ass, tell you how great you are all the time?" Lester squealed. "Not everything revolves around you, Amy! Remember what Elizabeth said to you: Humility and grat—"

"Oh *shut the fuck up*, Lester!" I closed my hand and the lightning around his body tightened. It cut through his clothes, into his skin. Red stains bloomed on his starched white shirt. Fuck, this shouldn't feel as good as it did. But it did.

"You don't get it, do you? Your narcissistic, close-minded brain doesn't have the capacity for self-reflection."

Movement flashed at the corner of my eye. Christopher was trying to inch past my back. He was dragging himself along the wall on his ass, like a mangy dog.

"Oh no, you don't," I muttered and extended my other hand towards him. The lightning enveloped him, and when I crooked my fingers, it wrapped around his neck and tightened. I smiled and it wasn't sweetly this time.

"What-what do you want, Amy?" Christopher whined. His face was contorted with terror, sweat beading on his forehead.

I gave his question thorough consideration. What *did* I want?

I wanted women to be empowered instead of being reduced to a green accessory.

I wanted the executive managers to look to their lefts and rights and realize that, among the thirteen of them, there is only one woman. And I wanted them to see that this is neither right nor fair nor a reflection of the staff of this company.

I wanted women's voices to be taken seriously. I wanted their ideas and input and suggestions and work to matter just as much as their male colleagues'.

I wanted superiors who weren't staggeringly incompetent yet believed they have the right or means to judge my performance.

I wanted to get full control over a fucking marketing campaign, as had been promised to me, *because I earned it*!

I shook my head and closed both hands into fists. The lightning-wire tightened, cutting deeper and deeper into their flesh. The men cried out in pain, and Lester went to his knees. Magic was racing through me like a drug. I felt it in every vein, every artery. My whole body was rage turned into blue fire. My hands were glowing with such intensity, I couldn't look at them without fear of being blinded.

They would never listen to my voice—so they had to listen to my power.

A few weeks ago, Lester had ambushed me when I was alone in the office, demanding "The Talk." Apparently, I had misbehaved by asking for one of my home office days to be moved to the next month. When Lester denied it, I gave him a blunt reply ("I'll remember that.

"). Granted, that was not the cleverest thing to write to my CEO, but, just as he had been, I was *pissed*.

Lester promptly reprimanded me for my transgression the first chance he got when we were alone. I was already on my last nerve that day, and he backed me straight into a corner, demanding an unannounced meeting.

"Why don't you go and find a new job if being in the office sucks so much?" he asked, all venom and incomprehension.

All I recalled is that I lashed out like an angry cat. Frankly? I don't even know what I said, or all that Lester said. If I even defended myself. All I remember is being emotionally gut-punched at being told I was no longer wanted. Hello my little triggers.

We parted shouting at each other. Entirely frazzled, I got into my car and drove around to cool down. I parked in front of some trees and thought that if I just floored the gas pedal hard enough, if I picked up enough speed, aiming for that tree—

For a few long, heart-pounding seconds of pure, distilled hatred, I considered ending it there and then. What right did a man have to drive me to consider suicide?

But they had sons. Both of them, young boys, not even kindergarteners yet. Perhaps those kids would grow into better adults without fathers like them. Perhaps then they would learn to stand up for a woman, instead of trying to keep her small. Perhaps they would defend her when she's roasted in a room full of entitled white men, instead of joining in with the pack.

But perhaps it would break them.

I unclenched my fingers and the lightning obeyed. Lester crumpled with a whiny moan, and Christopher sobbed like a child.

I shook out my hands, the magic retreating down my arms, sizzling out. I took a deep breath. They weren't worth it. Their deaths were not worth my future, nor the futures of their sons.

I closed my notebook, unplugged it, and pushed down the door handle.

"The key visuals stay as they are," I said over my shoulder, then left the room.

I Think We're Alone Now

Rue Ellewood

CW: reference to child abuse (physical/sexual, not descriptive), child grooming, hospitals, head injuries, adult language, loss of a sibling, suicidal ideation, blackout, CPTSD, manslaughter

Jessi gasped as her eyes snapped open. Her body was racked with shivers. She couldn't tell if they were from a dream or she was actually cold. She took a couple deep breaths. Her thin cotton robe had done little to keep her warm, especially since she hadn't dried off after her shower before getting in bed, and the fabric was sticking to her skin. Her hair was still wet and cold against her neck.

Still shivering, she stood and dropped the robe as she went to her dresser. She pulled on a pair of paint-stained sweatpants, an old t-shirt, and a Metallica hoodie. Pulling her damp hair back in a bun, she went out to the living room and closed the windows against the early September night before wrapping herself in a blanket.

She walked to the kitchen to make a cup of tea. She had no idea what time it was and she doubted she would get back to sleep soon.

She sat on one of her mismatched kitchen stools and rubbed her temples. The dream that woke her had started to fade but her brother's face stayed in her mind. He was so angry that day. Jessi shuddered, trying to shake off the memories that tried to grasp at her consciousness.

What had made her think of him?

"He did what?!" Matty's small voice was filled with fury. "That sonofabitch, I'll kill him, I swear!"

"No Matty — please, don't say anything. We could all get in big trouble," she begged.

"No, he will," he said through his teeth.

"Matty — we will get in trouble. Mom and Dad won't love me anymore." She hated the whine in her voice.

"That doesn't make any sense, Jess." Her baby brother sounded so much older than her at that moment.

There was a gap in her memory; she could feel it yawning open like a black hole, waiting to swallow her entire being. Her body felt like a live wire and her mind felt like sludge. It had been years since she felt like this. Her old therapist would tell her to write everything down to process it. She felt heavy at the thought of pulling out her journal to work through whatever had caused the episode.

Thankfully the kettle started to whistle. Jessi methodically prepared a cup of chamomile tea then sat back down on the kitchen stool before she noticed her phone on the countertop. She sighed as she pulled it closer. It was nearly dead, but she could see that it was almost 3:00 a.m. She had an unusually high amount of missed calls and text messages.

What the hell happened?

Jessi wrapped both hands around her hot tea cup and inhaled the calming scent. The steam from the tea started to warm her face as she closed her eyes, trying to remember what happened before she fell asleep.

Her current head doc told her to start from the beginning of the day and work forward. She remembered waking up, having her morning coffee, chatting with a friend, and checking in with one of the galleries she was working with. She had put on some music and cleaned up her apartment before having a small salad and sandwich for lunch. And then she started working on her newest painting...

She turned in her seat to look at the piece. Despite the minimal light coming from the stove light, she could make out the major details on the canvas. Her chest felt a little lighter looking at it, a bit of peace draping over her like it always did when she was proud of her work.

She shook her head to refocus her energy. There was a tug in her mind like she was getting closer. She felt a clenching in her stomach like she may not like what she finds. Jessi closed her eyes, and took a deep breath.

This is Helen from St. John's Hospital... your cousin Darren...

The memory came back in a rush. Working on her painting with Lana Del Rey in the background. The breeze coming in her windows. The phone ringing.

"Miss Connors, my name is Helen and I'm a nurse at St. John's Hospital. I'm sorry to disturb you on a Saturday but we have some news about a family member," the caller said gently.

"Oh?" Jessi replied coolly. This must be a prank or a wrong number... there was no one left to call family.

"Yes, it is regarding your cousin, Darren Thompson."

Jessi's breath caught in her lungs. Panic crept up her arms like vines, snaking around her throat. Her ears were ringing. Her palms were clammy. Her legs would not keep her standing for much longer.

No no no no no no nonononononono—

Jessi shook her head to try and clear the darkness threatening to overtake her again.

"I know this can be hard. Your cousin, Darren, was in an accident and sustained some severe head injuries. He is currently in surgery and will likely be recovering in the ICU if you would like to come see him. It seems you are the only family he has."

"Wait... I'm the only family? That can't be—" she trailed off.

The nurse cleared her throat before answering. "He only had his wallet and a piece of paper with your information on it with him. The officers at the scene were able to confirm that you are his closest relative. He will likely need a lot of care in the coming months."

"Yes, I'm sorry. This is just—a big surprise. We haven't talked in a long time," Jessi replied.

"I understand. Again, I'm sorry to be the bearer of bad news. I'm sure your visit will help him immensely."

Jessi blinked a few times, trying to keep hold of the present while remembering what happened after the phone call. It was foggy, but she recalled running to the bathroom and losing her lunch. Taking a bath. Staring at the faucet and watching the water drip and ripple.

Screaming under water until she couldn't breathe.

Her whole body felt numb, and her cup of tea slipped from unfeeling fingers and bounced harmlessly on the rug. She stared at it, watching the liquid soak into the fabric.

It was not surprising that she had an episode. The person responsible for every panic attack and black out had found her after she had done everything she could to disappear. She didn't have any social media accounts. She'd started going by a different name. Only a few trusted people had her real phone number.

Jessi looked down at the tea cup on the floor. Her insides felt sharp and jagged. It was a shame it took so little for her to shatter, unlike the cup. Broken pieces never fit like they used to. There was no chance of smoothing them out that night. The urge to drop everything and run crawled under her skin.

She soaked up the tea with a towel. Then she cleaned her brushes and put away her paints. She did the dishes and cleaned up the bathroom. Finally, she changed the sheets on her bed before crawling back under the covers.

"I think we're alone now —"
A hand on her thigh.
"Darren, I don't —"
A pinch inside her leg.
"Shhh... It's ok, Jessi. All the big girls do it."
"But I'm not a big girl yet..."
"Oh but you will be —"

Wet tears streaming down her cheeks.
"Shhh, Jessi."

Sunlight streamed through Jessi's window. She pulled the sheets over her head and tried to ignore it. Her mind was awake now. She peeked at the old school clock on her bedside table. It was a little after 10:00 a.m. She buried her face in her pillow and let out a noise of frustration.

While she was feeling better, she wasn't sure if she was ready to face whatever the day brought. She was still undecided on whether or not to go to the hospital. She considered calling her therapist, but decided against it. She hadn't actually seen Darren yet. Maybe he hadn't even made it through the night. Then she would have called her therapist for nothing. She decided she would call if Darren was awake and talking.

She groaned as she got up and started her usual morning routine. Sticking to an established regimen would prevent derailing; from washing her face to making her coffee, every step mattered.

While waiting for her coffee to brew, Jessi plugged her phone into its charger. Now she had even more missed calls and text messages. She made her coffee and sat down at the counter to go through her phone. There were a few messages from some acquaintances; she forgot that she said she would go to a gallery opening with them last night. She sent off a quick apology and then moved on. The phone calls were from the hospital. Apparently, they thought she needed to be apprised of every little change. After listening to the first few messages, she deleted all of them.

Jessi took deep breaths, trying to clear her mind and keep memories from creeping in. Some memories were from long ago, some from the day before. Her fingers started to tighten around the mug as she struggled with her mind. The silence in the apartment became deafening, the memories a thrumming noise in her head. She tried closing her eyes but that just gave the memories more room to play. Her body tensed as though bracing for impact.

Darren, stop! I don't want to!
You don't have to lie to kick it, J—

I'm not lying!
I know you like it—
Darren, I've been bleeding for days, my mom is asking questions!
Psh, prove it.
Don't fucking touch me!

The sound of glass breaking brought Jessi back to the present. She opened her eyes slowly, taking shallow breaths. Her hands were bleeding. There was glass and coffee and blood on the counter.

Bile rose in Jessi's throat. A memory flashed through her mind as she stared at her hands, watching blood drip from the fresh cuts. She swallowed the bile back down with great effort. She walked to the sink and started washing her hands, picking out pieces of glass. She wrapped her hands in paper towels before looking for her first aid kit in the bathroom. She poured rubbing alcohol over the cuts and covered them in gauze. Luckily, none were deep enough that she needed to go to the hospital.

The hospital... She doubted they would stop calling her. She might as well put her big girl pants on and go see what kind of condition Darren was in. She didn't know if his parents were still alive, much less where they lived. He broke everything he touched... The world would probably be a better place without him in it.

Jessi shook her head. That train of thought would only lead her to more darkness. She didn't need more than she already had. Not if she wanted to keep fighting it.

Opening the medicine cabinet, Jessi found a bottle of expired Xanax. She shook one out, dry swallowing it before putting on a bit of makeup and dressing in jeans and a t-shirt. By the time she was ready to go, the Xanax had kicked in and she felt nothing.

She grabbed a sweater, pausing for a moment to look at her new painting in the daylight. She was fucking proud of this piece of art. The thought gave her a boost as she headed out of her apartment. She walked to the bus stop, arriving just in time for the bus. After making a couple transfers, she stepped off the final bus and faced the front of St. John's Hospital. It looked like any normal hospital, though she had never been a fan of the institutions, and despite the Xanax, she felt her heart beating harder in her chest, a trickle of sweat starting to run down her spine.

At that moment, she wished she had someone to talk to. A friend. A family member. She wished she wasn't such a hermit. She wouldn't even be this way if it weren't for Darren. She used to be so social before....

The thought lit a small fire in her and she felt heat crawl up her neck. She was mad at him. She might have had a normal fucking life if he hadn't been such a fucking bastard. She took a breath of the cool September air, though it did little to settle her.

With renewed purpose, Jessi strode up to the front door of the hospital. She walked up to the visitor services desk and got directions to the ICU.

Her fingers tapped a continuous tempo on her thigh as she rode the elevator up to the fifth floor. As the elevator opened, she made a conscious effort to unclench her jaw, whatever good that was going to do.

The nurse at the nurses station had salt-and-pepper hair that was pulled back into a severe looking bun. Her cool blue eyes looked at Jessi when she stepped up to the desk. Jessi swallowed thickly, unable to speak.

"How can I help you?" the nurse asked.

Jessi checked the name tag. Helen. That gave her a small reassurance; at least she had spoken to the woman before.

Jessi cleared her throat before saying, "Hi, I'm Jessi Connors. Here to see—"

"Oh yes!" Helen exclaimed. "Darren Thompson, right? I'm so glad you could make it today. I was hoping you would be here last night. Most family members come over right away, you know."

Jessi was thankful she didn't have to say the bastard's name out loud. She was not thankful that this random woman felt it was appropriate to guilt trip her the moment she arrived. Instead of responding to the bait, she plastered a small smile on her face. And waited.

After a few moments of uncomfortable silence, Helen asked, "Would you like to see him?"

No, actually. Jessi merely nodded. She wasn't sure she could physically say yes.

"Please follow me," the nurse said as she stood and walked around the desk to lead Jessi down the hallway.

Jessi cleared her throat and asked, "Still no word on his parents?"

"Nothing that the police have shared with us, no." Helen replied.

At a room near the end, Helen opened the door, peeking in before opening it all the way for Jessi. But Jessi was rooted to the spot. Her stomach felt like cement.

"I'll let the doctor know that you're here," Helen said before walking back down the hall.

Jessi stood in the hallway. She could hear the machines in the room beeping and breathing for him. She could feel her nails digging into her palms through the gauze as her fists clenched. She could smell antiseptic and bodies. She closed her eyes for a moment before she was finally able to step into the room.

Darren looked peaceful, despite the wires and tubes. A few bruises had bloomed on his face. He looked older but very much the same as she remembered him. The hospital bed made him appear smaller. Maybe he wasn't as big and scary as she remembered. Her eyes caught on one of his hands. It was bandaged and bruised, too.

Go home, Jessi. I'll take care of this.
No, Matty, come with me.
No, Jessi. If I don't do this now, he will keep hurting you.

She shook her head. The memories kept creeping in, becoming more insistent.

"Miss Connors?" a male voice behind her asked, making her jump.

"Sorry, yes, I'm Jessi," she said as she turned to the voice.

"I'm Dr. Liam Carey," he said, holding his hand out for her to shake. He looked a few years older than her and his dark hair was swept to the side. His green eyes seemed to bore into her and she squirmed a little.

She shook his hand, forgetting that her palms were covered in gauze. His warm smile faltered.

"What happened?" he asked, turning her hand palm-up.

"Oh, I just dropped a glass the other day. Cut myself cleaning it up, no big deal," she replied with a small smile.

"Well, let me know if you need a doctor to look at it. I'd be happy to help," he said, sweeping his thumb across her wrist before releasing her hand.

She laughed nervously. Was he hitting on her? While her dickwad cousin slept right next to them?

"So, how is my cousin?" she asked, a little sharper than she intended.

"Ah, yes," he said. "He sustained a severe head injury from the accident. He had to have several surgeries over the last twenty-four hours, including one to stop some bleeding in his brain." He looked at her expectantly. What he was expecting, she wasn't sure so she just nodded. He frowned a bit before continuing. "At this point, we don't know what state he will be in when he wakes up. He could wake up tomorrow and be fine or he could remain unconscious for months. There is really no way to tell right now."

"Thank you, doctor. So we're just going to wait and see for now?"

"Essentially. It may be nice for him to have someone familiar talk to him, even if he is unconscious. Studies have shown that having a loved one visit can drastically improve the odds of recovery."

Jessi couldn't help the bark of laughter that escaped her mouth.

"Excuse me, I think I had something in my throat," she said as she faked a cough to cover it up.

The doctor started to lead her out of the room as he said, "We'll keep you informed of his progress."

Jessi nodded.

As they stepped into the hallway, there was a gasp behind them. Jessi's heart dropped as she turned to find Darren with his eyes open and gasping around the breathing tube. The doctor rushed back into the room, and Jessi took the opportunity to hurry out of the hospital.

She went back to her apartment in a daze. She fell onto her couch, exhausted from the day. She laughed to herself as she thought about how Darren was still an emotional vampire even when he was unconscious.

She stared at the painting she had been working on when she got the phone call. Memories came creeping in. The times she fought Darren, and the times she disassociated so that she didn't know what was happening to her body. The last time she saw him—she had wanted to hurt him. She wished she had. Things would be so different now if she had.

A burning feeling spread up her body as her rage caught. She stood up, not sure what her intentions were, but stomped towards the kitchen regardless. She wanted to break something, destroy something. She needed to release the rage before it consumed her entirely.

She didn't remember the first time it happened. And she didn't remember the last time. Most of her memories surrounding her cousin felt like electricity— too much of it and she might pass out from cardiac arrest. She had been good. She had gotten therapy. She was living her best life. And now he just showed up again. It made her furious. She wanted to scream. She wanted to disappear again. She wanted to fight.

Jessi's breaths grew shallower the deeper her thoughts went into the abyss. She remembered how her parents would leave her and her brother alone with Darren because he was older, how she told them she didn't like it when he watched them. How he would sometimes lock her brother in the closet.

I think we're alone now. I think we're alone now. I think we're alone ithinkwerealoneithinkwerealoneithinkwerealoneithinkwerealone

---

Jessi's neck was at an uncomfortable angle. She winced as she turned her head. Her eyes cracked open. She was on her couch. Had she fallen asleep there? What had happened? She might need to make an appointment with her therapist sooner rather than later if she'd had two black outs in as many days. She checked her phone and saw that it was Monday. She had slept like that for hours. No wonder her neck hurt.

She rolled over and gasped.

Her painting—it had been destroyed. All her hard work. Gone.

Mouth agape, she sat up and put her feet on the floor. She felt something under her foot. Looking down, she saw one of her kitchen knives. Her hands drifted to her mouth of their own accord as she looked from the knife to the painting and back again.

Her chest was in a vice and her eyes were burning. Her mouth opened in a silent scream as tears slipped down her cheeks.

Jessi stood in a hot shower. She had cleaned up the living room. She saved the canvas, thinking maybe she could make a different piece of art from the scraps.

She was losing her grip. She had spent so much time building a steel safe in her mind for all these memories, all these emotions. She needed to do something to lock them away again.

One therapist had suggested facing her fears to process them. Perhaps if she faced Darren, she would be able to process some of these memories. She let the hot water hit her face. She considered facing him while he was in his weakened state might be a good start. She didn't think he would be able to hurt her now.

Feeling renewed from the shower, Jessi got dressed and made two cups of coffee in travel mugs. She wondered if the good doctor liked coffee, and if she could use his interest in her to get more information.

Unfortunately, Dr. Liam Carey was not at the hospital when Jessi arrived. However, the new nurse at the desk appreciated a good cup of coffee and liked to talk.

Jessi learned a few things chatting her up. No one knew what kind of accident Darren was in. He was found on the side of the road without any obvious markers of the accident besides his head injury. He had a battery of tests scheduled for the day since he was stable overnight. They were still trying to find information on his parents.

Jessi kept her back straight when she went into his room. Despite the bundle of snakes in her stomach, she put on a confident front. He didn't know her like he used to.

"Hello, dear cousin," Jessi said with a wide smile as she walked up to the side of the bed. "It's been too long."

He could only blink at her.

"I hope you're comfortable."

He just kept looking at her, as though he was trying to read her mind.

"Oh, don't worry, I'm only here for a quick visit. Word is that you have a lot of tests coming up. I just wanted to wish you good luck."

A different nurse came in to the room to take him to his first test.

"Darn, looks like I arrived too late for us to spend any quality time together. Don't worry, I'll be back tomorrow." She pulled her cheeks even wider. She was sure she looked crazed.

She gave him a small wave as he was rolled out of the room. Now that the tables had turned, she wanted him to be a little worried, a little anxious. She wanted him to feel a little unsteady.

Jessi was about to leave when she saw the nurse had left his chart on the side table. She took a quick look at it, not sure what she was looking for. She didn't notice anything out of the ordinary and left quickly, not wanting anyone to get suspicious.

Maybe his parents would show up and free her of this potential moral dilemma. He had done so much to break her in the past. She couldn't let him harm anyone else. And maybe the accident was karma, and he would never progress beyond where he was now, and she could disappear again, leaving him for someone else to take care of.

She took a deep breath as she exited the hospital. She would just have to take it one day at a time and see whether or not he got any better. Then she could make a choice.

On her way home, she picked up some good stationary paper. It had been a while since she had written her brother a letter and she wanted to use the good, quality stuff.

September 25

Dear Matty,

It's been so long. I'm sorry I've been a bad sister. My art is going well. I have a few galleries showing my work. I feel like I'm closer to making it like we always talked about.

Oh, and you will never guess who I saw. Our good cousin Darren. Apparently, the poor boy was in an accident nearby and they called me as the closest relative.

They aren't sure if he will walk or even speak again due to his head injury. Please keep him in your prayers.

Love,

J

October 21

Dear Matty,

I hope you have been well since my last letter. I sold some more art! Soon enough, your sister might actually be able to buy a decent car. Imagine that...

Darren started his occupational therapy. He has been learning how to walk again and while the progress is slow, he is making small steps. I visit him almost every day. I think he is happy to be out of the ICU. I'm looking at nearby assisted housing options for him. Maybe you can come out for a visit soon.

Love,

J

November 25

Dear Matty,

It finally snowed yesterday. I know, it's nearly December. Late for the first snow. But at least we got some.

Darren is still working on walking. It looks like speech and writing will be a much longer process, if he regains those skills at all. The brain is so fascinating. I had to shave his face for him the other day because his hands were shaking too much. I'm sure he wishes it was you instead of me. But I'm the only one here so that's what he gets. Still haven't heard anything about our aunt and uncle.

Let me know when you can visit. I miss you.
Love,
J

Jessi sat at her kitchen counter, drinking a coffee despite the fact that it was 10:00 p.m. She had just finished her most recent letter to her brother and was watching the falling snow outside.

The last few months had had a lot of ups and downs between Darren's recovery and her own life—getting paintings done, selling them to galleries, looking for a car. Once he had moved into the assisted living facility, she had even gone on a few dates with Liam.

In addition to writing to her brother, she had started journaling again. It was helping her sort through the memories constantly threatening to ravage her mental state, as well as helping her sift through her thoughts about what to do with Darren. He seemed comfortable enough where he was. Because the facility was sponsored by a church, the fees for his care were low. But she had never planned to stay in one place for long. And she was starting to get the itch to move along.

She sipped her coffee. A memory flitted in. She was maybe seven or eight. They had gotten a bunch of fruit from the store and Darren had refused to eat some of it. She was racking her brain trying to remember why.

Jessi pulled out her journal and started writing about the memory to see if anything else came up. Finally, something came to her.

Allergies.

Jessi woke up the next day with a plan. She took a long shower, luxuriating in the warm water. She took the time to do her hair and makeup. She dressed in a pair of black slacks that she kept for special occasions and a pink blouse. On her way to the bus, she stopped for some juice at the corner store.

She arrived at the assisted care home just as lunch was being delivered to the patients. She chatted up the nurses on her way to Darren's room, smiling as though she didn't have a care in the world. She knocked on Darren's door just as one of the nurses was getting ready to help him with his lunch.

"Hello, Miss Connors," the elderly nurse said.

"Good morning. Or I guess it's afternoon now," Jessi replied with a laugh. "I'm happy to help with his lunch today."

"Oh, that's lovely. Isn't that nice, Darren?" the nurse asked even though he couldn't respond. He glared at Jessi in response. She merely smiled. The nurse kept chatting, "Thank you, dear, you know how understaffed we are. I appreciate the help."

"Of course," Jessi said with a smile.

The nurse started to get up as Jessi reached for the fork, knocking over Darren's juice in the process.

"Oh dear!" the nurse exclaimed.

"Oops! I'm such a klutz! I'll get another one from the cafeteria," Jessi offered. She picked the cup up from the floor, dropped it in the trash, and left the room. She walked to the cafeteria where the more independent patients ate. It was full and no one noticed her as she went to the juice fountain. Instead of filling the new cup with orange juice, she pulled a can of 100% mango juice from her purse and poured it in. She headed back to Darren's room with a little pep in her step.

Entering his room, she looked around. The nurse had cleaned up the spill and left to attend to other patients. A slow smile spread across Jessi's face as she closed his door. At the noise, he looked up at her. His glare could freeze ice. Jessi checked the bathroom just to make sure the nurse was gone before she sat next to her cousin, putting the juice on his tray where he could drink it easily enough.

"Ahh..." Jessi sighed as she sat back in the chair. "I think we're alone now."

Darren's eyes snapped up to her, a mixture of anger and fear in them.

"You used to say that a lot, you know? Do you remember? Oh, I'm sure you do. Anyway, maybe you're wondering why I'm all dressed up today. Well, dear cousin, I think today will be the last day I visit you for a while. Or forever. We'll see where life takes me once I'm done here."

She could practically see all the things he wanted to say flit across his eyes. But alas, he could say nothing.

"What's wrong, Darren? Not going to drink your juice?" He scowled. "I'd hate to have to force you to drink it."

He leaned forward and took a small sip. His scowl deepened. She guessed he didn't realize what kind of juice it was.

"Go on, drink up. I know all those meds make you thirsty," she said sweetly, as though she was talking to a child.

She kept her face carefully blank as he took a bigger sip.

"It's good, right?" she asked.

He frowned at her, but took another drink. She continued to gently urge him on until the cup was empty, then she sat back in the chair again, watching him carefully.

A few moments later, he started coughing. He tried to grab his throat even though his hands were shaking.

Staring intently at him, she spoke in an almost dreamy voice. "Do you remember back when you were, like, twelve, and one of the aunts brought fresh mangoes for breakfast? You took one bite and had to be rushed to the hospital." He glared at her even as he was gasping, trying to get air into his lungs. "Funny story," Jessi continued, voice getting harder as she spoke, "I don't remember a lot about my childhood. But last night, I remembered that breakfast. It was before I started to hate you, back when you were just my cool, older cousin." He continued gasping. Jessi let out a long sigh. "Anyway, I checked your chart and I noticed there weren't any allergies listed. Which means no one knows about your rare mango allergy." She shrugged before leaning forward, schooling her expression into a glare. "This may not change what you did to me and Matty, but it will be a weight off my shoulders."

Jessi stood and stretched her arms. Bending over, she placed a gentle kiss on his head.

"May God keep you," she whispered.

Then she walked out of the room, closing the door gently. She spotted the elderly nurse from earlier, and pointed at the door before she tilted her head with her hands on her cheek to let her know he was sleeping. The nurse nodded with a smile and wave. She waved back before heading down the hall, towards the exit.

As Jessi stepped out of the building, she took a deep breath of the frigid air. For the first time in a long time, she was able to take a full breath. She didn't realize that she hadn't been breathing until the air flooded her lungs.

Christmas Day

Jessi stood at the gates to the cemetery, taking in the iron scrollwork along the top. She had never been there before and was a little nervous. She took careful steps between the graves, looking at the various bouquets resting against the stones. Even though it was winter, it rarely snowed in her hometown and the ground was covered in dry brown grass.

She finally made it to the plot she was looking for. She took several envelopes out of her coat pocket before looking at the gravestone.

Matthew Collins
Beloved Son & Brother

"Hey, Matty," she said as she knelt down. "I wrote you some letters. I know it's silly—" She took a deep breath, trying to keep the emotion at bay for just a little longer. "I got him back for all those years. And that incident at the bridge. He won't hurt anyone ever again." Tears flooded her eyes as she let herself remember the day her brother was lost to her forever. "I miss you, baby bro," she whispered as they fell.

She sat there until the sun set, letting her sadness seep into the ground. She left the letters and a bouquet of sunflowers at the gravestone.

Finally standing, she said, "Say hi to Mom and Dad for me, okay?"

Then Jessi turned, hands in her coat pockets, and walked to her new car. She didn't know where she was going to go next, but wherever she went, the past couldn't haunt her anymore.

Of a Heart

Anna Scanlan

CW: blood, mental abuse, gaslighting, murder, ritual sacrifice

She didn't know he had a tattoo.

Adela was engaged to this man. They had been together for three years. How in all that time had she missed the fact that Dalton had a tattoo on the nape of his neck?

The pair stood on the bluffs that lined the bay. All around them the tall grasses and wildflowers rustled as the smell of sea salt washed over them. They'd been diving off the cliff's edge for the past hour or so. Adela's hair was wet and tangled from the water below and it stuck to her back uncomfortably.

Down the cliffside, about a mile away, sat a huge, stone, gothic castle. It looked to be abandoned, dilapidated. Adela had always been curious about it, but she had never gone in. Dalton said it gave him the creeps, and his gut instincts had never led her wrong. Even so, it never failed to capture her attention, or set her mind racing with stories and ideas of what it had been in its prime. It looked almost angelic in the late afternoon light and her heart longed to go inside.

And despite all of this, she couldn't tear her eyes off of her fiancé's neck. It was a peculiar thing, this newfound tattoo; it was a simple circle with a line through it, but Adela couldn't think of a time when she had seen anything like it.

Dalton whirled around. "You ready?" he asked, face plastered with the most adorable shit-eating grin she had ever seen in her life. The sun caught his blonde hair sending it into a golden blaze.

Adela forced herself to smile. "Duh!"

He frowned. "You good, Dela?"

She had hated that nickname her whole life and desperately pleaded with him to stop when he started using it years ago. But she had lost that fight and convinced herself that it had grown on her, otherwise it would drive her mad.

"Did you get a tattoo?" she blurted.

His nose scrunched up, puzzled. "Huh?"

"On your neck. I haven't seen it before?"

His eyes lit up in recognition. "Oh, that old thing? Had it since college."

Adela frowned. She never pushed Dalton on anything, their relationship just worked better that way. But this felt different. "I don't think I've ever seen it before." It was no longer a question.

"It's been there for years." He shook his head and sighed. "Stop being dramatic."

But the thing was, it hadn't been. And she wasn't being dramatic.

"C'mon. Be a good little girl and forget about it."

Adela tried to shake away the sense of unease forming deep in her gut. She smiled, trying to do so with her eyes this time. "Let's go." She reached for his hand. It felt cool and clammy in hers.

The two of them ran across the rocky edge, their footsteps pounding in unison with the beating of her heart. They jumped off of the cliff and cut through the air, waiting for the icy embrace of the water below.

Adela jolted awake in a cold sweat. Panting, she reached over and pulled the chain on the bedside light. It flickered to life with a worn-out click.

Adela slowly held her shaking hands to her face. Through her sleep-coated gaze, and the shadows of the night, the red of her nail polish looked like blood slowly seeping down her fingers. She blinked rapidly a few times and when she looked at her hands again the bloody mirage was gone.

Carefully, so as not to wake Dalton, Adela propped herself up against the headboard, supporting herself with her shaking hands. Last time she had woken him up she'd heard about it for weeks on end. Dalton's sleep schedule was very delicate and if she so much as breathed in his direction he'd grow restless. So she didn't look at him. She lifted her tangle of hair off her sweat-soaked neck. The cold air that rushed in came as a welcome relief.

What had she been dreaming about to cause such unrest? Adela wracked her brain for answers, but all she came up with was a knot of fear that settled deep into her stomach. It felt like the same uneasiness from earlier in the day.

Five years ago, right before they had left, her mother warned her that going off-grid was a bad idea. That she'd wake up one day and regret it. Was that what this feeling was? Regret?

Adela dismissed the thought as soon as it appeared. The last thing she wanted to do was leave this life they built for themselves behind. Dalton was right, this life was best for them. Best for her.

But the unease remained. It wrapped its spindly fingers around her soul and refused to let go. Dalton would probably have something to say about the dream, even though she couldn't remember a lick of it. He'd always had this deep belief that dreams meant something beyond the surface. That they had insight into your life that not even you yourself could possibly know. He believed it with such an intense ferocity that Adela almost wanted to believe it too. In fact, she let him believe that she believed in it. She sighed and looked over to his side of the bed.

Dalton was not there.

Adela shoved the covers away and got out of bed. She walked around their small A-frame so quickly that her feet seemed to glide over the hardwood floors, the hem of her white nightgown fluttering as she went. The bathroom was empty, as well as the kitchen and living room.

She turned her attention to the door, which was slightly ajar. She froze. That door was closed and locked before they went to bed, she was sure of it. She had only forgotten to do so once in their relationship and had been careful to make sure it would never happen again.

Adela's heart pounded as she slipped outside, carefully closing the door behind her. She stood there on the stoop facing the rest of the world.

"Dalton?" she called out.

The breeze picked up her words and carried them into the wood where they were promptly swallowed by the vast night.

She sighed and began walking through the forest, towards the seaside. Twigs snapped and leaves rustled under her feet as she moved. Something was poking through her slippers. She looked down. Her feet were bare; she must have forgotten the slippers in her hurried frenzy.

The cliffs were only a few hundred yards away and she had done the walk barefoot before. So Adela trudged on through the dark along the makeshift path that had been worked into the ground through the years..

A misty shower of seawater welcomed her as she trod towards the edge.

Looking down, she watched the water crawl up against the edge of the rocks and its foamy spray leap into the air. Out in the bay, the reflection of the full moon rippled as the waves ebbed and flowed.

Her eyes landed on the abandoned castle to the north. Except it looked far from abandoned.

Every window was aglow.

She rubbed her eyes frantically. Surely she was seeing things. Surely this was just another mirage, like the blood dripping down her hands. She was just tired, that was all.

But when Adela put down her hands, the lights were still there, perhaps even stronger.

She felt an all too familiar burst of excitement and a small smile pull at the corners of her mouth. A sense of wonder and curiosity washed over her as strong as the winds that lapped at the waves.

Adela felt alive.

Although, she shouldn't. The love of her life had vanished without a trace.

But since he was missing in action, she could finally take a look at that castle without any backlash.

She walked along the bluffs, careful to not get too close to the edge. After a while, the rocky ground shifted into soft, patted-down grass. The wind continued to blow, and she paused, tilting her head towards the sky, letting the breeze roll over her and pull her hair back.

As Adela neared the castle, she could see that not only were lights flickering in the arched windows, but also along the path. Carefully, she scampered over to where it started. Along both sides of the cobblestone walkway sat candles encased in tall glass jars.

Despite the shiver that ran down her spine, Adela gingerly walked along the path. The further and further she tread, the brighter the lights became. She was washed in their glow, and its pull was hypnotizing. She looked over her shoulder, back towards home. From here it looked cold and empty.

The flames danced against the inky night, and the only distinguishable piece of the bay was the moon, proud and full as it hung above a sea of nothingness. It was eerie the way they reached towards her, beckoning her to follow their call. But Adela still obliged. The thought of exploring such a majestic structure excited the little girl inside of her that still dreamed of adventure, whose head would be spinning with ideas at the mere thought. She'd left those dreams, and her Archeology degree, behind to come out here with Dalton. They had seemed like childish whims at the time, but she couldn't deny the way her heart was now pounding with excitement.

Soon, Adela was standing at the base of the structure. It was more beautifully intricate that she had imagined, stone crumbling away from gargoyles and windowsills. The doors were majestic, probably three times her height. She looked them up and down with admiration, but on closer inspection, her heart dropped to the floor.

Etched into each of the doors was a symbol: a circle with a line drawn down the middle.

She thought back to the lie about the tattoo, his aversion to the castle and began to realize that maybe she didn't know Dalton at all.

Adela didn't dare walk through the front doors. Instead, she walked around the perimeter of the building until she happened upon a broken window. She shimmied inside, but her nightgown caught on a raw edge of glass. She tore it away, cursing under her breath.

All of the hallways had the same vaulted ceilings and grey stone walls that seemed to go on forever and ever into the ether. They were all heavily lit with brass candelabras that were just taller than her.

Adela crept against the wall, making sure to stay low so her hair wouldn't catch on fire. While she didn't know where she was going, she didn't quite care. Just being in such a grand place was exhilarating enough.

Chatter echoed from around the corner, and Adela jumped behind a nearby tapestry, hoping it would be a good enough cover to hide her from whoever it was.

The fabric was certainly worn and it pained her to have to disrupt it in this way. It was some sort of woven pattern, and an old one at that. It was falling apart, and she feared that if she breathed too hard, the whole thing would come crumbling to the ground. She could see glimpses of the hallway through spots that had been completely worn away.

A group of men donning floor-length red and black robes, slowly made their way down the hall, laughing. One of the laughs soared above the others. It's all too familiar warmth squeezed at her heart.

It was Dalton. It had to be.

She peered through another weak place in the hanging and squinted at the group.

The robes were beautiful. They had an inky black base, and the red was from embroidery. Intricate images and scenes and symbols lined the bottom hem, front closure, and sleeve cuffs. They were stunning works of art.

"We knew as soon as we saw you that you were destined for this. Having you here for the past two years, it's been a blessing," an older man said. He clapped Dalton on the back as the group made their way through the corridor, closer to Adela's hiding spot.

Her breathing stopped. They had lived in the area for that exact amount of time.

A younger, dark-haired man nodded his head in agreement. "You looking forward to your ascension? Being our Leader is a huge honor." His eyes shone as he looked up at Dalton. In this circle, Dalton was revered. Respected.

Dalton grinned, but it was nothing like his usual smile. The corners of his mouth appeared forced upwards and his eyes were cold, blank. A shiver flew down her spine. "It's going to be the best day of my life." His voice was harsh, cutting through the air unlike anything she had ever heard from him.

He had certainly been lying to her. About the tattoo, about this castle, why they were here, who he was, even. She remembered when he first approached her with the idea. "It'll be just you and me, Dela. You and me and the forest and nothing else will matter. Because you are all that matters to me."

She had melted at those words. That was the moment she knew she loved him, that she would do anything for him despite anything else.

But those words now felt like a lie. The person she had become for him felt like a lie.

Red-hot rage flooded her senses as she stared at him through the tapestry's holes. She clenched her fists and jaw and thought she just might explode.

The group walked further down the hall, and soon all that was left of them were the echoes of their footsteps lingering in the air.

Before she could process what she had seen and heard, a gloved hand clasped her mouth. Another wrapped itself around her throat.

She was too shocked to scream.

Muscular arms jerked her back and she let out a sharp gasp.

"You think you can get away with snooping?" a deep voice asked.

Adela tried to squirm away from the man's grip, but only got pulled tighter against his chest.

"Not around here, you can't."

Adela struggled against him to no avail. Her breathing picked up and she struggled for air between his fingers.

"Never think you can outsmart The Dreamers," the man laughed. "Never, never, never."

He pushed his head closer to her ear. She could feel his cold, wet lips brush against her earlobe with every word as he whispered, "Do you know how many have met their end trying to outsmart us?"

Adela gulped. His black leather gloves pressed against her skin and she felt cool and unbelievably warm all at once as he tightened his grip.

The flames of the candles, colors of the fabric, and texture of the stone walls started to blur together as the world spun. When the man next spoke, it sounded as if the hallway was under water.

"You're just going to be the next."

That was the last thing she heard before the world went dark.

Adela's head pounded as her eyes fluttered open. She was splayed out on a cool stone floor. Her neck throbbed, and she reached over to rub the sore spot. The hazy memory of a man came back to her in flashes.

She scanned the room, looking for him, but it was no use. She didn't know what he looked like. All she could remember were his thick, leather gloves. There were quite a few people in the room, either that or she was seeing double. All the people wore the same robes they had on in the hallway. And black gloves. They were murmuring amongst themselves, too caught up in their own world to notice her.

Adela moved as little as possible, trying to keep it that way. Her head throbbed with every slight movement.

The room had no windows, at least none she could see. It was more of a dome than a room with a high, arched ceiling covered in ornate drawings. It was a scene of figures wearing the black robes that Adela was starting to dread. They were surrounded by red and gold runes, one of which was the symbol that had been haunting her life as of late.

The same brass candelabras circled the room, the only source of light. Their shadows danced on the wall like phantoms trying desperately to escape their anchors.

Towards one edge of the space was a rather large table made of cracking grey stone. Moss crept up its sides, covering the jagged edges. Adela squinted at it, trying to get a better look. The stone and moss was also covered in staining that varied in color from black to brown to red.

Very dark red.

She thought she remembered reading about tables like this in one of her classes but couldn't for the life of her recall any details. By the looks of it, it couldn't be anything good. Adela closed her eyes, hoping for this to all be a dream.

When she opened them, one of the cloaked figures was staring directly at her. He raised his hands and softly clapped them together.

In an instant, the mumbling around the room ceased. Everyone glided to the edges of the room forming a circle. Adela could now make out the intricate patterns of the mosaic floor. She wished she were in any other situation so she would have time to admire them. They were certainly old; quite the find. A find that would have been hers to write about if she had just followed her instinct and came here years ago.

Her train of thought was shattered as the wind was knocked out of her. Two of the cloaked people had grabbed her from behind and forced her to her feet. They dragged her across the room, closer and closer to the table. She struggled to catch her breath and elbowed them away and they stumbled back reeling.

Frantically, Adela looked around the room, trying to find a door. There were none. She pushed her tangled mess of hair out of her face and tried her best to breathe. They had all gotten in here somehow. There was bound to be a way out. But her heart fell as she continued to twist and turn, looking around the space. There truly seemed to be no way out. The cloaked figures stood as still as statues, watching her as she spun into a frenzied panic.

Her gaze landed on the stone platform and she froze. Sitting on the heavily stained surface was a dagger. Long and gold with blood-red rubies on its hilt.

She heard footsteps behind her. The two were coming close to her again. She threw herself backward, clawing at them, forcing them away. One of them stepped on the hem of her nightgown, now crumpled and smeared with grime. She ripped it away before he had a chance to grab it.

"It's not worth the fight."

Dalton.

Shakily, Adela turned around to face him. His expression was stone-cold and he looked paler than usual. His blue eyes pierced daggers into her soul.

"What's going on, Dalton?" she breathed, though she already had a guess.

"I need you to do this for me," he continued in that eerie monotone voice. "I can't do it without you."

She crossed her arms. "What does that mean?" she asked. "No, really. What's that supposed to even mean at this point? You seem to be doing just great without me."

He gave her a sad smile and for a second, he was the Dalton she knew. But it was gone as quickly as it came. "It's a part of the ascension ritual. I need this for my future. For us. For all of our futures. You understand, don't you, Dela?"

"Don't call me that."

He stared at her, blankly.

"The blood shall stain our very foundation. And a new dawn will rise," the others chanted in a low, droning tone.

Adela couldn't tear her eyes off Dalton. "What happened to you and me? What happened to forgetting everything else? What happened to nothing else matters?" Hot tears pricked at the corners of her eyes and she furiously blinked them away. She couldn't afford to cry and let the devastation suffocate her.

"Nothing else matters," he said. "No one else. Without you, this wouldn't be possible."

All the warnings and red flags her mom and friends and sisters had brought up flashed through Adela's memories. All of the things she had refused to believe.

"So that's why you brought me here," she spat. "For this? To..." her voice trailed off and she couldn't bring herself to finish the sentence.

"To kill you," he flatly finished for her, picking up the dagger. "A sacrifice from the heart, of a heart. It's the only way."

She had done everything for him. Been everything for him, been the person he had wanted. And this was how he repaid her for that?

"I can't believe you," she hissed as she lunged forward, ready to strangle the daylights out of Dalton.

But someone held her back, picked her swiftly off her feet and tossed her onto the table. She cried out in pain from the impact. Her head was still pounding from earlier. Adela had to force herself to swallow the bile rising in her throat. It burned. She refused to believe that this was how everything was going to end. It was so ridiculous that it couldn't possibly be her reality.

Dalton towered over her, raising the dagger. The others in the room began chanting a series of latin phrases that grew louder and more powerful as they continued.

"Dalton, please" she whispered. But there was no remorse in his face. No sign that he even recognized her.

The chant grew in intensity and a soulless grin spread over Dalton's face. "It's my time," he told her. "My time to take over, to rise to the top. Thank you for everything."

He pulled his arm back, preparing to thrust it down onto her.

As he did so, Adela shot out her throbbing arm, grabbing his. She yanked him down onto his side. He was now laying on the table beside her. There was no way in hell she was dying today, especially not like this. Not because of him. Dalton still reeled from the impact and Adela used all of her strength to hoist herself upwards, on top of him. He twisted, using his free hand to grab at her skin, her fat, her hair, her dress. She wrangled herself free and knelt over him, keeping most of her weight on his lower torso, trapping him down.

He flung the dagger towards her face. Instinctively, she reached out and yanked it away by the blade.

Adela winced as it cut through her skin and quickly grabbed onto the hilt with her other hand. She winced.

Dalton lurched at her again, but this time she was ready. With every remaining bit of strength she had left she plunged the dagger towards him. She felt it go into his chest, resisting as it slipped through flesh, his bones, his back. Finally, she felt it hit the rock underneath.

Blood pooled out of his mouth and he sputtered, blinking at her, confused. The coughs didn't last long though, and soon he was staring at the ceiling, lifeless.

She couldn't help but feel relief. Relief that she was alive. A sense of pride that she hadn't let him use her again.

Adela let out a shaky breath and slowly unfurled her fingers from the dagger's hilt. It remained stuck in his torso.

Her fingers were coated with a layer of thick, shiny blood, a mix of hers and his. She looked down at her nightgown, now in tatters and spattered with little red droplets.

Her gaze lifted to look at the rest of the room. Everyone had moved in closer and was bowing towards her. Up and down their heads bobbed as they bowed and bowed and bowed. The latin chants resumed once more, but they were calmer now. Subdued, even.

"All hail our new era!" one of them shouted. The rest murmured in response.

"Hail the sacrality of our ascension, the sacrality of The Dreamers."

Adela's face scrunched up in confusion. Dalton's sacrifice had failed, so there should be no ascension. Her gaze fell once again to the body below her.

The dagger had struck Dalton directly in the heart. *From the heart, of a heart.* The sacrifice that he had needed of her so he could be the leader of The Dreamers.

Instead, he had been the sacrifice. The blood that poured out of the wound, despite the dagger still holding strong, now seeped further into Adela's dress, further into the stone below.

"All hail Lady Adela," the voice cried.

The rest chimed in with agreement. "All hail Lady Adela!"

Adela took one last look at her blood soaked hands, at his lifeless face, before looking back up at the sea of figures. They were slowly taking their hoods off one by one, slowly standing back. A few of them stared at her in shock. Others with admiration. A few soon sank back to the ground in a mix of awe and fear.

Adela gave them a tentative smile. Whoever these Dreamers were, in their eyes they were her people. And maybe that did make her one of them now. Their faces were bright, shining, hopeful. Looking towards their new era. At her.

This was absurd.

But here they were, and here she was, and she was and something about it felt right, put her at peace. Finally, she was in control of herself again. The feeling hit her so suddenly that she let out a laugh of relief. She hadn't realized how far she had gone until now, how Dalton made her twist and turn to his every whim. She was no longer Dalton's fiancé, Dalton's girlfriend, Dalton's love, Dalton's life, Dalton's good little girl.

It was as if a weight had fallen off her shoulders and sunk underneath the thrashing waves, never to be seen again.

She had killed her fiancé in self defense, but she had still killed him. In cold blood. Yet, she couldn't bring herself to feel remorse about it. This man she had killed, he wasn't Dalton. He was someone that she had never met in her life. He was the one who had killed Dalton. He had killed her Dalton long before today.

And in return, she had taken everything from him—from this stranger who had ruined her life.

It was time to finally have it back.

Pretty Little Bird

Lily Kent

CW: sexual harassment, sexual assault, blood, gore, death

Blood is not as warm as I thought it would be.

In the back of my mind I'm vaguely aware that this should not be my biggest concern, but the sentiment is crystal clear, easy to grasp, almost grounding.

I clench my fists tightly until my nails dig deep, pointed grooves into my palms that are sticky with sweat. No, sticky with blood.

I can feel my lips moving, my mouth falling open and closing in tune with my heaving chest. Strained breaths escape my lips as my heart beats a frantic rhythm, as if it wants to escape from my rib cage. My erratic gasping is bordering on hyperventilation, but my panting pools into silence and is absorbed by the wooden walls of the lifeless home. Not that I'm alone.

My black dress clings uncomfortably to my pale skin. The once itchy material is now damp and sticky. Tendrils of untamable, deep orange waves have escaped from the haphazard bun I threw my hair into minutes ago. My baby hairs cling to my forehead, slicked down with blood. No, this time it's sweat.

Liquid seeps down the staircase before me. The velour carpet lining the steps has turned an even deeper shade of red from its descent.

I drop the solid brass candelabra from my grasp and distantly register the dull thud as it dents the wooden flooring. I'm sure the small crater of damage would cost a fortune to repair in an authentic Victorian house like this, but splinters and wood chips are laughable compared to the red sea before me.

I feel my feet lift from the ground and begin to carry me up the stairs. Blood seeps between my toes with each step as the soaked carpet squishes audibly under my weight. The substance coats the soles of my feet and drips off my toes as I continue my ascent. I raise a shaky palm to glide along the wooden banister, painting it a glistening red to match the floor below.

When I reach the first body I pause my ghostly trek and bend at my waist to gaze into my Professor's eyes, now dull from the lack of life behind them. He's splayed on his back with his arms thrown wide and his head hanging off of the step I stand before. The ends of his hair tickle my toes and are dipped lightly in his own blood.

His mouth hangs agape, exposing his perfectly straight teeth that I tap a finger on.

"Pretty little bird," I coo, and run a hand through his soft, thick hair. My fingers catch in the wet ends and I have to tug with extra force, yanking his neck so that the back of his skull bangs against the step. A hollow thud radiates from the impact.

A high-pitched giggle fills the air and I tear my gaze from his. I straighten and whip my head around as the laughter continues to echo before I recognize it as my own. I quiet myself abruptly and return my cold stare to my Professor's even colder one. I cock my head and smile, satisfied, before stepping over his crushed torso.

His ribcage is cavernous. Skin mottled and sunken into the crater formed by his cracked ribs. Pride consumes me.

I had never considered myself strong or powerful until I cracked the candelabra against the skull of his friend. That body is in the hallway at the top of the stairs. He went down with one strike. My Professor put up more of a fight when he realized what was going on, but it wasn't enough.

The third body is in the study. He was too drunk to fight.

I reach the top of the stairs and turn to observe his lifeless form. The events of the past day haven't registered so I wait. I wait for the tears, for the regret that will no doubt flood my system. I blink and half expect the scene to melt away.

It doesn't. The bodies remain.

And I don't regret it.

12 hours earlier

The collar of my wool coat itches against my neck as I peer up at the magnificent estate. My duffel bag rests on the ground beside me as I wait for the door to be answered. My hands are balled into fists and shoved as deep into my coat as my pockets will allow. The mid-December wind is a brutal bite against the exposed skin of my cheeks.

After what feels like hours, but is only a few minutes, the door swings open to reveal a grand entryway and the warm face of my professor, Dr. Lancaster.

"Ah, Clarise, I'm so glad you could make it." He smiles in greeting.

"Thank you for the invitation, Doctor. I didn't even consider turning it down." I grin back politely. My statement is more than just flattery, it's the truth.

From the moment I was accepted into the University of Virginia's MA program a year ago I started imagining myself as one of the few students to receive an invitation to Dr. Lancaster's elusive winter "retreat." It was no secret that he was the most renowned and beloved of the English literature professors in the program. Students practically worshiped the ground he walked on while the other professors tried simply to follow in his footsteps.

If you asked any one of us grad students what exactly was so special about him, I doubt we could pin it down. From the moment you entered one of his enigmatic lectures you were swept into the Lancaster wave and all you could do was drown. None of us brought life vests, and none of us wanted them.

There are very few people who genuinely possess that level of charisma. Dr. Lancaster is magnetic, and I feel his pull now as he beckons me into the house.

"Your room's just upstairs," he remarks as I step into the warmth of his house and his presence. "I'll grab your bag." I don't realize I left it until he steps outside and bends down to retrieve it. As he does so his hair falls over his eyes. I've always thought that for a man in his 40's he was unfairly blessed with thick, shiny hair, but up close I can see the blunt ends and the true dullness of the brown.

When he straightens I take notice of his unusually casual outfit, jeans and a beige sweater that compliments his tanned skin. It's odd seeing my professor in his natural environment. It makes him appear almost childish, like a teenage boy instead of the accomplished writer and teacher that I know him as. In a way it humanizes him, makes a god mortal.

While the graduate program prioritizes its members' autonomy, the hierarchy between student and teacher persists. Dr. Lancaster is my professor and I his student, but here that boundary is null. We are both human and the field is level. This week isn't about what I can learn from him, but rather how we can work together to breathe life into my thesis before its defense.

"I printed out the current version of my thesis," I say to the back of his head as he re-enters the house and leads me to my room. I take note of the extravagance of the foyer with its tapestried walls and grand spiral staircase. Even tenured I wonder how a professor can afford such an estate in the Virginia countryside.

I don't think I've ever stepped foot in a building this expensive, excluding my university's libraries. This type of luxury is not something I'll ever get used to, or feel comfortable in. My life up until higher academia was spent moving from apartment to cramped apartment, my family barely scraping by. As soon as I received my first stipend check I moved to a modest apartment of my own that's a considerable commute to campus, but it's affordable and for the first time in my life I have a space of my own. Moving out was the last step in cutting ties with my family and the first in starting my new life. It was a choice I thanked past me for every day.

Dr. Lancaster stops when we reach a door near the top of the staircase.

"I have it on my laptop as well," I continued, thinking he didn't hear me. "I know you prefer physical copies so I brought both."

"Right," he says absentmindedly while pointing towards the door before us. "This is my study. Your room is the one to the left." The doors to his study and my room are separated by about ten feet and I immediately head to mine.

He watches me open the door and I involuntarily gasp at the sight before me. A magnificent four poster bed outfitted with pristine white sheets sits opposite the entrance. Mahogany nightstands sit on either side of the bed, each adorned with large brass candelabras, and a matching armoire big enough to fit all of my belongings three times sits to my left. Next to it is a baroque-style, full-length mirror that I can only dream of owning myself.

"Thank you, Professor," I whisper in awe. "This place is amazing and the room is lovely. I really can't thank you enough for inviting me." I tear my gaze from my room for the next week to look him in the eyes. His own gaze is fixed upon me and he leans against the doorframe with his arms crossed. His stare is cold and intense, a contrasting expression from his usually jovial demeanor.

"It's my pleasure, Clarise." His baritone raises goosebumps on my arms despite being clad in multiple layers. "There's something special about you." My cheeks flush red at the compliment and I hope he attributes it as being a leftover effect from the cold.

"I guess I'll unpack my things and bring my manuscript to your study after?" I struggle not to stutter under the seriousness of his still unbroken stare. He sighs and pushes away from the doorframe.

"Take your time getting settled. We don't start for another few hours. The bathroom is the door across the hall and your uniform is hanging in the armoire." I open my mouth to ask what he means, but he turns away to head to his study. From the hallway I hear him add, "And burn your manuscript. You won't be needing it."

After I unpack my things and shower long enough to turn my skin a blotchy red, I finally work up the courage to approach the study. Dr. Lancaster hasn't explicitly stated as off limits, in fact he hasn't said much of anything since I've arrived, yet I get the feeling that I'm encroaching on sacred ground by entering.

I opt for an outfit to match the casualness of his. A plain green sweater, black leggings, and thick wool socks. I don't want him to think I'm over-excited for this opportunity even though in reality I'm ecstatic, but also terrified. Everyone has heard the rumors of the students invited to his retreats who drop out of the program entirely because they couldn't handle his blunt honesty towards their work. Luckily bluntness is something I'm used to from my harsh upbringing.

I also have my doubts about those stories. From the couple of classes I've taken with Dr. Lancaster, he's been nothing but encouraging and supportive of the ideas I bring to lecture. Still, no matter how much I tell myself I can handle whatever he throws at me, the underlying imposter syndrome rampant in almost every literature student begins to creep in.

My grip tightens on the thick stack of pages that is my manuscript and I can feel my palms growing sweaty. My hair hangs in still damp waves just past my shoulders and my face grows warm. I take a few deep, calming breaths and knock on the door before my courage vanishes entirely.

"Come in," is his muffled response so I grab the cold, brass handle and turn.

Dr. Lancaster's study looks like a projection of the man himself. Every wall is lined with shelves that are filled with books shoved haphazardly into rows and stacks. If there's a specific organization system it isn't immediately obvious. A large, brick fireplace is the only interruption in the shelves other than the doorway I now stand in. A fire emits a satisfying warmth I can feel even from the other end of the room. Mismatched rugs cover the hardwood floor, creating a chaotic collage of colors and patterns in stark contrast to the maroon carpet lining the stairs and hallway just outside. A purple couch and other gem-toned chairs form a circle with his large desk that is also stacked with books and papers. He sits at the desk now with his head down, intensely focused on the paper before him.

I tread into the room with uncertainty and he looks up to meet me with the same assessing stare as before. As I falter in my approach I realize that nothing could have prepared me for being the sole focus of his unwavering attention.

"You're not in your uniform," he states bluntly. The uniform he's referring to is indeed hanging in the armoire like he mentioned it would be. After my shower however, I assumed it was a lighthearted joke, albeit an inappropriate one given the nature of our relationship.

I laugh in an attempt to dispel the intense air that has suddenly filled the room, but it comes out forced and I have to clear my throat before speaking.

"The maid outfit?" I mean for it to sound sarcastic, so that he knows I'm playing along with his joke, but his expression remains unchanged. "It's okay, Professor, I'm not offended. It was funny." I don't even sound convincing to myself.

Anger flashes quickly through his deep, brown eyes but he recovers quickly, taking a deep breath and leaning back in his chair.

"I can assure you, Clarise, that I do not play games on my retreats. By accepting my invitation you agreed to follow the rules of my house."

Flustered, and worried I've offended him, I quickly apologize.

"I'm sorry, I'm very grateful for this opportunity, and I absolutely will respect your home since you're kind enough to let me stay in it." The words tumble out in a torrent of anxiety. "I'm just confused, Professor. I don't know how this week is going to work exactly, so maybe walking me through how you usually structure your retreats would be helpful? I would hate to cross any boundaries you might have." I didn't expect the people-pleaser in me to come out so quickly, but old habits die hard.

He pushes his chair back and stands. Framed by his belongings he appears bigger than usual. I've always noticed his height, but it's emphasized in the low lighting that seems to be a staple for the estate. His humanity melts away as quickly as it had appeared upon my arrival, and I'm reminded of my true status among him. Unconsciously I take a step back.

"How I structure my retreats," he says sharply while walking around the desk towards me, "is I give the commands, and you obey."

I furrow my brows and part my lips in confusion. I clutch my manuscript as an anchor as his presence floods the room around me. For the first time in my two years of knowing him I don't want to be drowned.

"I still can't tell if you're joking," I admit because I don't know what else to say. He crosses the room to where I'm standing in a few short strides and plucks the manuscript from my hands. The loss of weight is uncomfortable and I don't know what to do with my hands so I cross them over my chest and tuck them tightly against my sides.

"What did I tell you to do with this?" He's only a foot away from me and I can feel the warmth of his breath as he speaks. Up close his eyes are even darker and more all encompassing. I can see how easily one could get lost in them and dragged farther out to sea.

"You told me to burn it." It comes out as hardly more than a whisper. I'm trapped in his riptide.

"I don't joke, Clarise." He stares at me for a few more seconds before turning towards the fireplace and throwing my manuscript into the flames. All I can do is watch as the papers catch and the corners curl in on themselves. I'm frozen and utterly speechless. The students liked to joke that he had that effect on girls, but now I understand with terrifying clarity.

"The guests are arriving in two hours. Go change and meet me in the foyer." He returns to his desk without another word and it takes more intention than is natural to get my body moving.

I make the short walk to my room, which felt luxurious mere minutes ago, but now looks like a cell glamoured to distract me from the mental prison I suspect this week will be.

The maid outfit mocks me from the floor where I tossed it. I pick it up and rub the thin black fabric between my fingers. It's at least one size too small given my ample chest and I can already tell that the skirt will hardly cover my ass. I'm only a few inches above five feet tall, but my long torso makes every dress I wear risque by only leaving a few inches to cover my legs.

I consider not putting it on, but I want this to be a joke so bad. If I play along I'll earn his favor more than I already have. He's always complimented me in his lectures, saying how I have valuable ideas and unique perspectives. If I wear the damn outfit then he'll see I'm funny as well as smart. I don't always have to be so serious. I pestered him too much already with my manuscript so the least I can do is put on the dress for a few minutes and play along.

I throw the outfit onto the bed and shed my current one. The dress is itchy as I slide it over my arms and I can feel the cheapness of the fabric. It smells stale as if it's been sitting in the armoire all year waiting for me. I douse myself in my vanilla body spray to counteract the aroma and peer quickly at my reflection in the mirror.

My breasts strain against the bodice's square neckline and a considerable amount of my cleavage is on display. I turn and see that I was right about the length as well as the size. While the skirt covers my ass fully, I know without a doubt if I bend over even slightly that will no longer be the case.

My wool socks match the white lace accents of the collar and sewn-on apron. My thick hair still hasn't completely dried and as a result darkens the fabric around my shoulders with water. A small giggle escapes my lips at the bizarreness of the situation, and because the only other sound I can currently produce would be a scream. I know there will be questions from the other grad students about the retreat when I return. There always is, that is when the student actually returns from the retreat and doesn't drop out. There's been a recent trend the past few years of the latter and I know my peers are dying for details from someone who actually survives the apparently brutal process.

Although right now the experience doesn't seem brutal as much as degrading. Maybe this is his way of reminding me of my role as his student rather than an equal. Either way, Lancaster certainly seems to have an interesting sense of humor.

After examining myself in the mirror one last time, I leave my room and head to the staircase. I can hear a voice as I start my descent so I call out.

"Alright, Professor, I changed into your uniform," the words echo back to me. "Is this like an initiation thing? Are you gonna take me into the basement with candles and make me swear never to reveal the advice given to me here?" My steps falter and I stop dead in my tracks. Dr. Lancaster has entered the foyer from I'm assuming the kitchen off to the side, but he isn't alone. A shorter man stands beside him wearing a dark blue button up and black slacks. He has close cropped black hair and eyes as dark as his skin. Both men are holding glasses filled with singular ice cubes and amber liquid.

I grab the banister to ground myself. Clearly I'm not as in on the joke as I thought I was.

"Well, Mark," the new man exclaims while unapologetically looking me up and down, "she's certainly better than the girl you chose for us last year."

I feel my breathing quicken and my eyes widen.

"Clarise, nice of you to join us," Lancaster drawls. He makes his way up the staircase and stops on the step below me. "Usually the help pours our drinks, but as you had an issue with your wardrobe I'll excuse the offense." He lifts his drink as is to emphasize his point and the powerful stench of alcohol wafts towards me. The almost antiseptic aroma snaps me back to the present and I draw myself up to my full height.

"Professor, what is going on?" I bite out between my clenched teeth. He ignores my question and takes my arm with his free hand to guide me effortlessly down the staircase.

"This is Thomas," he manually extends my arm towards the man when we reach him, "and, Thomas, this is Clarise, the help and entertainment for this year's retreat." Thomas extends his own hand to meet mine in a handshake.

"Well it's a pleasure to meet you, Clarise," he smiles, flashing white teeth. I have a strong urge to snarl back, but I'm in too much shock to muster any kind of retort.

"Thomas, why don't you head up to the study. Nathan should be arriving shortly and I don't want our pretty little bird here making the same mistake with his drink."

Thomas chuckles. The sound grates my ears.

"Alright, I'll be waiting." His eyes make a final sweep over my exposed body before he leaves us.

Lancaster watches his retreat and when we hear the door to the study close he turns to me. "Kitchen, now."

I have no choice but to follow him. The kitchen of the house has been completely modernized and it almost feels like stepping into a different world. A world with no retreat. A world where I'm not being forced to wear a provocative outfit in front of my professor and his friends.

Except I look down and I am.

Lancaster sets his drink down on the granite countertop of the island and turns to me so fast I hardly have time to blink before he's holding both my wrists in his icy hands.

"Welcome to your retreat, Clarise." He has to bend down to bring his face level with mine. "You're a smart girl so I'm sure by now you've figured out what's going on?" The question feels more like a statement. Lancaster was always good at validating me academically. His compliments towards me in his lectures combatted my imposter syndrome, but this one has me thrown. My skin crawls where his hands form vises around my wrists.

"I'm confused, Professor," I can barely get the words out and I stutter as I do. He loosens his grip and sighs.

"Not Professor, call me Mark." He drops one hand as he says this and uses it to tuck my hair behind my ear. My eyes sting with the threat of tears and I have to tell myself to breathe before speaking again.

"Please, Mark. Tell me exactly what is going on."

"Every December break I host a retreat for a couple of my close friends. A week of drinking and talking about God knows what." He stops and I nod to let him know that I'm listening. "But you see, little bird, we men get lonely, and we get bored so quickly by just each other's company. So a while back we got the idea of inviting a girl along, and I thought who better than one of my dedicated students? Someone eager. Someone special." He smiles as he says this and I can see how age has taken a toll on him. Wrinkles form on his forehead and his teeth are slightly yellow. I cringe away from him.

"I'm leaving," I claim with more confidence than I feel. I turn on my heel but he still holds my wrist.

"Nobody is concerned about you, Clarise," he shouts sharply. "What do you think the other requirement is for the bird whose wings I clip?" The tears I've attempted to tame suddenly break free with an audible sob, but this doesn't deter him or damper his harshness. "A loner. You're the first to come to class and the first to leave. I've checked with the school and your emergency contacts are listed as distant relatives. Your housing is a single unit with no roommates. Nobody is waiting for you, and nobody will come for you."

The ferocity of his words stun me but he finally lets go. He knows I won't run. He knows he has me. He knows he has me because nobody else does.

"It's all just a little bit of fun, little bird. Pour our drinks and give us a show. We'll be gentle." He picks up his glass and turns to leave. "Clean yourself up and greet Nathan when he gets here."

And with that I'm left alone.

Nathan arrives at 7:30.

I spent the past thirty minutes in my room sobbing and trying to devise a plan to leave. Lancaster had insisted on sending a personal driver to pick me up from my apartment. I thought the treatment was just part of his extravagance, but now I know it was another barb in his carefully set trap.

I consider calling a taxi, but when I search for my phone in the pocket of my abandoned coat I find it missing, no doubt taken by him. I remind myself that he's been doing this to students for years. By now he has every base covered, and I don't kid myself by thinking that I'll be the one to outsmart him.

Walking is also out of the question as the nearest neighbors are miles away and I'll certainly freeze before reaching them if I can even locate their houses in the pitch black.

My eyes are swollen and my cheeks red and splotchy when the knock comes from downstairs. I can hear Thomas and Lancaster in the study next to me and the pause in their conversation.

I wait a moment and let the silence stretch.

The knock comes again and this time I surrender. As quickly as possible I bounce down the stairs. If it's entertainment they want from me then they can certainly have it. It won't be the first time I've bitten my tongue for a man and played the part he's asked of me.

I worked my ass off to make it to this point in my life without the support of my family. I'm in one of the most competitive graduate programs in the entire country and I'm not going to throw it all away because I can't lighten up for a week. I'll do what they tell me to, be the perfect little maid for them, and then when it's over forget it ever even happened.

This I can handle.

I quickly slip into the kitchen and pour a generous glass of the closest whiskey. I smooth the front of my dress as he knocks a third time and I hear the door to the study open. As I approach the door I look up to see Mark, his face a mask of annoyance. I meet his glare with my sweetest smile and open the door.

A few hours and countless drinks later and the men are thoroughly wasted. At some point in the night I gradually started giving them stronger and stronger pours. I thought that if I could just get enough alcohol in their systems they would eventually tire, but each drink only seemed to bolster their attitudes.

Now they lounge around the study, lazily sprawled on the various chairs while I stand near the desk, patiently waiting to retrieve more drinks. The only "entertainment" I've been asked to provide is twirling around the middle of the room to give them a good view, and reaching to the highest shelves for books they subsequently would discard to the floor.

Each time I extend my body onto my tip-toes I feel their violating stares like daggers. Nevertheless, I perform each task with no complaint and a tight lipped smile that they're too drunk to notice is fake. When they laugh, I laugh, and when they ask for something I oblige.

Nathan, however, has been noticeably more difficult to please. When I welcomed him, his eyes had shot immediately to the drink in my hand which I held out in offering.

"Is that Johnnie Walker?" he asked. He stood at least a foot taller than me with dark, slicked back hair and emerald eyes. He wore sweats and a ragged Yale sweater, the casualness which made a stark contrast to his uptight personality.

"Yes, sir." I handed him the glass which he took nonchalantly and sipped slowly while never breaking eye contact.

After emptying the glass he licked his lips and sighed. "You lied." And with that he shoved the glass into my chest and walked past me to the study.

Now he rests in the chair directly across from me, drink in hand. I haven't refilled any of their drinks for a while and I know it's coming so I'm extra alert. As if on cue Nathan calls out my name.

"Clarise, pick that up," he drawls while motioning with his empty hand to the ground in front of his chair. The other men look to him then to me.

"Pick what up, sir?"

He rises from his chair and walks to the nearest shelf, plucking a random title from the top of a stack and returning to his seat. After lowering himself into it he straightens his arm out and drops the book with a thud.

I clench my teeth and take a quick breath before pasting my smile back on.

"Of course." I saunter to his chair and bend my knees.

"Turn around," he commands. I pause. Slowly I turn around so that my backside is facing him. With the level he's at I'm almost certain he can already see up my dress. I glance at Thomas and Mark to find them smirking, enjoying the show as much as Nathan clearly is.

I start to bend my knees again but hear him clear his throat.

"Bend at the waist darling." I feel my lips start to tremble and a small sob nearly escapes, but I manage to swallow it down. I can handle this.

Following his instructions I bend at the waist and immediately feel a cold hand cup my now fully exposed ass. He squeezes painfully hard then releases as I swipe the book from the ground and essentially run back to the desk. Blood pounds in my ears and my chest rises and falls in rapid succession. I drop the book on the desk and slam my palms onto the surface with my head down. I squeeze my eyes shut as I attempt to get my breathing under control. I will not let them see me fall apart. I can handle this.

I take one last deep breath and straighten. I turn around while tugging the hem of the dress down only to find the men in hysterics.

Mark's head is tossed back, his mouth wide open from laughter. The other two are in similar states and Thomas slurs his words.

"That never gets old," he exclaims while extending his glass to cheers Nathan's.

"I love how they jump," Mark adds and raises his own glass. Nathan is quiet but the expression on his face is no less content.

I turn my gaze from him to Mark to see him already staring at me and for the first time in hours, I let my smile fall. He notices and immediately barks out a command.

"Get some candles, little bird, it's too dark in here."

"We need to see you properly," Nathan remarks, his smirk one of satisfaction.

"There's some in your room I think, and more in the kitchen," Mark adds. I stand frozen in place until he snaps his fingers, making me flinch. I exit the room as quickly as possible and make the short walk to mine.

I slam the door behind me and rest my back against it. The study door opens and I worry Mark is coming to reprimand my performance, but then another door closes and I know it's just Thomas using the bathroom for the hundredth time.

The only other sounds are that of the blood roaring in my ears and their continuous laughter. I clench my fists, digging crescent moons into my clammy palms. A sob finally breaks free from my lips and I slap a hand over my mouth to smother my cries. I can't let them hear me. I know it's what they expect, what they want.

I shut my eyes tightly and run my hands through my hair, counting my breaths. I tell myself for the millionth time that I can do this, that it will be over before I know it. Their laughter rings in my ears and when I reopen my eyes I see clearer than I have the entire evening.

I look to the candelabras on the nightstands to see that they are devoid of any candles. When I walk towards the closest one I catch my reflection in the mirror and stop in my tracks. I don't recognize the woman staring back at me. I take a step towards her and see how scared she is. But there's something more under it, something stronger.

Rage.

It finally registers that the feeling I have been biting back with a smile, and the sobs I have been suppressing are not ones of sadness, but of anger. All that time I spent craving his validation, eager to be one of his favorites, was time he spent laying his trap. Manipulating and weaving me into his web of charisma with waves of compliments until he knew without a doubt that I would abandon ship to swim to him.

I played right into his hand.

Their laughter pierces through the wall and I snap my gaze away from this new, angry version of myself. I grab a hair tie from my bag on the floor, throw my hair into a bun, and snatch the candelabra from the night stand. I take a last look in the mirror and smile, then I leave the room and follow the sounds of their laughter.

Thomas exits the bathroom across the hall at the same time and stumbles into me.

"Whoa there," he exclaims as he leans against the wall to steady himself. Before he can say another word I raise my arm and smash the candelabra into his head.

Secrets of the Moon

Kassandra Morgan

CW: sexual assault, domestic violence, suicidal ideations, violence

THE BEGINNING

No one envisions their life will be one long stream of night. The stories that are weaved and passed on through the next generations occur in the light. It is a reminder that every day is a chance to begin anew. The light is the place we all want to live in.

Well, unless you're me, that is. See, I've never touched the light. Well, I suppose that is not true in its entirety. I have felt the light cast shadows upon my skin, but not without drastic consequences and not in the same way you have. My hand still burns at the thought of it. What I mean to say is that my existence has never occurred in the light.

I've read about the light. I've seen it in shows and movies. I've watched it rise from my windows on mornings after I stayed up too late dreaming about a different world than the one I live in.

I'm sure you're wondering how we ended up here and what you've gotten yourself into. The truth is both incredibly simple and far too incredulous for most people to share in these sentences of our brief introduction. If you're patient with me, however, you'll find the answers you seek.

I suppose that for this anthology, we can explore the overarching portion of my story that created the person I am. After all, you can't marvel at a finished masterpiece without understanding the craft of sacrifice that created it. Besides, what great legend do you know that is spoken of without the hands that molded it, touched it, brought it to life? In that same way, this is my story-my legend.

My name is Kamaria and should you go looking to the great histories, you will find no mention of Kamaria the Amaurotic. If I'm being honest with you, I prefer it that way. Even now, after all these years, I find no reason for my story to be recounted for the masses except like this.

My mother aptly named me Kamaria, seeing as the sole meaning of my name is "the moon." She has been my one true friend in each lifetime of my never-ending existence... the moon that is, not my mother. She has never failed to show me kindness and she has always led me home.

I was born in Old Bohemia within the Holy Roman Empire in the year 818 and lived there nearly eighteen trips around the moon. I had the privilege of watching as the empires of old rise and fall. There are many things I should tell you about my existence, but I do not have the space to share it here. So, for now, I will simply tell you these four truths:

I have traveled the world and marveled at its beauty. I have also wept blood red tears at the cruelty it shows to humans and creatures alike. I've known the touch of a person that loved me and felt the wrath of a man that despised me. I've lived throughout centuries, re-inventing myself, trying to embrace the light but sometimes fully descending into the darkness of my depravity.

What you should truly know. However this is the first time I've shared this unfiltered tale of Kamaria the Amaurotic with anyone who was not alive to witness it. No soul has come before you that I have deemed worthy to entrust with my secrets... with my truth. What you do with it after is no longer of my concern. I do not think I will be around by then in any case.

PART ONE: THE BOY

I remember vividly the year I turned fourteen. It was during this time that I should've been budding into my womanhood, but everything is different when you're a vampire. My body isn't like yours or any other human for that matter. But, unluckily for me, I still got to experience hormone fluctuations, out of control emotions and existential dread.

It was also during this time that I felt the first tug of love on my heartstrings. I don't have to recount the idea of feeling butterflies in your stomach because I feel you are intelligent enough to know of what I speak. For me, this just so happened to be during the autumn equinox when Lahahana noticed me for the first time.

Before I tell you of that night, I need to explain that I enjoyed watching people from their windows as they slept, listening in on whatever they were dreaming about. It was an interesting way to pass the time. This might make me sound like a psychopath, but I've come to terms with it.

I spent most nights that I wasn't hunting with Fahim in Lahahana's window. He always had interesting dreams and I enjoyed hearing them. I suppose it didn't hurt that he was beautiful when he slept, almost as beautiful as when he was awake. There was something calming about watching the rise and fall of his chest as his light snores filtered through my ears.

I had been listening to his dreams for years by the time of the festival. If you asked me to

recall the first time I'd done so, I don't know if I could give you an accurate answer. I

believe, however, that it was one night in the summer that I'd just turned eight. I'd recently been given the knowledge that I could hear the dreams of everyone around me, and not just the people I loved. I remember it was especially interesting to me because while I could hear their dreams and thoughts, they couldn't hear me speak to them telepathically unless I had an emotional bond with them.

Perching in windows to listen in as people dreamed was risky. But the closest I'd ever come to getting caught in someone's window was roughly three months before the festival by Lahahana himself. His dream that night was especially harrowing. Something had been chasing him through the mountains, but it only manifested as a dark cloud of smoke. He was running as fast as he could when he tripped on a tree branch and landed face first onto the mossy earth floor.

His skin was pale and clammy, sweat dripping from him onto the ground below. He was screaming at the apparition as it came to a stop above him. He tried to move away, but the tree branch he tripped on snaked around his wrists and ankles, binding him in place.

Just as the apparition reached out for him, he began to stir. I quietly lowered myself off the window frame and tiptoed to where he lay. I slowly reached my fingers out, brushing

the tips lightly against his skin. I trailed my fingers down his jaw, noting the way it clenched from my touch, or perhaps from the dream invading his mind. Even in that state, he was beautiful.

He yelled, startling me out of my daydream. I barely made it to the window and off the ledge onto the ground below when he began to pant as he sat up in bed. I could hear Lahahana as his dream-addled thoughts began to describe what he believed was a dark, looming figure in his mind. His thoughts were trying to make sense of the presence that seemingly leaked evil in the aura that surrounded it. Each thought raced through his head as he tried to work up the courage to see if the figure was real.

"It wasn't real." I heard him think as he wrung out his hands. *"Dreams aren't real."*

"They could be." His thoughts answered, confirming his fear. *"Maybe the apparition was real and coming to eat you as punishment for all the evil you've done."*

He made up his mind in that moment, telling himself that he had to face his fears. The soft sound of his feet hitting the floor shook me from listening to his thoughts and I raced into his family garden and hid behind a small tree. I watched him approach the window, looking out cautiously to see if his dream had manifested into reality. He sucked in a deep breath as he scanned the world outside before releasing it in the relief that it wasn't real. Thinking that he would be fine, he turned from the window and climbed back into his bed where he quickly drifted to sleep.

He never saw me that night as I hid in the shadows of the garden, and I only ever visited his window twice more.

The air was full of music the night of the festival and I felt its electricity in the air around me. I loved night festivals because it was the most interaction I was allowed with the human world. Of course, I heard the silent whispers of "*the cursed Bartak child that only comes out at night,*" but I told myself they wouldn't ruin the night for me.

I was allowed a seat with other girls at a long wooden table while we wove together florals that we would later wear as a crown. The whole time, I kept a close eye on Lahahana. I practically willed him to look in my direction as I tried to manage not speaking to him through his thoughts... just in case he secretly loved me. Teta Salma and Maminka Lucie had already warned me several times about being careless with my gifts tonight.

Just as I started to give up, Lahahana tipped his head in my direction, hair swaying with the breeze as his eyes met mine. They were light blue, and they were exquisite. They were the kind you could get lost in, and that's exactly what I did. When he stood and started walking toward me, my stomach flipped. I was frozen in the moment. If I had any breath to hitch, it would've, as he stopped in front of me.

"Hi, Kamaria," he said, his voice smooth as my name vibrated off his lips.

My voice shook as I replied, "hi, Lahahana."

I cursed myself internally, begging myself to get a grip. *He's just a boy*, I protested. *Yeah, a boy that looks like beauty in the flesh. Not to mention, a boy you've watched sleep from his window.*

"Want to get some kolach with me?"

It's not my favorite, but it was a human tradition to eat these small cakes at Obzinky once the harvest for our village was complete. I stood and he grabbed my hand, his skin soft against mine. My cheeks flushed as he interlaced our fingers.

I followed behind him as we walked, his warmth leaking into my cool palm. If you believe in love at first sight, fourteen-year-old Kamaria would've sworn this was it. I had longed for someone my age that would make me feel normal, and that's what it felt like being with Lahahana.

"Where are you, Zlatíčko?" My Strýc Fahim's voice filtered through my thoughts. When I didn't answer, he tried again, *"please, Zlatíčko, be careful."*

I pushed his voice out of head as Lahahana and I came to a stop. I didn't want my god-uncle to ruin this for me. Lahahana handed me a piece of kolach, and I took a small bite.

He watched me closely, scrutinizing the miniscule amount I had eaten. His voice was almost accusing as he asked, "Do you not like it?"

I sighed lightly and gave him a small smile, "Just savoring the taste."

My answer seemed to be good enough to appease him because, without saying anything else, he finished off his slice and took my hand again. I casually dropped my slice behind a bush, careful not to let him see. I let him pull me closer toward the sound of the music saturating the streets. As we got closer to the musicians in the main area of the village, he led me into a side alley.

His eyes scanned mine as he whispered, "Kamaria, have you ever been kissed?"

His words stunned me. He was so forward, and I'd never even been this close to a boy before, unless you count the time I touched his face while he was sleeping. I knew if I had a pulse, it would've quickened as he searched my eyes, and I wouldn't have been able to breathe. If I had been smarter, I would've made myself aware of his thoughts and would've seen his plot unfolding. But that wasn't what I wanted when he was standing in front of me because, for once, I felt like a normal girl in a normal moment with a normal boy.

I shook my head no and shrank into myself. Why had I told him that? I didn't owe him an answer, but it felt like he would know if I was lying. Why was I suddenly so embarrassed? It's not like I got to play with children during the day or go on trips to the fields with neighbors. My life wasn't normal, and it wasn't fair. If it had been normal, maybe I would've been prepared for this.

"I could show you, if you want?" he suggested and I nodded yes. He smiled and continued, "Okay, but first you have to close your eyes."

I don't know why I did as he said, but I did. I shut out the noise of the world around me as my eyelids fluttered closed. That was my second mistake of the night. When nothing happened after I stood there for several seconds with my lips stuck out, I opened my eyes and felt my heart drop. What little kolach I had eaten began to sour in the depths of my stomach.

Tears welled in my eyes as I saw Lahahana join his friends, and they all began to laugh at

me. Bloody tears welled in my eyes as I saw Lahahana join his friends. They stained my pale cheeks crimson as I tried to make sense of what was happening. I have always loathed the fact that my tears were crimson instead of clear. The look on their faces quickly changed to fear as I sprung through the air and sent Lahahana crashing into the building behind him.

"I hate you, Lahahana!" I screamed, my fists pounding into his chest.

Before I knew what I was doing in-between my rage and shouts, *it* happened. My razor teeth pierced through my gums, and I saw the horror as it began to flood in Lahahana's eyes. My rage was insatiable, and I moved to crash my mouth onto his exposed throat.

Before I could make contact, I felt strong hands grip me and pull me away.

"Dcera!" My father screamed, wrapping me tightly in his grasp. "Dcera, stop it! You're okay, my sweet daughter!"

I couldn't feel anything as I sobbed in the arms of my father. I could hear Lahahana's racing thoughts about what had happened. I could hear the terror and confusion that laced through each thought. and that made my shame increase once my rage began to subside.

"You don't understand, Tatinek!" I yelled through my tears. "You'll never understand because you're not like me!"

He held me close and let me sob against him in the darkness. He didn't try to argue with me or tell me I was wrong. He knew there were no words for the cruelty I had experienced, or for what would come. What could he have said anyway? Instead, he held me as I shook with tears from my broken heart until I had nothing left to give.

Once I had exhausted myself, he scooped me up in his arms and carried me home. I don't remember making it there, as I must have nodded off in the safety of his warmth. He laid me gently on my bed, pushing the stray hair out of my face.

"Am I ugly, Tatinek?" My voice shook with all the resentment and humiliation I carried within me for what I was. "What's wrong with me?"

He gave me a small smile as he stood and walked to the water basin at the other end of the room. He was silent as he wrung out the cloth, but his thoughts were loud as I listened to him attempt to find the right words to string together to console me. As the last drops of water hit the bowl, he moved back toward me with a sadness clouding his eyes I hadn't seen before.

"My love," his voice was gentle as he began to wipe away the crimson on my cheeks, "you are as beautiful as any moon. You were created to be different, special. That doesn't mean something is wrong with you."

I scowled at him, "I don't want to be special, Tatinek!" My voice grew softer, "I want to be like you. Like Maminka. Like Salma and Fahim. Like Jindrich and everyone else."

Placing the cloth over his knee, he put his hand to my cheek. His eyes searched mine with something I'd never seen before... an expression I didn't know.

"Kamaria, you will never be like us. You were not created to be just another person who is born and lives and dies." He kept his eyes locked on mine, love radiating from him the entire time. He chuckled lightly,

"You burst into this world unlike anything we'd ever known. You are brave and beautiful and courageous. I couldn't bear it if you were anything less than what you are now. I don't think any of us would know what to do with you if you were any less extraordinary."

He placed a soft kiss upon my forehead, rubbing my cheek one last time before he stood. He walked toward the doorway, pausing once he reached it.

He took a deep breath, turning to look at me once more, "I love you, Dcera. Exactly as you are."

I felt the truth in his words as he walked away, cloth in one hand and candle in the other. As the darkness waned outside my window, I felt love and what could only be described as his light wash over me.

I was safe.

I was home.

What I wouldn't give to have that same feeling now.

PART TWO: THE WEDDING

Candles adorned the small sanctuary making a path of light in the dark for our wedding. Lahahana, the boy that caused me so much pain, stood looking at me. My future waited for me at an altar with a boy I'd grown to hate.

He stood tall and proud, his blue eyes watching my every move as he ran his hand through his light brown hair. He wore a white shirt and pants with what looked like a white skirt trimmed in lace over them. His black vest matched my corset but was bursting with colored filigree and floral designs on the right side.

The church was eerily silent as I made my way toward him. I reminded myself to time my breathing so that it appeared natural and real. The kastel was full of more questions than answers about the night wedding between the demon girl and the village golden boy.

I felt my father's absence as he left my side, Lahahana and I then turned to face each other. He smiled at me, as if it would offer me some kind of reassurance that things were okay. I smiled back only out of politeness. I still wanted to rip out his throat.

The priest had Lahahana speak his vows first. Then it was my turn. Each word spoken excruciatingly painful to my soul:

"I, Kamaria. surrender to you, Lahahana, and accept you as my husband. I promise to keep your love, respect and loyalty, to never leave you, and to bear with you all the good and the bad until death. May God help me to do that. Amen."

As the last word left my lips, it felt like the final nail in my coffin. It was the death sentence that had finally come to carry me into oblivion.

Our reception was small and quiet. I spent most of my time hiding in the shadows, away from the prying eyes of villagers and family members whispering about the devil Lahahana had married. From where I was hiding, I could see my siblings, Jindrich and Pipulak, dancing. Jindrich was spinning her in circles until she was too dizzy to stand.

"Zlatíčko," Fahim spoke as he came to stand in front of me, "why are you hiding at your reception, my little gold?"

"You know better than anyone I didn't even want to be married... least of all to that monster of a man."

"Ah," he smiled sadly, "but here we are. Your Teta would've thought you were beautiful. She would've loved that you wore her headpiece in honor of her."

I reached up instinctively, running my hands over the jewels. I thought it was a family heirloom, I suppose in a way, it was. It both filled me with sadness and a sense of peace that I got to keep her with me that day.

"I hope she's proud of me." I whisper to him. "I know she would've loved this."

He embraced me and held me tightly. "She would've loved this almost as much as she loved you."

I heard someone clear their throat and opened my eyes to see Lahahana standing there. I scowled at him, but he only shrugged.

"I'm sorry to interrupt," he starts. "But we..."

"Then don't," I retort, cutting him off. "Go back to whatever you were doing."

His cheeks burned red from embarrassment at my words. I could hear the anger rising in his thoughts at the idea I would dare challenge him, but he doesn't show it here.

"We have to share the soup." He finishes, extending his hand to me.

Today, you would cut a cake and feed each other a piece, but at my wedding it was different. We sat together in front of a bowl of soup our parents had prepared for the day. Together, we picked up our individual ritual spoons and simultaneously ate a spoonful.

I didn't know what I saw in his eyes as he watched me swallow, but I had a feeling it wasn't something I should be optimistic about. Everyone rejoiced as we solidified that we were sharing life together. But as Lahahana and I stared at each other, we only shared a look of contempt.

We were the only two there that didn't feign excitement for our journey ahead.

In a lot of cultures, you'll find that the wedding night is often consummated under a watchful eye. Luckily for us, our wedding had taken place during unusual circumstances and since I wasn't someone of importance to the village, we were allowed to be alone. Although, if I'm being honest, I don't think anyone that would've watched would've gotten any pleasure out of it. I know I didn't.

I was shy; he was awkward. There was a silence that lay heavy in the space between us on the bed. I untied the bow to my headwear and placed it on a small table next to me that Fahim had crafted for us. I sighed, not wanting to ask Lahahana for help but knowing I would need him if I wanted my corset off.

"Will you unlace me?" I asked, my voice louder than I meant. "Please?"

He didn't speak as he stood from his side of the bed. I turned with my back toward him and brushed my hair to the side. I groaned in relief with each unlacing of the string. When he was finished, he didn't move.

"What?" I asked, sliding the corset up and over my head.

"It's not like I wanted to marry you either." His tone was sharp and his words stung. "You act like you're going to kill me anytime I'm around. I'm trying, Kamaria, and you're forcing us both to be miserable."

"Oh, so I'm just supposed to fake being happy so you can live in whatever world you've dreamed up for us?"

"It's preferable to how you're acting now."

I scoffed at him, standing to remove my wedding chemise. He grabbed my arm, harder than I was used to someone touching me. I tried to yank it out of his hand, but he tightened his grip.

"Let go of me!" I hissed.

"You can't scare me anymore, Kamaria." Darkness radiated in his eyes as they searched mine. "You're my wife and I can make the rest of your existence miserable."

I wrenched my arm free and glared at him. Just because we were married didn't mean I would allow him to treat me however he wanted. I cocked my head, giving back as much loathing as he was radiating in my direction. I walked toward him, his demeanor beginning to change as he stumbled backward. That strong show of force he had been putting on had merely been a farce I was now watching crumble.

I stopped only once I had him pressed up against the wall. I could hear his breath hitch as I pressed my face into his. We'd played this scene out once before in my bedroom, but now it could have a very different ending.

I trailed my finger down his cheek, nicking the bottom of his jaw with my fingernail. It wasn't enough to hurt him, but he let out a hiss. I chuckled as I wiped the small droplets of blood from his skin onto the tip of my finger.

"I may be your wife, Lahahana," I said, looking at his blood dripping onto the floor, "but don't forget that you're married to the demon girl of our village."

I licked the blood off my fingertip and moved away from him. I needed to hunt and, if I didn't get out of this house soon, Lahahana would be my prey.

PART THREE: ECHO OF REVERBERATION

Lahahana had thrown me over his shoulder, my face dripping with blood. A trail of it followed us as he walked, and I was proud that at least some of his had been mixed in with mine. I thrashed in his arms, fighting him all the way, but I had lost a lot of my own in the fight and was weak.

"I'll kill you for this! I'll rip your throat out!"

He dropped me, kicking out swiftly before I could stand. His foot connected with the bridge of my nose and there was a crack. Pain blistered throughout my face. I hissed at him, but I forced myself to stand. He wasn't going to lock me in here without a fight.

"You will give me children, Kamaria!" he screamed, wrath radiating from him. "One way or another you will."

I knew there was truth in his words. Aside from being the monster that he was, he never lied about what was to come. Whatever horrors he had planned, he always told me beforehand.

I charged forward, leaping on his chest and knocking him to the ground. I bolted to the doorway, praying I could make it in time. His hand wrenched around my leg and pulled me back down to the floor. His nails dug into my flesh as he began to yank me towards him.

I whipped my body from side to side as I kicked at him, but it was no use. As he pinned my body beneath him, he wrapped his hands around my throat. My fingers dug deep into his skin, my gasping begging him to stop. My eyes welled with tears as they met his. They were dark orbs, devoid of emotion.

He tightened his grip until I was seeing spots. He was going to kill me. Could he kill me? He released my throat and sprinted out of the room. I rushed to the door, coughing, trying to make it out but I failed. The lock clicked and I was entombed.

I spent the next hours doing whatever I could to try and get out of that room. I charged the door, throwing all my weight on it, but it wouldn't budge. I pounded my fists against it, wood splintering into my knuckles as I screamed. After what felt like hours of self-brutalization, I sank down to the floor with my back against it.

Was he still here? Was he waiting on the other side of the door, listening? What little light had escaped through a tiny crack under the door was now gone and the world around me was silent again. My eyes adjusted to the darkness of my new home but there was nothing to see.

It was an insignificant room that would become my mausoleum. A pallet was on the floor for me to sleep on, but it was devoid of furniture. Apart from the cot, all I had was four walls of impenetrable clay, mud, and the door that was meant to keep me imprisoned.

I crawled to the cot and rolled myself onto it, my body singing with pain. The only comfort Lahahana had afforded me was leaving behind the blanket Maminka had knit for me. I clutched it close to my chest as I began to sob.

I had to get out of here.

My fingers dug at the small bit of earth beneath the door, but it was no use. I couldn't get enough traction to increase the hole much in size. I screamed out in frustration and started clawing at the door again with fingernails that were broken and bloody.

I knew I'd been in here three weeks when I lost count. It was already too long. I began to bang on the door again, screaming at the top of my lungs.

"Let me out of here, Lahahana! I'll cut out your tongue if you don't! Let me out!"

But he never came. Not even when I would bellow for hours. He would leave me to panic in the darkness, anger and fear mixing inside my chest. How long did he plan to keep me locked in here? What had I done to deserve this type of cruelty?

Maybe I would try a different approach this time when he came to see me. Maybe if he thought I loved him, wanted to have his children, he would let me out. I could play the dutiful wife if it granted me my freedom. I could sell that part of myself.

So, I waited.

And I waited.

But, he never came.

After several days without him, I crawled back to the door, barely tapping it with bruised fingertips.

"Please, Lahahana," I sobbed softly. "I'll be a good wife. Please let me out."

Still, there was silence. I wept against the door until my body fell into a slumber. I don't know how long it was before I was jolted awake by the door being pushed open against me.

"Lahahana?" I whispered, scrambling backwards.

He walked into the room, candle in one hand and my dinner plate in the other. The smell made me nauseous. It wasn't his fault I had trouble keeping down the food he made for me. It just wasn't what my body wanted. I needed blood. I needed to hunt. I needed to feed.

He sat the candle down followed by the plate. As he turned toward me, I flung my arms around him, tears falling onto his shirt and staining it crimson.

"I thought you'd left me here to die."

He stroked my hair gently, unflinching at the crimson tears he'd grown accustomed to seeing since our childhood, "Kamaria, I would never."

His words were a lie, but it didn't matter. I leaned in gently, my cracked lips melding into his. He pulled me tighter, his lips pressing harder into mine. I reached for the string on his pants, quickly untying them.

"Are you sure?" He asked, the irony of his words dancing thick in the air. "I want you to want me like I do you, Kamaria. You're my wife. I love you."

Here he was, my husband, asking me, his wife, that he assaulted and locked away, if I was sure I wanted him to take me as he dared to utter his love for me. The obvious answer was no, and anyone could've seen that. If he had been anyone else, if he had been any normal man in our village, perhaps he would've known that too.

"Yes," I whispered, trying to convince myself of my plan more than him.

I laid down on the cot, pulling him down on top of me. His lips found mine once again as I snaked my hands up his shirt to push it over his head. He stood, just long enough to remove his pants, as I removed my torn dress.

Had our circumstances been different, I would've found him handsome as he stood in front of me in the dim candlelight. Each part of his body was highlighted as the flame flickered near his skin. He was beautiful but he was a monster. Maybe even more of a monster than me.

He lowered himself back onto the bed, pushing my legs open with his knees. I willed my breath to hitch as I stared deep into his soul. There was nothing there I could ever love. There was once before but that time was long past.

He was gentle at first, his hand reaching down to caress my face. As much as I hated myself for it, I leaned into his touch. I truly had been afraid he was never coming back. Now, I just needed to get out.

He ran his thumb gently over my bruised, cracked lips. It tasted of dirt touched by sunlight and herbs he'd used to cook dinner. He watched me closely, studying my lips as a smirk began to creep across his.

Without warning, he pushed his shaft into me, and I let out a moan. Due to the fact that he'd kept me locked away without being able to feed, my healing had slowed dramatically so I found myself still torn and sore from the last time he violated my body. My heart felt heavy with every nail each of his strokes hammered into it.

He gripped me by the back of my hair, wrenching my head up so that I would look at him. I wanted to know what he thought as he looked at me, my body covered in sweat as I felt the ruminations of pain scorching my skin where he touched it. When I looked at him, I could only ever see a monster that I was allowing to steal away parts of me.

"I want you to look at me while I fill you Kamaria," he said, his breathing uneven. "I want you to know that it's me inside of you as your belly swells with our child."

His words disgusted me. My body screamed in pain. I couldn't do this. I had taken so much from the man on top of me. I had held his resentment and his anger deep in my soul. I had allowed his words to mutilate my skin, but I would no longer let him have this. I could no longer let him have me, not if I could salvage any part of who I had been. So, with every ounce of strength I had left, I yanked my hair free and flung my head at his face.

There was a crack as I made impact.

Find more of Kamaria's story in Kassandra Morgan's upcoming novel *Secrets of the Moon.*

10 Minutes: A Tale of Violence, Justice, and Healing

Melissa Martin

CW: domestic violence, sexual assault, suicidal ideation, abortion, deportation

For Christy; I'm here today because of you.

Ten minutes—I can do this. Todd will only be gone for ten minutes and everything is ready. My cat is safe with a friend. My cash stash, my new phone, clothes, sentimental items, and valuables are all in a duffel bag. I just have to get it to the car.

"Cass? Sweetie? We gotta move," Sam says, looking at me from the now mostly empty living room of the apartment Todd and I have shared for two and a half years.

We've been planning this for months. Down to the tiniest of details, with every second accounted for. My cat—Bilbo—has been at the "vet" for a few days now, for an "emergency surgery," but really, he's been at Sam's, living his best life being spoiled with attention and affection.

To rid the apartment of Todd, I ordered Chinese food for dinner, using the excuse that we hadn't had takeout in ages, and how I could really use the comfort food. Todd bought it, and went to pick it up, buying me ten minutes to get my stuff together and get the hell out. The last time he and I went for Chinese, I had counted the seconds to the elevator, then to the car in the parkade, then out to the stop sign at the end of the street. That had taken three minutes. I set myself a timer and once three minutes had passed, I texted Sam one word: "*Go.*"

She knew to head upstairs with Caleb and Alex—two good friends of ours—in tow. They'd been parked directly in front of the apartment building in Alex's dad's truck, one that Todd would never recognize.

As we loaded the last two boxes into the truck bed, I took one last glance back. For two and a half years, that place had somehow been both a sanctuary and a prison. Full of anger, passion, violence, torture, love, fear, and hatred.

"I'm free," I whispered. "I'll never come back here."

"You know what they say," I state confidently, before taking the shot Sam just placed in front of me, "the best way to get over one"—I cheers her on the next shot—"is to get under another" we shout in tandem.

It's been roughly a month since I fled. In that time, I have been trying to find myself, heal a bit, and rediscover who I am without Todd's poison in my system. Now, I'm ready to get back on the proverbial horse, and go for a ride. It better be one hell of a ride! Sam and I are going to karaoke. I don't know how I let her talk me into this, but here we are. I'm dressed in a knee-length emerald swing dress. It's my favourite. It has off-the-shoulder straps, a simple corset top, and the skirt flows out like the petals of an amaryllis when I twirl. Sam, on the other hand, is wearing a skin-tight, black, backless jumpsuit, striking red shoes, and is looking rather like Sandy at the end of Grease.

Entering the bar, my eyes crash-land on the walking definition of dangerous. He's tall and handsome. Admittedly, something does feel a little bit off with this guy, but we pregamed too hard for me to care. I nudge Sam, and we take the table beside him. "I'm Cassie, she's Sam, and you're pretty," I say sloppily.

He looks from me, to Sam, and back again before responding with a laugh. "I'm James. Do you girls actually participate in this mess, or are you just here to class up the joint?" He nods towards the stage.

Sam giggles and says, "She sings! I'm just here to make sure she doesn't chicken out."

James's hazel eyes settle on me, and I begin to sober up as I see the ravenous look behind them. Mercifully before another word can be spoken, the DJ calls my name.

> **"You've got one hell of a set of pipes."**

I'm staring down at my phone like it's going to explode in my hands. What the hell was I thinking? I'd spent all night and this morning with the mysterious James from karaoke. I had spent half the time sobbing into his shoulder about the abuse I had endured from Todd, and the other half on that ride I mentioned earlier . . . I could already tell that one little taste had me forming a habit. There I was, in the backseat of an Uber heading home, smiling down at my phone like a teenager.

> **"Thanks, I hope the private concert afterwards was satisfactory too."**

I cringe at myself. I'm out of practice and rusty, even with flirting via text, but hopefully James finds it cute and endearing.

When I get home, Sam is waiting for me in the foyer. "Well?! Give me the dirty details lady!" She's standing with her arms crossed, tapping her foot impatiently—like a TV Mom.

"Well, nothing *really*. We stayed for an hour after you left, walked to his apartment, I broke down crying over Todd, and he . . . you know . . . cheered me up . . . " Sam is still looking at me incredulously because I haven't given her the filthy play-by-play. "He's great. I think I'm going to see him again." Before she can ask anymore questions, I turn and walk into my room with Bilbo following close behind.

The truth is? James scares me. He's charismatic, says all the right things, makes me laugh, and he's great in bed; he's everything Todd was at the start. Too good to be true. However, I chalk my apprehension up to trauma and push the what ifs from my mind, getting ready for bed knowing I'll call James tomorrow to arrange a proper date.

"Come on, let's go in the back!"
"Babe! We can't go back there!"
"Sure, we can—I'm staff."

James takes another bump, following it up with a swig of beer. It's his birthday, we've been together for five months now, and we're at the bowling alley he works at on a weekend when he doesn't have his son. He's drunk and high, and all I want to do is leave. I should have listened to my instinct from the start: tall, handsome, and *dangerous*. Everything in me was screaming for me to run, but I ignored it. Suddenly, he's taking me by the arm and pulling me back into the area behind the lanes, where all of the ball return machines are, and I'm pulled away from my wandering thoughts . . . and the public eye.

I watch as he whispers something to his friend who's working the back, and I watch as that friend leaves. I watch as his eyes darken, and that same ravenous look comes over him. The one that scared me when we first met. My stomach drops as he messily crushes his lips against mine. "James, no. You're drunk—and people might see us. We should get back to your party."

"It's my birthday, I want my gift."

My body grows cold, already knowing what my brain has yet to catch up on. As James is fumbling with my pants, I freeze. Then, just as his hands are forcefully tugging at my bra, my brain catches up. My body comes alive with adrenaline. He has me pinned against a ball return machine, but I still manage to wrestle an arm loose. I throw a quick jab, catching him square between the eyes. It's enough for him to stop what he's doing and stumble back, allowing me to get free of his grip. I quickly pull my pants back on and bolt for the door we came through.

Turning back, I see him trip over his own pants and land on his ass. I giggle in spite of myself. On my way out the door, I stop in front of Jessi, James's best friend. Jessi lives just across the street from James, she's your classic girl-next-door and follows James around like a lost puppy. Loudly, I tell her "James just tried to rape me behind the ball returns. I punched him in the face and he fell pretty hard on his ass with his pants around his ankles. You might want to take him home to sober up."

Jessi doesn't respond, she just fixes me with a glare and turns to run to the back to see to James. It isn't until I'm halfway home in the cab that the tears finally roll.

The next morning, I wake up to no less than 33 texts from James, and 6 missed calls. I'm not interested in his excuses or empty apologies. He hasn't been sober a single day in the last four months, and he's growing angrier and more aggressive by the day. Things are going south in his custody battle for his son, and it's turned him into a monster. I should have ended things by now. I shouldn't have started dating him in the first place. I'm ending this. Today—right now.

"James, we need to talk."

"No. I'm sorry. Let's go for a drive. I need to pick some stuff up anyway, and Jessi wants to play games . . ."

"No. I'm done, James. We're done. You tried to rape me last night. You're using coke and drinking all day every day. You're angry; you never laugh or even smile anymore. I can't keep doing this to myself, I deserve better."

"You'll change your mind."

"No, I won't. Please don't call or text me anymore."

My cheeks are wet from crying, and I'm shaking. He sounded so sure, so confident. "You'll change your mind," he'd said, as if I'm helpless to resist. Well, he's wrong. I'm resisting. He's Todd 2.0, Addict Edition, and I will not subject myself to this pattern any longer.

My car comes to a stop in front of the all-too-familiar apartment complex. "Fuck. I'm an idiot." As I open the car door, I hesitate. Todd is angry and violent, but he's familiar. There's safety in the familiar. Todd has never tried to rape me.

Before I even make it inside the alcove of the apartment building I swore I'd never return to, an eerily familiar voice calls to me from somewhere up the street. I turn to see James running full tilt towards me. Before I can react, he's got a tight hold on my arm and is dragging me away from the building. I'm fighting, and finally manage to scream "TODD!" but it's useless. James has me over his shoulder and there is no one around. I assess my options and decide that it's better to just fawn (Go with it, blend in. My therapist taught me that one! It goes with fight/flight/freeze.) until I can make a break for it. I'm in his car, and he's calling me a cheating whore.

"James, we haven't been together for more than a month. You do know that, don't you? After you attacked me at your birthday party, I broke up with you."

"No. You're mine. You belong to me. I'm about to remind you. You can't end this. I won't allow it."

"You're scaring me . . ."

"Good, *bitch*."

We pull into his driveway and he orders me to get out of the car. I demand he take me back to my car so I can just go home. Instead, he throws me over his shoulder again and takes me inside.

"See, Cassie, the thing is, I fucking love you"—he pauses to snort a line of what I assume is cocaine on the table—"and you belong to me. You're my woman, my property. I'm going to teach you." As he stalks towards me, there's something in his face I don't recognize. Before me, coming at me like a hungry lion, is a broken and unhinged man. When I realize there is no reasoning with this person, I try to run for the door, but he catches me by my hair and drags me down to the floor. I try to scream, but it's stifled by his hand on my throat. He's pushing too hard, my vision is narrowing and my head feels swollen. The last vision I have is him forcing my jeans down to my feet.

When I wake, James is passed out on his bathroom floor. I'm bleeding, I'm not even sure where from. Everything hurts, it's as if I've been sandwiched between two trains going full speed. I gather myself and my belongings. My phone is beside James, unlocked and open to a message from Todd asking where I am. My movements are slow and almost robotic—I'm on autopilot. I need to get to my car. How do I get to my car? Uber? *Call an Uber.* No. *Call Sam.*

"Cassie! Are you at Todd's?! He said you never showed!"

"Sam . . ." My voice breaks.

"Where are you? I'll be right there."

I give her James's address, but I tell her I'll wait at the park up the street in case he wakes up. Then, holding myself like I'm cracked porcelain about to shatter, I limp my way to the beach front park and wait for my best friend.

It has been a month and a half. I've told no one what happened with James that night, and he hasn't tried to reach me. I didn't even tell Sam the whole story. Only that James basically kidnapped me for the night. I'm embarrassed. I should have fought back, fought harder. He shouldn't have been able to do that to me. In the span of ten minutes, that monster turned my world upside down. He left me hollow and broken.

I roll over in bed and feel a twinge of pain run up my back. A reminder that as mentally broken as I am, I'm also still physically broken. As I stare up at the ceiling, Todd grumbles in his sleep beside me. I moved back in shortly after James attacked me. I think they call that a trauma bond; he's a monster, but he's my monster . . . or something like that. I know it's stupid; I know I shouldn't be here, but I'm grasping onto anything familiar right now. My own body feels foreign, like it doesn't belong to me and I'm just operating it like some kind of avatar. Familiar is safe, at least for now. Besides, Todd promised he'd change. He's taking anger management classes, and he doesn't drink anymore. Maybe we have a real chance this time.

"Todd? Love? I'm not feeling well, can we go pick up some Gravol and tea from the store?"

He grunts and shakes himself awake, propping himself up on his elbows and looking over at me. "Sure babe, you do look a little pale. What time is it? I'll get dressed and we can go to Shoppers, then we'll go get a chicken noodle soup from Timmies, I know you like those."

While we're at the store, I think to myself that I should pick up a pregnancy test. There's no way it'll be positive, but I'd rather rule it out. When I place the test on the counter at the till, Todd looks at me incredulously. "I'm just ruling it out, babe—don't worry."

"Well, it wouldn't be so bad if you were. Things aren't perfect right now, but we're working on it. We could get there in nine months, easy. Speaking of working on things, I need to renew my PR card." He's changed the subject, but also reminded me of something I'd forgotten; he's not a citizen. He's a Permanent Resident. He's been here long enough he should really apply for citizenship. I say as much when we climb in the car. Todd just brushes it off by stating, "It doesn't make that much of a difference."

Back home, I'm impatient, so I immediately take the pregnancy test. It shows a very prominent positive before I've even had a chance to set it down on the counter. Shock rolls over me. There's no way . . . this must be a mistake. "Todd! You're not going to believe this."

Todd bursts through the door "What happened? Are you alright?"

"I'm pregnant."

I've now taken no less than five tests. They all say the same thing. In nine months, I'm going to be a mom. It's everything I've ever wanted, and the single most terrifying thing I've ever faced. Todd is thrilled; he's already told both of his brothers and his mom.

Over the weeks that follow, I get hit with all the usual symptoms: Nothing smells good, everything makes me sick to my stomach, I'm exhausted, everything hurts, and I'm an emotional mess. The excitement is building, however, and I find myself telling people close to me all about the good news, as well as one manager at my job who asked about my frequent sprints to the washroom. True to form though, the Powers That Be have other plans waiting for me after work that day.

"Care to explain what the fuck he's talking about?" Todd is angrily shoving his phone in my face, there's a message open. Grabbing the phone, I see it's from James. A pit forms in my stomach as I read the words on the screen.

> **"Ha ha ha, could be mine."**

My knees buckle, and I grip the back of the couch for support. "Todd, it's not . . . I can explain—"

My words are cut off by a sharp slap across my face.

"Fucking cheating whore. Get out of my apartment. I'll pack your shit."

My face is still stinging from the slap. "No, Todd, you don't understand. He raped me, and it was before we got back together, not that that should matter since it was rape . . ."

Todd is standing across the room with his hands in fists at his side.

Suddenly, a memory comes slamming into me like a truck. "He finished in my ass, Todd! It can't be his!" I scream, using all the strength I can muster. "Please, you have to hear me!"

The next words out of his mouth shatter all that was left of me.

"You kill it, or I will kill both of you."

"No." It's the only word I can manage.

"What did you just say to me, you bitch?"

I try to steady myself and steel my nerves, understanding full well that what I am about to say may indeed be the last thing I ever say. "I said *no*. You can throw me out, but I will do this with or without you." No sooner have the words left my mouth, and he's across the room. I take a backhand across the face with such force it knocks me back and I trip over the couch. Seeing an opportunity, he comes forward again. This time, as I'm on the floor, it's a kick to my side. I don't think he cracked my ribs, though he certainly tried. I fight my way to standing, using the couch like a climbing wall. Through broken breaths, coughs, and sobs, I stand to face him. He lands one more blow to my mouth, splitting my lip, before taking his keys off the counter and leaving me alone in the dark.

The following day, with an ice pack on my face, I phone my parents. I haven't told them, and won't tell them, not the full story. I'll just tell them enough to get some sort of encouragement.

I tell them that when Todd and I broke up the first time, I started seeing someone, things didn't work out, and now I'm back with Todd. I tell them I'm pregnant and that the guy I was seeing between the breakup and getting back together is claiming that the baby is his, Todd is demanding I get an abortion, and that he is kicking me out.

To my dismay, rather than encouragement or support, I'm met with, "We think Todd is right and you should abort it. You don't know who the father is, and you can't do this on your own. You are not capable of doing this on your own."

Too stunned to respond, I just hang up the phone. I dial Sam's number. I'll fill her in and seek comfort in her, the difference will be that she knows I was raped. She is the only one who knows. Aside from Todd, but the jerk doesn't believe it. Classic.

"Hey lady!" Her voice, always so warm and soothing, breaks me.

"Hey Sam."

I fill her in; James claims it's his, Todd doesn't believe me, he wants me to abort, my parents want me to abort, but that I don't want to abort. True to form, she gives me the reminder that I needed, but already know.

"I'm in your corner, whatever you decide. You've got me."

I sigh, "Thanks Sam. Love you." The call ends, and a single tear trickles down my cheeks. After nearly twenty years of friendship, she is the only solid and consistent presence in my life. I can always count on Sam.

I recognize all at once that while I may have the "Right to Choose," this is not going to be my choice. I'm going to get an abortion, whether I want it or not. I suppose that's something I'll work through with a therapist later on. That, and the rest of this mess.

The procedure takes place a week later. Todd agrees to take me and bring me home again. He tells me I can stay while I recover, but after that, he never wants to see or hear from me again... at least we agree on that point. On our way out, I change my mind. This is still my choice.

I tell Todd as much, but he grabs me by my throat, holds me against the apartment door, and tells me it is not my choice. The rest of the walk to the car, he's gripping my arm firmly enough to leave marks. I struggle to break free of his grip, but he's stronger than me and I don't want a scene in the halls. I'm not ready for that.

At the hospital clinic, they do an ultrasound to make sure it's safe to perform a surgical abortion. I both see and hear my baby's heartbeat. A nurse is getting ready to start my IV, and, noticing the tears now streaming down my face, asks if I'm sure.

"Once I start this, love, there's no going back. Are you absolutely positive?"

I nod and say in a breathless whisper, "Yes, I'm sure."

It's a lie, but it's the only option I have. This is very literally a life-or-death situation. The nurse starts the IV, and I am plunged into a haze. I'm awake, technically, but I am not present. The room is spinning vertically, the surgical light I'm looking up at looks like it's movie credits scrolling over and over. It's like I'm inside the wheel of a slot machine, and I am desperate to get out.

Todd is waiting for me after the procedure. He asks the doctor if everything went okay. I know what he's really asking. The doctor assures him everything went well, they just need to keep me under observation for an hour or so.

When we get back to the apartment, I fall asleep on the couch.

It has now been one year since James assaulted me, and a little less than since Todd forced me to get an abortion. Every life changing event last year happened in the span of ten minutes each. It's amazing how much ten minutes can change your life. I'm a fraction of who I was then; a thin shell, full of cracks. I need to start building up the shell again, make it tougher, less hollow.

I snap back from my daydream to see my therapist, Angela, looking at me quizzically.

Shit, she's asked a question I've failed to answer. "Sorry, I spaced. Can you repeat the question?"

"I asked if you want me to go with you?"

"Oh. That? No, I think I'll just have Sam take me. You've helped me prepare and cope, that's more than enough."

"Okay. As long as you're sure. Then, I guess we're done for today. I'll see you next week. Let me know how everything goes."

Constable Caitlyn Granger takes my reports and statements. For both the violence I suffered at Todd's hands, and the sexual assault by James. Sam literally holds my hand the entire time.

About six months after my initial report, I learn that Crown has approved charges against both men and warrants have been issued for their arrests. There is a mountain of evidence, but the justice system is slow, so I shouldn't expect any immediate results.

Months turn into years. Before I know it, nearly three years have passed. All the while, I've been going to therapy, I went to school and got a paralegal degree. Somewhat ironically, I'm working in criminal defence. I want to make sure everyone gets real justice—even if I'm just a small cog in a big machine. Real justice also means innocent people don't go to prison, hence working in criminal defence.

I've been seeing someone wonderful. His name is Zack. He's kind, and gentle. He puts me on a pedestal. We're going to have a baby soon! A little boy. Sam can't wait to be an aunty.

I'm healthy and happy for the first time in a long time. Everything is going my way. Then, my phone rings. *Private Number.* Uh-oh, that's Constable Granger.

"Hello?" I answer the phone, my voice noticeably shaking.

"Hello, Cassie? It's Constable Granger here. I just wanted to let you know that you're being called to testify at the trials."

"Oh. Okay. When are they?"

"In about a month..." She starts to sound further and further away as my ears start ringing.

I have to face them.

The trials are each scheduled for two days, but I only have to go to one. They asked if I wanted to testify behind a screen and I declined. I want to look them in the eye when I describe the atrocities they committed against me. I want to see them break as they realize how fucked they are. It's my turn to scare them.

My turn on the stand comes. James's lawyer is trying to discredit me using the fact that James and I had been seeing each other. Neither the Crown, nor the Judge, are having any of that nonsense. James is found guilty and sentenced to ten years for aggravated sexual assault. A weight lifts off me. I'm free of at least one monster.

During Todd's trial, things feel different. He's smug, and that makes me nervous. They take the "no witnesses, and she's clumsy" approach. Thankfully, I gave Crown pictures, videos, audio recordings, and medical records. No one is *that* clumsy, and how do they explain the circumstances around the forced abortion? Answer: They can't.

Todd is found guilty of six counts of aggravated assault, and two counts of coercive control. Since he's a Permanent Resident and not a citizen, he is deported back to Holland.

I'm free. I'm finally free. Each sentencing trial took ten minutes.

It took ten minutes to break me, then ten minutes to save me, and now ten minutes to win my happy ending.

Zack and I have our baby. He's a beautiful, perfect little boy, who we name Noah. At our wedding, he's our ring bearer. Meanwhile, somewhere, James is rotting in a jail cell, and Todd is who knows where—and who cares?

I'm free, and I'm happy.

These Lunar Bonds

Holly Dunwall

> CW: misogyny, mentions of homophobia, self-harming urges, cursing, blood, gore, mentions of parental neglect, emotional abuse,
> violence against abusive family members

Her therapist always told her that people hellbent on bringing her down were discontent with their lives. It was hard to remember that when she felt like she was being smothered by condescending laughter.

For Mara Silver, escaping to the bathroom during her family's Thanksgiving argument was like watching Super Bowl trailers—a perfect escape from having your brain turn to soup. She would compare the current state of her brain to cranberry sauce, the one her mother insisted on having by the turkey. It was all liquid with a few chunks and a hint of zest. The zest represented her brain cells clinging to sanity.

"Just imagine never having to leave my room . . . " she whispered, momentarily pressing her hands against her face. A migraine was beginning to throb in her left temple, more intense than normal. "That's the dream."

Mara had a tough time during the holidays. Relatives she didn't care about bombarded her with questions about her life. Her parents didn't defend her and seemed to *enjoy* putting her on the spot in front of the whole family. Just a few minutes ago, her aunt and uncle made a comment about her appearance being 'frumpy,' which her parents laughed at.

Fuck. Taking a deep breath, Mara nodded to her reflection. "You got this. I fucking got this." Tucking wavy brown strands of hair behind her ears, she splashed some cold water on her face. *You fucking got this. It's one more day of this, then back to business as usual.* Pushed herself off the sink and emerged from the bathroom, rejoining the fray.

Mara was an only child. There were no siblings to bitch to. She did have cousins but she wasn't close to them. They all chatted amongst themselves. Mara caught pieces of conversation as she passed their section of the table.

"Mara!"

The sound of her name brought her back to the present, tugging her out of the tunnel vision. She lifted her head, meeting the cold, stern glare of her father.

"I was telling your Aunt Susan that you'd turned down that nice boy from church last Sunday."

Her aunt's little round glasses made her look like an imposing, evil librarian. "Why would you go and do such a thing, you silly girl? You're of the age to find a man and marry! Lord knows your twenties are the best time to conceive."

Mara gritted her teeth. She kept a serene, polite smile on her face, acutely aware of her father and mother glaring daggers. "He's just not my type. He's nice, but there's nothing there."

Aunt Susan scoffed. "Nice? Is *nice* going to provide for your kids? No."

Kids? Absolutely the fuck not. Mara plastered a pleasant smile on her face, forcing out a laugh. "Oh don't worry Auntie, the right one will come along."

She heard her father scoff, grumbling under his breath as he cut up his turkey. "You said that about Dylan Waters, too."

"Dylan was a jerk," Mara can't help the bite in her words. That asshole was a bully through and through to anyone he didn't deem worthy. "I would have rather drank acid."

"See, that right there," Aunt Susan pointed with her fork, a green bean attached to the end of the prongs. "That's why you can't find a man. You're too damn opinionated, it doesn't do you any favors."

"And what would you have me do, Susan?" The venom coats Mara's words, the migraine in her head throbbing. It all comes out before she can't even stop herself. "Marry some asshole who just likes my face? How did that turn out for you?" she snaps. It was no secret her uncle was a belligerent bully.

The room goes silent. Aunt Susan gapes at her.

Mara can't keep the smirk off her face. *About time she shut up.* She takes her glass of juice, downing the remaining contents before rising, plate in hand. "I'm turning in for the night."

The bravado died in her chest as quickly as it rose at the darkness in her parents' eyes. Her mother was the first to stand up. "Apologize to your aunt!"

Mara scowled, walking out of the room and into the kitchen. She placed her plate in the sink, turning the water on to rinse the remaining sauces off it. Heavy footsteps followed her. Then, hot breath brushed her face as her father bared down on her. "The fuck is your problem?" he snarled.

"The fuck is *your* problem?" she growled back, matching his temper. "Every time they come over you let them tear into me."

"Oh don't be stupid," he scoffs. "You—you always say these things. We look out for you, Mara. Don't we do enough for you? Pay for your therapy? Give you a roof over your head?"

Mara gritted her teeth. It was true. They did do that. But it was the bare minimum. "I would be more than happy to contribute if you fucking let me." *Let me out of this damn house! Let me be a person.* "Why can't you just accept I don't *want* any of the pricks in this town?" Her father riles her up so much that she forgets all about the soapy plate still in her hand. One little squeeze of her fingertips and it falls to the floor, shattering on impact.

Time seemed to slow. Both her and her father stared at the plate, equally dumbstruck in the moment. The scrape of a chair comes from the dining room, followed by quick footsteps. Mara and her father make eye contact, mirroring each other's dread. A hurricane was coming.

When her mother's eyes zeroed in on the broken ceramic plate, her gaze darkened with pure fury. "What did you do?" she roared, looking directly at Mara.

THESE LUNAR BONDS 167

Mara froze. Her heart thundered in her chest, in tandem with the growing migraine brewing in her head. Yelling. Whether it was her parents yelling at each other, or at her, it always made her feel so small. She wasn't twenty-one anymore. She was Sweetie Mara again, the little girl with a stuffed Clifford the Red Dog toy, playing alone in daycare.

"Mara Maree." Her mother's tone was icy. "Look. At. Me."

"Honey, it—it was an accident—"

Her mother silenced her father with a death glare before turning her ire back to her.

Mara fought to say something. "I was washing it and talking to Dad, and I dropped it. I'm sorry. I'll clean it up." Mara moved quickly, a lump in her throat as she grabbed the broom and dustpan from the corner, moving with haste to sweep up the mess.

"I've had those plates since the nineties. Irreplaceable." Her mother moved within her personal space, halting her movements. Her small frame shook with fury. "You fucking klutz," she hissed.

"Mom, I'm sorry. I'm so sorry—" Tears began to form in her eyes.

"Keep your voice down." Her mother's eyes widened, emphasizing her words. "Don't you fucking start crying, or I'll *really* give you something to cry about."

Mara stared, unseeing, as her mother took the broom from her, sweeping away the shards. Her eyes darted to her father, silently begging him to say something. *Do* something. But he just stood there.

Out of the corner of her eye, Aunt Susan peered around the corner. "Everything okay here, Lisa?" she asked, looking at the scene before her.

Her mother's entire demeanor shifted before Mara's eyes. The fury was gone, replaced with a serene expression. Bending down to pick up the dustpan and discarding the contents in the trash can, she said, "Oh it's fine, Susan! Mara just broke one of my turquoise plates."

Aunt Susan gasped. "No, the one we got you as a housewarming gift when you moved in here?"

Her mother pouted. "The very same."

Mara's aunt shot daggers at her, a cold sneer on her face as she looked her up and down. "What a *mess*."

The older adults in the room laughed—loudly—at Mara's expense.

How fucking could you? Despair washed over her, accompanied by an anger that set her veins on fire. *I'm done,* she thought. *I'm done, I'm done, I'm done.*

Mara's head pounded with a throbbing intensity, as if shards of glass were piercing her temples. Her vision blurred. The world around her became hazy and distorted. With a sudden jolt of determination, she pivoted on her heel, her body propelled forward by a surge of adrenaline towards the back patio door. The urge to run won.

It swung open with a creak, releasing a gust of cool air. Ignoring her mother's voice calling out to her, Mara's feet hit the ground with a resounding *thud* as she leapt over the porch stairs. The backyard stretched out before her, a vast expanse of greenery bordered by rolling hills and dense woodland. Running downhill, the ground beneath her feet became a blur, the wind rushing past her ears like a roaring waterfall. Each step she took sent shockwaves of agony through her skull, a relentless assault on her senses. The cold air bit her skin, leaving a tingling sensation in its wake. The migraine intensified with every stride, as if her head was being split open, a fiery agony consuming her every thought.

She heard her father yelling behind her. She was almost at the treeline, the forest dark and foreboding. Gritting her teeth, she forced her legs to carry her faster and let the darkness swallow her as she vanished into the woods.

The deeper she went, the more her head fucking throbbed. The anger only made it worse.

Mara grew up exploring these woods. She knew the land, its twisting roots and towering trees like the back of her hand. Racing through the thick woods, she moved with grace. It had always been a safe place. Always.

But her head! God, it hurt. She'd gotten migraines before, but nothing *this* bad. It clawed at her brain, sinking its claws into the burdened flesh. Each step sent a shockwave through her head. Step forward, misery. Another, agony.

Mara spotted some moonlight up ahead. She stumbled towards it, gritting her teeth. Pushing some bushes aside, she stepped into a small, circular clearing surrounded by tall, ominous trees. Spinning on her heel, she looked around her. Part of her felt some anxiety at having wandered so deep into the forest at night—she had never seen this place before—but another part of her felt good. It was just her. Just Mara. Alone in the moonlight. The real, raw and fucked up version of herself she'd tried to shove down exposed under the stars.

Lifting her head slowly to gaze at the moon, she exhaled. Her eyes closed, a gentle breeze kissed her eyelids, lips, and nose. It was as if the forest was comforting her, telling her it's going to be okay.

Mara opened her eyes, gaze fixed on the moon. It was full. A beacon in the darkness with stars scattered around it like freckles in the night sky. Another breeze wafted over her, making her twitch. Her neck jerked to the side. And again. And again with more force, enough to make her eyes roll to the back of her head.

The fire in her brain erupted, spreading like wildfire devouring her body.

Doubling over in pain, she clawed at the ground, crying out in agony as she felt her bones shift under skin and muscle. She was being stretched, her limbs contorted and lengthened. Deep breaths didn't help. Something was wrong. Very, very wrong. She pressed her face into the cold dirt and sobbed.

The moon shone above her, casting an ethereal glow. As its light enveloped her hunched form, the pain subsided. She heaved a sigh of relief. "It's over," she breathed, "It's over . . . Thank God."

A tearing sound, followed by the worst pain she had ever felt, more than her bones shifting, shot down her spine. A breathless gasp left her lips, and then *fire*. Fire, coursing through her veins, rampant and unforgiving and angry. It consumed her. She heaved, rolling onto all fours. Her heaves became deep, guttural growls with each exhale. Her hands went to her shoulders, reaching for her back and sinking into the soft flesh there.

With a jerk and a snarl, her pallid flesh gave way underneath newly grown claws, skin tearing to give way to new flesh. *Stronger* flesh. Russet fur—the same shade as the hair on her head—took its place, a thick, muscular hide formed. Her mouth hung open as shooting pain ebbed in her face. Her soft, heart shaped face stretched outward, full lips and button nose shaping into a furred snout with sharp, deadly teeth.

After what felt like eternity, the pain went away. Standing on her hind legs, the remnants of her clothes fell away from her body. Her shoes had torn, large, furry feet took their place. Emotion rose quickly and fast in her chest, like a tidal wave forming in the ocean, rising and rising, higher and higher.

Mara opened her mouth to scream for help. A howl echoed across the countryside, reverberating off the trees, and sent a nearby flock of birds fleeing for safety. The last shred of her sanity tore apart, and all she saw was red, red, red, and the silhouette of something large and black in the shadows.

When she came to, she felt comfortable. Eyes flickering open, she realized she was lying on a soft, plush couch in what appeared to be a garage. A fuzzy blanket draped over her small frame, Mara slowly sat up, clutching it to her naked chest. *This is a . . . garage.* She saw the metal door , taking in the hot pink graffiti of a naked woman with a wolf's head.

"Hey, you're up," a high, feminine voice said cheerfully to her right, making her jump.

Mara wrapped the blanket around her tightly, eyes wide. A young, thick-bodied woman stared back at her, smiling with excitement. She was blonde and had a round face like one of those old paintings from the Renaissance era. She looked tired. Bags were under her blue eyes, but she remained chipper.

"Whoa, easy!" The blonde raised her hands. "You're okay. You're safe." She looked toward the garage door, which led further into what Mara assumed was a house. "Sloane! Get in here!"

"Who are you?" Mara whispered, voice trembling. "Why—why am I naked?"

The blonde scowled. She made frowning look pretty. "You don't remember anything?"

Mara shook her head, trying to bring herself clarity. She remembered being angry. So, so angry it rocked her world.

The blonde sighed. "It's okay if you don't. We can fill you in."

At that moment, the door swung open. A tall, muscular looking copper-skinned woman with tousled, chin length black hair stood in the doorway. Her sharp eyes locked with Mara's, and she felt a jolt of *something* go through her. Not necessarily fear, but something that made every nerve in her body wake up. She was utterly gorgeous.

"Gina . . ." The woman said slowly. "Does she remember anything?" The blonde—Gina—shook her head. "She doesn't. She's scared, Sloane."

Sloane's gaze drifted back to Mara, making the petrified girl's stomach do somersaults. "Hey there, what's your name?"

Her voice was like honey. Lower register, but sweet. Mara shivered. "My name's Mara," she breathed.

Sloane bit her lip, a flash of emotion in her eyes before they became steely. Focused. "Hey Mara." She walked over in two long strides to kneel in front of her. "I'm Sloane. This is Regina. We're new in town."

Gina waved, a grimace on her face. "Please don't call me Regina, by the way. Gina is good."

"We found you in the woods, by our place. What do you remember?" Sloane was the picture of patience. Calm. Grounding.

Mara thought back to last night. *Thanksgiving dinner was going on, I remember that much. I remember... an argument with my mother. Dad didn't help. I'd... dropped a plate. And the yelling.*

The yelling. The insults. Her mother's furious, unhinged glare. Even picturing it sent chills down her spine, her mind blanching at the memory of the threats made. Her shiver doesn't go unnoticed by Sloane or Gina.

"Someone hurt you, didn't they?" Gina spoke softly, her voice a sweet Southern drawl.

Mara nodded, gritting her teeth. "Shitty family."

Gina looked at her with a sad smile, almost like she was recalling a long-forgotten memory. Sloane, on the other hand, snorted. With a bitter smile on her face, she shook her head.

"Cunts," she snarled. Her tone made Mara's hair stand on end.

A steady silence fell over the three women. Mara was the first to break it, surprising herself by doing so. "So you were going to fill me in?"

Sloane's gaze was unwavering, sending a wildfire through Mara's veins. "Right. So, there's no easy way to say this, so I'm just gonna say it. You're a werewolf."

Mara blanched at that. *Werewolf?* She scoffed. "Be serious."

"I am, Mara."

Another damn rush of nerves ran through her at the sound of her name on Sloane's tongue. "You can't seriously expect me to believe you? Werewolves aren't real. I just . . . had a mental breakdown or something. I must have."

Sloane looked at Gina. "Gina, grab the laptop."

Gina got up from her seat and left the garage. She came back after a few minutes with a small, black laptop. She sat next to Mara, tapping on the keyboard.

"We have security cameras around our property. You should see this."

Mara leaned forward, peering at the screen as footage began rolling. The green nighttime haze of the security camera flickered. Nothing at first. Then, she saw herself appear on screen, falling over onto the ground. Her body twitched on camera, jerking like she was having a seizure. Anxiety crept up her spine as she watched her body writhe and then go still.

Then she watched as her body contorted. Her limbs stretched and snapped. Her clothes ripped off her body as she grew, *grew*, in size, fur sprouting over her now bipedal wolf-like body. The sheer size of herself, when the creature—when *she*—rose from the ground and threw her head back in what looked like a howl, astounded and terrified her.

"I . . . that's *me?*" Mara croaked, mouth hanging open. "I turned into *that?*"

"Yeah, that's you."

"What the fuck?"

"I know."

Mara leaned in closer to the screen, amazed. Horrified. Confused. "This shouldn't be possible. This is like something out of a horror movie." She saw more movement to the far corner of the screen. A big, black bipedal wolf emerged from the shadows, slowly circling her. "There's another one!"

Sloane chuckled. "That's me."

Mara's eyes bugged out of her head. "You're huge!"

Loud laughter erupted from Sloane, accompanied by soft giggles from Gina. "Why thank you." Sloane flexed her muscular arms. "Put a lot of work into getting big."

Mara's gaze lingered on Sloane's biceps. Blinking rapidly, she dragged her eyes away from the woman's arms to her face. "So, what, I'm a werewolf?"

Sloane nodded, her arms relaxing, expression turning serious. "Yeah. Do you . . . have any family with lycanthropy?"

Mara quickly shook her head. "No. I mean, not that I know of. I've never seen my parents turn into giant wolfmen." A sense of trepidation crept up her spine. "What am I going to do now? I'm a werewolf. A literal werewolf. None of this should even be happening." A frown creased her brows, eyes turning downcast. Just the thought of her family made her stomach turn. Mara shifted in her seat, arms wrapping around herself.

Sloane raised an eyebrow. She cocked her head to the side. "Mara, are your parents kind to you?"

Mara looked up. Her rich brown eyes fixed on her, piercing her with their intensity. "I, um . . ." *Lie. Lie so you don't look like a whiny bitch.*

"Tell the truth," Sloane breathed, eyes going hard.

Mara's breath hitched in her throat. This woman was reading her like a book. "They're . . . pretty bad."

"Do they hurt you?"

"No."

"I'm not talking just a beat down."

Mara paused, her eyes turning glassy. "They . . . they yell a lot. At me. At each other. They get on my case a lot."

Sloane's eyes narrowed. "Go on." Her voice held command, and Mara found herself complying. *Needing* to comply.

"That I'm useless, don't know better. They don't give me independence even though I'm old enough to leave home. They won't let me leave, insisting I must stay with them forever until I find a church boy, even though I'm pretty damn sure they *know* I don't like men." Mara's voice trailed off. She'd addressed an elephant that followed her into every room. She held her breath, wary of Sloane and Gina's reaction to that piece of trivia.

The corner of Sloane's mouth lifted in a smirk. "Join the club."

Mara's brows shot up, reaching her hairline in disbelief. Meeting another queer girl was a first for her. Shock coursed through her caused her lips to part involuntarily, much to Sloane's delight; the woman's smirk only grew wider. Determined to maintain composure, Mara quickly pursed her lips, attempting to regain control.

When she found her voice again, her tone was laced with suspicion. Trepidation. "Forgive me. I don't mean to look a gift horse in the mouth, but I can't help but feel like there's a catch."

Gina wrapped an arm around her. "No catch. You know the worst already. We're werewolves. Painful transformations and bloodlust galore. But it's not all bad. *And*, you have us!"

"But you don't know me," Mara countered.

"We do *now*," Gina replied. "Duh."

Sloane got up from her crouch and sat on the other side of Mara. She rested her chin in her hand; Mara caught sight of a tattoo on the side of her wrist. A moth between two crescent moons. "Gina's right. Look. We're strangers. I get it. But we'd like to help, Mara. We've been exactly where you are. Being a lone wolf sucks serious dick."

Gina hummed in agreement, rubbing Mara's arm. "You should be part of our pack."

Pack. Something deep within Mara ached for it. Was this her new-found wolf side coming out? If it was, she yearned to be part of a pack. "You'd really do that?" She looked between the two women. "You'd help me?"

"More than that." Sloane's low, calm voice sent a shiver down Mara's spine. "We even have shitty movie nights. It's fun."

"I bake!" Gina chimed in, grinning brightly.

Mara smiled. The muscles in her face stretched. Like she'd forgotten how to genuinely smile. Try as she might by biting her lip, the joy won, her tired stormy blue eyes shining in the dim ochre light. "Baking and shitty movies sounds amazing."

Sloane and Gina exchanged glances, mirroring each other's grins. Sloane was the first to speak again. "Run away then. Join us."

Mara's heart raced in her chest. "I—I want to. It all sounds amazing. But, my parents . . ."

"Don't worry about them." Sloane's tone left no room for discussion. "As far as I'm concerned, it sounds like you're better off without them. Join us." She leaned in closer, her voice dropping to a whisper. "Join *me*, Mara."

Tempting. It was all too damn tempting. A dream come true. Mara had prayed for a way out. And these two were handing one to her on a silver platter. It was a no-brainer. Nodding, Mara stared into Sloane's eyes. "Okay. Okay, I'll join you."

Gina's squeal made the pair jump. Mara and Sloane found themselves wrapped in an eager embrace. "Oh, this is going to be so exciting!"

Mara and Sloane giggled. A bit nervous, Mara was still shocked by the rapid, 180-degree turn her life had taken.

"Give it a week. We'll come and get you. Just be ready to bolt." Sloane shared a glance with Gina, who nodded and hummed in agreement with Sloane's words.

A week. A week and then I'm fucking gone. A big grin light up Mara's face,

The next week went by in a haze. After returning and getting an earful from her mother and father, Mara spent her days holed away in her room, save for when her mother had made dinner. The waiting was killing her. It took a toll on her mind. The wolf wanted out. It wanted to tear down these bedroom walls and run free. To her pack.

Her head jerked as a shudder ripped through her. *Please don't*, she begged her wolf. *Not now, not now. It's not time.*

Her inner wolf—which was what she'd taken to calling the restless beast that dwelled within her—was a storm brewing overhead. A tempest. Before, she could withstand her parents trying to control her life. Her body. How she presented herself. The wolf? She didn't like it one bit.

Looking out her bedroom window, the fall landscape that surrounded her family home had begun to lose its pretty colors. The trees dropped their leaves and a perpetual fog lingered over the grass. Winter was on its way.

The window glass was icy against her cheek as she leaned against it. She wanted to see Sloane and Gina again. It wasn't just her wolf that missed them. Gina's happy demeanor was infectious. And Sloane . . . Sloane made Mara feel alive. She was intense. Intriguing. Beautiful. Despite knowing her only for a brief moment, something about the woman ensnared Mara.

Her palm rested on the glass, feeling the coolness of the window under her clammy skin. "Where are you?" she whispered. "You promised you'd come."

Interrupting her melancholy, her bedroom door swung open. Her mother stood there, an eerie calmness about her. "Mara, we need to have a talk."

"What about?" Mara found herself asking, immediately regretting her word choice when her mother's eyes narrowed.

"You've been acting weird since Thanksgiving night."

"I have?"

"Yes, you have. After your little dramatic exit—"

Mara turned to face her mother fully, anger building up. "Dramatic exit? That's what we're calling it?"

"There you go again." There it was. The eerie calm broke, the last little thread containing her mother's ire snapping. "You don't make this easy. We've done everything for you! Fed you, given you a place to stay, provided for you. Don't you trust us to know what's best for you?"

"I—Mom, come on, that's not fair—"

"The least you could do is listen for once. And give that nice boy a chance."

Mara's face contorts into a glare. She stood up, the wolf rearing its head. Egging her on. Telling her 'Don't take this lying down.' To get fucking *mad*. "Mom, I don't want a boyfriend. Or a husband. I don't want to be some guy's broodmare!"

"Oh boo hoo, you don't wanna get married? Have kids?"

"Is that so hard to believe? I'm not *you*. I don't want some bullshit picket-fence life."

Her mother took a step closer. "Take the chance while you can, Mara. Say yes. No other well-rounded young men are lining up for you. Might as well buy the first car to call you pretty while you can."

A sharp pang clenched Mara's heart, squeezing it tight. A storm brewed in her blue eyes, a small, shocked exhale leaving her lips. Suddenly, she felt like a small, scared little girl all over again.

Before she could even respond, a smile tugged at her mother's lips. She placed her hand on Mara's cheek. "Mara Maree, you will thank me for this one day. Once you start listening to us—to *me*—you'll understand."

Like hell I will. Mara could only glare in response, her heart hammering away.

Her mother withdrew her hand with a soft scoff. "Dinner will be ready in an hour. Clean yourself up before then, it looks like you have a bird nesting in your hair."

Mara's eyes widened, a hand reaching up to run through her hair. It didn't feel frizzy, or frumpy. Just soft and poofy.

With a self-satisfied smirk, her mother left her room, leaving the door ajar.

Mara growled, stalking toward the door and closing it quietly. Her hand clenched around the doorknob, her heart raving wildly. She had this indescribable urge to bite. To tear someone apart. It possessed her, tunnel vision taking over. It downright frightened her how bad she wanted it.

"God help me." *I need to get out of here. I need to get to Sloane and Gina. They're going to be waiting for me. My girls. My . . . my pack.* The thought of the girls was a lifeline for her. An anchor.

Striding over to the window, she attempted to open it. It was jammed shut, the wood swollen from the damp weather.

With a string of muttered curses under her breath, Mara desperately pulled against the wood. Gritting her teeth, a surge of anger washed over her. Strength flowed through her arms, and with an ear-splitting *crack,* the window gave way.

Blood pumping in her ears, Mara grinned. *Sweet, beautiful victory.*

She moved away from the window, moving about her room like a tornado, throwing clothes into a backpack. She could find new clothes. New things. Most of her belongings in her room were pretty old.

To add to her stress, she heard footsteps approaching her bedroom door. "Mara? We need to talk." Her father's voice came from the other side.

Shit. Go, go, go! She chanted to herself in her mind, zipping up the bag with haste. Approaching the window, Mara's bedroom door opened, and she moved as quickly as her feet could carry her to her escape. She heard a muttered curse, and loud stomps. Clambering to the windowsill, she had managed to hitch one leg outside before her father dragged her back.

"What the hell are you doing?" Disbelief was evident in his tone.

"Let go!"

"Like hell I will!" He grabbed her by the straps of her backpack. They bit into her shoulders as she was yanked backward and thrown onto the hard floor. She let out a cry on impact, landing on her wrist awkwardly in an attempt to catch herself.

Her father loomed over her. "You're not leaving this fucking house!" He roared, chest heaving with angry, labored breaths.

I'm coming.

Mara froze. A voice was in her head. Sloane's.

I'm coming. She heard it again. Louder, echoing in her mind.

"Sloane?" *Where...? And how can I hear her?* Her breathing became unsteady. Her father narrowed his eyes. "Who the fuck is Sloane?"

The house shook from a loud crash downstairs. She heard her mother scream. The next time she blinked, a large black blur rushed past her, obscuring her vision. Within another blink, her father was no longer standing over her. Turning her head, Mara's mouth fell open at the sight of her father being held up to the wall by the throat. Sharp claws dug into his throat, puncturing the flesh. He choked on his own blood.

Sloane lifted her head. Snout to his ear, she spoke—*spoke*—in a deep, guttural voice. "Don't. Touch. Her."

Mara watched her father struggle. His eyes flickered to her. For a moment, a brief moment, she saw a glimmer of the dad she once had as a little girl. The one that stood by her. Protected her. Loved her, even. His lips moved, bloody spittle flying. "Mara . . ."

Mara slowly stood up, eyes trained on the scene before her. Words couldn't come out, no matter how hard she tried to speak.

She heard more screaming coming from downstairs. Another roar.

Slowly, in a daze, Mara stood up, turning her back on her father as he bled out. She heard a thump as something heavy—his body, she figured—was dropped to the floor. She felt Sloane's presence behind her, following her out of her room, down the stairs toward the commotion. Tunnel vision took over. She saw rubble from a destroyed section of wall scattered across the living room floor, pieces of drywall and wood scattered everywhere.

A squelching sound caught her attention, followed by crunching. Bones snapping. Turning toward the sound, Mara's eyes widened. She'd turned her head in time to see another white and brown werewolf—Gina, she presumed—gnawing at the joint of her mother's arm. Her mother dropped the knife she was holding, screaming in agony.

"S—Sloane . . ." Mara's hand reached out to her, feeling the black fur under her fingertips. This was surreal. A numbness washed over her. She should be upset, shouldn't she? She should be screaming, begging Gina to stop. That's the morally sound thing to do, right?

With a jerk, Gina tore the arm clean off, blood coating her jaws. Tilting her head, she went for the jugular, biting down hard enough that Mara could hear the bone snap.

Mara felt a hot breath against her ear. "We take care of our own." Sloane's voice left no room for arguments.

Time slowed. The heavy thudding of her heart echoed in Mara's ears. She watched Gina release her mother's corpse, turning toward her. Gina cocked her head to the side. She approached Mara, gently bumping her snout to Mara's chest, letting out a tiny whine. Blood and viscera dripped out of her mouth. "You alright?"

"I—" Mara couldn't find the words. "I don't know."

Gina blinked slowly. Then she nuzzled her enormous head against Mara's shoulder, letting out another whine.

Sloane copied her movements on the other side of Mara. A silent display of comfort.

The two wolves nudged Mara forward, toward the hole in the wall. A chill winter breeze had spread throughout the house. Mara let her packmates gently lead her out of the wreckage of the home, her hands resting on each of their furry shoulders like a lifeline as they stepped out into the darkness. To freedom.

Mara didn't look back once.

The Blossoms of Twilight

R.K. Devon

> CW: death of a loved one, graphic violence, blood, mental health, PTSD flashbacks, gang violence

The Debt

I always knew I would die young. One by one, death had come calling for my friends long before old age could leave its withering mark, and I thought the same short life would be in the cards for me. Which hand would smother my pathetic existence was the only difference. I always suspected Fate would be cruel when she decided to end me.

Fate has never favored me, no matter how bold I've been.

I never considered what would happen if I didn't die first.

Espen's glassy eyes mocked me, and I could almost hear his familiar baritone berating me for my carelessness.

Always have a plan, Azura. Be ready for every possibility or else Fate will find a way to punish you for your negligence. Fate. Such a volatile bitch.

How could I have possibly anticipated she would come for him first? Ice-cold skin met my fingertips, crimson trailing in their wake as I traced my hand down Espen's unnaturally pale face. The stench of iron hung heavy in the air, coating my tongue with every violent heave of air I forced into my quaking lungs. My heartbeat wouldn't slow, couldn't steady itself as I took in the blood soaking both Espen's clothing and the wooden floor underneath him. Blood roared through my ears. His frightened face blurred as tears obscured my vision and I hastily wiped a sleeve over my eyes, only to stifle a cry when it reopened the gashes on my scuffed knuckles.

Shame scalded my throat and I hurried to bite back the sobs that ballooned my chest. *How can I cry over banged-up hands when Espen doesn't even have hands anymore?* My stomach twisted as I took in the wounds that marred Espen's lifeless body. I didn't want to look, but I needed to know. To see for myself how he'd been savaged. The cost he had paid to protect me.

A sacrifice I would never have the chance to repay.

Espen had always been so full of energy. Seeing him lying there, still and silent, just seemed so *wrong*. He didn't even look like he was peacefully sleeping. No, his mouth was widened in horror and those grey eyes that had always looked at me with warmth were hardened chips of ice.

I wiped the blood off Espen's face with trembling fingers. I couldn't stand to see him like this, garbage carelessly tossed away. He'd always been meticulous about cleanliness in life. If he knew his clothing was drenched in blood, that dirt coated every inch of him, he'd be livid.

A manic laugh bubbled up in my chest. Espen would never be angry again. He'd never be anything, because he was *dead*. Another friend I'd failed to protect.

My eyes drifted to the dead body beside him, replaying in my mind the moment I'd returned home and found the intruder standing over Espen's lifeless body, greedily rifling through Espen's pockets to take that which didn't belong to him. He hadn't heard me approach. Didn't even know I was standing behind him until my knife slid between his ribs.

Sloppy.

He'd fought like an idiot too. My knuckles ached with the reminder of the fight he'd put up before the life had finally leached from his eyes. He'd been a wild animal, fists flying in a furor that I'd struggled to dodge. There'd been no calculation behind his moves, nothing to assess or parry. No anger either. Just an animalistic fear that propelled him into a frenzy of movement as he faced his impending demise. Espen must have been taken by surprise, because there was no way the man who'd trained me to always be on guard had been caught unaware by such a weak fighter.

I kicked the assailant onto his back, my heart dropping as my fears were confirmed. Under his body was a stunner, its sleek metallic body sitting innocently amidst the gore as if it weren't a deadly weapon capable of incapacitating a full-grown man.

But the attacker's neck was what sent blood raging through my veins. A small tattoo was inked into the flesh. I hadn't noticed it in the blur of the skirmish, but now it stood out like a beacon against his bronze skin. I had the same mock bite mark engraved into my arm. A mark placed on me against my will. A brand I'd been forced to accept.

The Scavengers did this.

And it was all my fault.

I wanted to scream at the injustice of it all, my lungs swelling with the need to do *something*, anything but sit here and witness how I'd failed Espen. He'd always been a staunch cornerstone in my life, and this was how I repaid him? What would I even be without him? I'd never considered what would happen if he left me behind.

Frigid realization descended in a crushing wave, smothering my rage until all that was left was a numbing fear that shook my shoulders in violent heaves. Who would I be without Espen? Without our friends? We'd always been together, ever since the day a young Espen found me scrounging in the garbage and pulled me into his crew. We'd grown up together, learned everything we needed to know to survive the streets together: which alleys to avoid, how to read gulls, how to pick pockets. Before I knew it, Espen's crew had become my crew, and together we'd terrorized the streets of Labec. That little ragtag group of orphans and street rats was the only home I'd ever known.

We'd always had each other's backs. What little food the group scoured the streets for was shared amongst us, and our love for each other made even the chilly nights seem warm. The dusty wastelands we called home were less frightening to me knowing that we'd face their trials together. Everything had been a golden dream; fractured, sure, but wonderful all the same.

I should've known that nothing beautiful lasts in this world.

The Scavengers had descended on Labec with a violence we'd never seen before. Their old hunting grounds had run dry and they'd turned their greedy gaze to our small enclave. They absorbed all the local gangs with honeyed words of glory, and when that didn't work, their brutality ensured that no one would be brave enough to cross them. We were just fodder to their cruelty. Like carrion, they'd taken what they wanted from our broken bodies. Our little crew didn't stand a chance, and we'd been snatched into the Scavengers alongside countless others.

Then the tests began. I don't know if it was a desire for sadistic punishment or if they truly believed they could instill loyalty into us through fear, but it didn't matter. We did what they asked of us, or they killed us. And they killed so many. With each friend that fell, my anger burned hotter and brighter.

My eyes narrowed on the letter that had been tossed carelessly on Espen's mutilated corpse.

Your debt is paid.

Four little words were all Espen's life was worth. Every measure of his breath, every twinkling moment of triumph and every heartbeat of misery, boiled down until all that was left was his connection to me and the quota I'd failed to fulfill. As if Espen had been nothing. As if I was nothing more than what I could earn for the Scavengers. Just another body to milk dry.

I was so tired of it all. The constant struggle to survive, always looking over my shoulder, waiting for the death blow I knew was coming my way. Living was such a tiresome burden. At least with Espen and the crew, I hadn't suffered alone. Without them, I was looking down a bleak future spent serving fuckers who weren't even fit to clean Espen's boots.

What's the point of it all?

The letter slipped numbly from my fingers. Fatigue settled in like a heavy fog as the strength left my body all at once. I found myself lying beside Espen on the bloody floor as if it were any other night, one of many where we'd laid down together and exchanged stories about how we'd spent our time apart.

The pain in my chest tightened and grew spikes.

I reached out my hand for Espen's, remembering at the last moment that I wasn't going to find that familiar warmth against my palm anymore. *Why couldn't they have attacked when I was home?* It was a cruel irony that they had killed Espen for my failed hunts when I had been out doing exactly that.

Dread curdled in my belly. If I continued to live under the Scavengers' thumb, it would be me lying here dead one of these days.

Fuck that.

Rage burned in my veins, smelting away the indifference until all that was left was boiling fury. I wasn't going to roll over and let them do whatever they wanted to me. They'd done that for long enough. My life may have been worth nothing to me, but Espen's had been worth something. So had Mara's, and Anthony's. Even little Rhea's life had been worth more than what she had been able to contribute. They hadn't deserved any of their ends.

My eyes snapped to Espen's. My life was going to end anyways, but I would make it count.

For the family they'd taken away from me, they would pay in blood. They wanted me to hunt? I would be the carrion bird that feasted on their rotting corpses.

Resolve hardened my muscles and I paced frenetically, looking around the threadbare hovel that our crew had called home. My choice was made for me.

The Scavengers would regret the day they came to Labec.

The Reckoning

No matter how many times the smell of burning flesh caught in my nostrils, the acrid odor never failed to surprise me with how repugnant it was. I stepped back from the greedy blaze that strained towards me with blistering flames, and took shelter from the rain under the awning. The clouds had broken open with a vengeance the moment I trudged outside to cobble together Espen's funeral pyre. The inferno that licked across his skin roared with an unholy anger that resonated with the wrath swelling within me. I didn't even glance at the smaller pyre beside Espen.

Warmth trickled down my fingers. I looked down in surprise to see red droplets rushing towards the ground. I unclenched a fist I didn't realize I'd made, revealing four gouges in my palm. It was almost poetic really, each a physical manifestation of the wounds in my heart that the Scavengers had carved into me with every member of my family they had taken away. The sting grounded me, and I relished the pain knowing that I would be delivering my retribution soon.

I wasn't dumb enough to think I could take down the Scavengers alone. But I'd seen the infighting. They were held together by a shared need for food and survival; there was no loyalty to be found except among the little clans that had been absorbed. The gangbangers were kept in line through fear alone. Without the threat of death hanging over them, they'd scatter with the wind.

I needed to take out the threat at the source.

The Scavengers were led by the Karreri brothers, a bloodthirsty trio with deadly reputations and the personalities to match. Akton the Arrogant was the eldest, a brawny behemoth laced with scar tissue from his days spent in the brawling cages. His rage was legendary, second only to his bloodlust. I'd personally seen the destruction he could unleash with his meaty fists.

The second brother, Kieran, was a wisp compared to the eldest, his willowy frame misleading in its frailty, but the stain of cruelty was apparent once you gazed into his flat eyes.

My skin prickled as my thoughts turned to the last brother. Thane the Butcher. His brutality far outweighed his brothers, and his propensity for weapons would make him the hardest to kill. But his death was the one I yearned for the most. He'd earned his moniker in alleys filled with severed limbs and sightless eyes.

He's the one who put the hit out on Espen.

The hands had been a clue. Thane's own hand had been lost in his youth, and he'd made it his personal mission to ensure that those who opposed him knew his pain. But the Karreri brothers were too proud to send their lackeys to do their dirty work. They heralded themselves as "men of the people," unafraid to get their hands dirty for their fellow members.

So why did he send that prick after Espen?

I racked my brain for answers, and only one conclusion presented itself. Something else had come up. Something more important to the Karreri than building their reputation.

I rubbed my hands along my arms, trying to force some semblance of heat into my chilled flesh. It was useless. Something inside me had died alongside Espen and the others, and now my body was as cold as my heart. A stranger to warmth.

A feral grin curled my lips. I would take what was precious to them until their lives were as cold as mine.

I planned under the light of the waxing moon, unable to stand the thought of being inside where Espen's life had spilled out across the floorboards. I didn't bother to clean it.

I knew my chances of surviving were dismal.

So I remained outside, warming my body with the heat of the pyre—the last time that Espen would be able to keep me warm—and

I plotted. Wracked my brain for remembered rumors and whispers of details until the rain let up and I could put my murderous plans into action.

I grabbed my dagger from the dining table before making my way into the slums. The moon was the only witness to my moral descent as I crept from shadow to shadow down the streets. It was easy to stay out of sight, second nature to a thief like me. I didn't mean to toot my own horn, but I was an excellent thief. The only reason I'd failed to meet the Karreri quota was because of this damned heart of mine that wouldn't let me steal from those who obviously didn't have much to lose. I may have had the moral fiber of a rat, but I wasn't a monster. Not like the Karreri.

The Karreri's greed was legendary. It had decimated mountains, savaged hundreds, and nearly wiped entire towns off the map. Each brother's hand had personally shaped the lives of every person in Labec. For them to leave their punishment to be doled out by another meant it was more important to them than their reputation—so it must be related to their greed. And there was only one thing left in Labec that they didn't have their filthy hands on already.

The Griman.

I grimaced as my stomach soured.

There were other dissenters to the Scavengers' rule whom I would need to find. Other clans broken up by the Scavenger's avarice and undying quest for power.

Skid Row was wide awake despite the late hour. Huddled bodies sheltered around makeshift fires, smoke blooming in the chilly air and wafting upwards towards a colorful array of loose fabrics that had been strung together into a makeshift ceiling.

Any other night I would've stopped and spoken to the familiar faces I could make out, but tonight only one destination blared in my mind. The only place left for those who did not yield to the Scavengers.

The Lowers.

It was one thing to do nothing when the Scavengers came looking for prey. Skid Row was full of people who only looked out for themselves. But it was another thing entirely to naysay the Scavengers. The ones who had fought their overtaking, who cried out when the Scavenger came to steal and claim their belongings, became the hunted.

I was about to join their ranks in the only place safe for those hunted, a series of sewers and underground tunnels that had long ago been abandoned.

Exactly as Anthony had described.

Sweet Anthony had joined our crew only two short years ago, but he'd made a big impact. His bubbly personality was at odds with his bulk, but the way he'd been able to see the silver lining in everything had been his biggest strength. He'd come out of the Lowers as a youth, and despite what was no doubt a horrible childhood, he'd always been quick with a smile or a helping hand. He'd tell us stories about the life he'd left behind, never knowing that one day I'd use his tales as the basis for a coup.

The slums backed up to a massive wall that supported the Erimon bridge, and there I stood before the entrance, a gaping hole as tall as four men, my palms sweating as my heart danced a rapid beat. There was no light down the long tunnel, only darkness that whispered dangerous murmurs on the rancid breeze pushing past me. It was almost as if there were a veil of impenetrable blackness, and I took a step forward to see if I could touch it. I gagged instead, raised a sleeve to my mouth, and hastily breathed through the bloodied fabric. The cloying scent of dried blood on my sleeve was distasteful, but far better than the rank smell of bodily fluids that clawed at my nose.

Am I really doing this?

My pulse fluttered wildly as I gazed into the darkness of the tunnel. But when I thought back on Espen's lifeless body, my mind settled with a hush.

"I'm here to meet with those who wish to see the Scavengers fall," I shouted into the gloom. Espen had always said my bluntness would be my doom, but I hoped he was wrong. Time was not on my side.

An eerie cackle sounded from the thick darkness as a match was struck. A lantern flickered to life, illuminating a dirt-speckled face and red, wiry hair that reached in all directions. Blue eyes came into view, crinkled in humor, the face of a young woman who watched me warily. She looked me over, her discerning eye traveling up and down, and I realized I hadn't changed out of my blood-soaked clothing. I cringed and wafted an embarrassed hand over my clothes as she let out a huff. If I hadn't been staring right at her, I might've missed the shadow that drifted by. My eyes latched onto the motion, following it as it trailed towards the side of the tunnel. Sweat slicked my palms as I became aware of the weight of dozens of eyes on me.

"Only a fool would shout that sort of nonsense out loud. And we don't suffer fools here." The woman moved to put out the lamp, sending panic rampaging down my spine. I rushed forward before she could snuff out the flame.

"Wait!" I swallowed a lump in my throat before stepping into the darkness. Despite my instincts screaming at me that the sewers were dangerous, I knew my courage was being tested. "I know the type of person who gets sent to the Lowers." I met her steely gaze with my own. "I know there was nowhere else for the people of Frissia to go after the Scavengers drained them dry. Nowhere but among the refuse." I took another step forward, aware that the woman wasn't alone before me. "I know how the orphans of Bera came to be. How the revenants of Ilis came to lose their limbs. How so many more were driven from their homes by the Scavengers. And I know they ended up here."

The air was heavy with tension. I took a steadying breath, only to choke back a cough as rancid air met my lungs.

The woman's face remained passive as she watched me gag. "We may have a reason to hate the Scavengers," she said quietly. "But hatred will not keep us alive. Grudges will not see us live for long."

I scowled. "The Scavengers may number in the hundreds, but their leadership is only three men."

"Those three men are the Karreri. And they cannot be defeated." The deep, hoarse words reverberated through the tunnel, echoing in the tense silence. I squinted, but my weak eyes couldn't pierce the thick darkness.

"Who's there?"

The lantern tilted to the side, giving birth to another flame and another illuminated face. On and on, little fires came to life until the tunnel was filled with disheveled faces and haunted eyes.

"Even if we could get past their foot soldiers, the Karreri are fearsome warriors," another voice called. Low mumbles rang out. My eyes darted around, but I couldn't locate the source. Judgement pounded down on me, invisible hands shoving against my body and pushing me away. But I'd had enough of being forced into a corner.

"My name is Azura. I don't know what suffering the Scavengers have subjected you to, but I know your pain. It lives within me as well, its roots planted in the graves of my loved ones." I raised my gaze and looked into the eyes of the person nearest me. His suffering was written clearly across his face and my heart panged with sympathy. "The Karreri took the last of my family today, and I want them to suffer. I know the brothers are alone, and I know where they are." I snarled. "Now is our chance to strike."

A figure staggered into the light. The man limped closer and as the gloom melted away, I realized the cause of his limp. I looked away before I could offend him, but not before the image of his ruined body seared into my mind.

"How do you know?' his broken voice rasped.

I'd tried my whole life to stay away from the memories, but my mind wouldn't let me forget. I used to think the nightmares were just that, nightmares that a child's mind had made up to rationalize the horrors that had scarred me. But as I'd grown, pieces had shifted into place and I'd come to realize the startling truth that had teased the back of my mind for years.

"Before I was a waif running the streets of Labec, I had a family," I said softly, my eyes downcast as I recalled the image of a woman's smiling face. She must have been my mother, because who else would've looked down on me with such an indulgent smile? "A blood family. I was probably a handful, because my parents would bring me to work with them to keep me out of trouble. I used to love it, exploring the ruins with them. I'd show them all my finds, and they'd graciously pretend like I'd found the most important artifact they'd ever seen. My best find, however, was a shiny yellow statue that sparkled in the sun."

Gasps rang out but I pushed on, bulldozing my way through the memories that threatened to drag me under. "Things changed after that." I scoffed lightly. "My mom stopped smiling. We moved." I pushed the words through the tightness of my throat. "We moved a lot, actually. Looking back on it now, I think we were running from someone."

I swallowed past a lump in my throat. "They were hunting the Griman that I'd found."

A relic of the past, from before the world began to eat itself. They say that the ruins we wandered used to stand tall and proud, reaching towards the sky with shiny hands and see-through faces. What a children's tale.

"The night our luck ran out, my parents hid me before they died. I saw the man who killed them, the one who stole the Griman. He had one eye and a jagged scar that ran through his ruined socket deep into his cheek." Murmurs erupted. They knew what I did. There was a man with those distinctive markings, high up in the Scavengers' ranks. And somehow the Karreri had found out about what he had.

"They'll come for him this night," I shouted. "And we can be there to meet them with blades and steel!"

Silence met my declaration. I pressed on, fueled by the knowledge that this was our chance. "We will never have a chance like this again. This is your opportunity for vengeance, to escape the Lowers!"

A soot-streaked hand shot into the air. "Name's Mary. I'll join," the red-haired woman said. It was as if a dam broke, one that had been holding back years of anguish. Hand after hand reached towards the ceiling like blossoms in a field.

The Remittance

There was a quivering in the air, and for a moment I worried that my nerves were getting the best of me and it was actually *me* shaking. *Way to promote confidence.*

A staccato shrill sounded in the distance, vibrating the air with a dull shriek.

"It's begun," someone hissed quietly.

I took a steadying breath, inhaling the dusty wind and the faint scent of ozone. Tension coiled in my muscles. I shook my hands out with a sigh, but kept my gaze focused on the darkened home ahead of us. "Give it time," I answered roughly. "We need them to take each other out first or else we chance them joining forces against us." The house was sizable, two floors of fabric-covered windows that could easily house three families. As expected of a top-earning member of the Scavengers.

Murmured sounds of approval sounded only to hush moments later when pops of light reflected behind the curtains.

I eyed the pale moon hanging low in the sky and discreetly reached up to wipe away a tear. *This one's for you guys. I'll see you soon.*

Our group numbered in the dozens and realistically our chances of victory were slim, but the element of surprise would play a giant factor in our survival. Excitement thrummed in the air and as I looked at the weary faces around me, I saw the same determination that I knew was reflected in my own features.

A muffled shout of victory rose from the home. There was a collective inhale as we all held our breaths, and I almost laughed at the silly reaction before remembering that the next moment would decide if we all lived or died. We waited, hiding behind the refuse that lined the streets, blending with the darkness as best we could. I went over the plan in my head, counting out the steps to the front door over and over until I could see the distance with my eyes closed. *Thirty paces before they reach our hiding spot.*

After what felt like hours, the front door crashed open with a bang and out walked three men. Dark patches covered two of them, and even from this distance I could tell they were dripping with blood. The third was spotlessly clean, but I knew that wasn't an indicator of innocence. Kieran Karreri was just as cruel as his brothers; his sadism lay in the poisons that left their taint on his victims.

He'll be the easiest to kill.

The brothers walked into the street, a burlap sack carried between them as they excitedly talked over each other. Undisguised glee practically rolled off them in waves. My hand shook as I raised a fist in the air, preparing to signal the start of the attack. I wet my lips nervously as I counted their steps.

Twenty-nine. Thirty.

The unclenching of my fist set off a ringing in my ears.

As silent as specters, we stepped into the moonlight. It was a dirty move to attack them while their backs were turned, but fair fights were for those who hadn't been tortured, tormented, and victimized. Street cred was nothing in comparison to freedom. And it was more than freedom on the line, it was our existence as something other than shackled workers, bent over in subservience for people who thought themselves our betters.

Mary's blade sank into Akton's massive back before the Karreri even knew we were there.

Everything seemed to move in slow motion. A howl of pain left Akton's lips before he crumbled to the ground. Kieran darted to the side, his hands diving into the pockets of his muddied trousers. There was a flash as Thane drew his daggers, his eyes narrowing with a sneer as he surveyed his attackers.

"This is for the Strays," I yelled as I charged towards him.

A chorus of shouts echoed in the night air as my cry of vengeance was mirrored. Dimly, I heard a woman wail her outrage for the pillage of Bera. The thundering scream of a man rang out with the name of the revenants of Ilis, but my mind snapped to attention as Thane dodged my knife strike with one of his own.

His eyes brightened with delight as he towered over me, skimming down my body in a caress that sent revulsion careening into my sour belly. "Sweet Azura," he purred indolently. "I wasn't expecting a visit so soon." Mirth cascaded across his features as he took in the scowl on my face. "How is your family, dear?"

"They'll be better once I wipe away the stain of your existence." I sneered as I jumped out of reach.

My fingers ached with how tightly I gripped my dagger, but my dance around Thane was fluid, dashing forward in slashes and pokes that had him reeling backwards defensively. He may have been bigger and stronger, but his size would be his downfall. I was smaller, faster, able to skip below his guard with one well-timed rush.

Adrenaline flooded my veins, feeding the wrath that swelled my muscles with every patient breath. *I can do this. For Espen and the others.*

Annoyance flickered across Thane's face as I scored a cut across his left shoulder. "Such a pretty dancer," he hissed between his teeth. "Why don't you come closer and let me show my appreciation?"

I ignored the jibe, though irritation sparked hotly across my skin. My stamina was quickly waning. I needed to end this soon. Thane bolted forward in a flash, his speed far greater than it had been moments ago. *He's toying with me.* His knife dragged deeply across my side before I could dodge, and I bit back a cry of pain as I jumped away. Satisfaction twisted his lips. He raised his blade into the moonlight, revealing the blood that coated the metallic length in a sickening display that sent my belly writhing.

"My my, how clumsy of me." His ebony eyes darkened with cruelty.

I gritted my teeth as my wound pulsed with agony.

How do I get out of this?

As if in answer to my silent plea, a figure appeared behind Thane. *Mary.* Her red hair blazed around her head like a flame as she crept closer. Thane was too busy admiring his handiwork to notice, so I kept my expression carefully neutral as I gripped my side. We'd have to play this smoothly or we were both going to die.

I faked a stumble, only to groan as I fell onto my knees when pain wracked my body. My side burned hotly, and I had the nauseating realization that his blade had been poisoned. Why was I surprised? Kieran was known for his toxins. Espen would have yelled at me anew for not taking their brotherly bond into consideration. Thane shuffled closer with a smirk, no doubt eager to finish me off.

"It's not often that someone has gotten the jump on us," Thane mused as he stopped a foot away. "How did you know where we were going to be?"

I stayed silent, glaring at him with all the enmity I could muster.

Thane chuckled as he crouched before me. His lips parted to speak, only for a choke to emerge. He whirled and I saw my chance. My blade catapulted into his belly with a dreadful thud. I jerked the knife upward, relishing the feel of blood spilling across my hands even as a horrible stench exploded from him.

We did it.

Thane collapsed in front of me, his head swiveling back to face me with accusation in his eyes.

Victory sent energy coursing through me and I scrambled to my feet, only to fall as dizziness slammed into me. Hands turned me onto my back, but I couldn't see who. Everything was starting to drift away. Words passed over my ears, but they were meaningless, just sounds that pricked my eardrums in rapid succession. Warmth touched my lips and I gasped. Liquid trickled down my throat. A hand covered my mouth as I started to cough, forcing me to swallow despite my thrashes to get away. Pain wracked my side, the energy draining as quickly as it had arrived. Slowly, I became aware of faces peering down at me.

Recognition struck. I pushed myself to my feet with a grimace, surprise lashing me as Mary came forward.

"He had the antidote on him. Probably in case he ever nicked himself, the fucker." Mary spat at the corpse at her feet.

Bewilderment threatened to drag me back onto my ass as I looked around. Kieran lay dead a few paces away, his face savaged beyond recognition. Akton sprawled where we had first struck him, a crimson puddle cooling around his body.

Only a handful of us were left, but we'd done it. We'd survived. Mary clapped me on the back as she went to the others, their low voices pulsing with relief. Someone opened the sack, and with trembling hands raised a small yellow figure into the air. Eyes turned to me, waiting for my answer to the unspoken question.

"That's it," I choked out. A hushed cheer broke out, smiles fluttering to life across faces that probably hadn't smiled in years. The first rays of dawn crested in the distance, highlighting each figure who'd stood beside me on this momentous night, each one willing to die for the chance of retribution. I took in each scarred face, each distinctive body, and marveled at how so many dissimilar people had mustered their strength and gathered together to take down the threat of death that had hung over us for years. Silence rang out as we absorbed the ramifications of what we'd done. But we couldn't stay here for long, not if we wanted to avoid the other Scavengers discovering who we were. A nod to the others was all the goodbye we needed. We would carry the secret of this night to our grave.

But I would never forget it.

I left the Griman with them, knowing they needed it more than me. Maybe it could help them escape the Lowers. With my mind turning over what we'd done, I walked into the twilight, my side aching stiffly as the weight of my sins settled heavily on my shoulders, and yet for the first time in years, a bittersweet euphoria bloomed to life in my chest.

The Infinite Ethereal

Sunny J Rowley

CW: violence, blood, guns, shooting, implied sexual assault, mentions of torture and abuse

A hollow sound echoed through the silence of the back alley as Crescent blew away the smoke drifting from her revolver's barrel. The smell of charred flesh lingered in the air, floating through the mist that filled the alleyway. She looked at the young woman who had pressed herself against the wall, eyes wide as she stared down at the prone form, mouth moving as if trying to speak but unable to find adequate words for the current situation.

"I find cursing helps in times like these," Crescent said with a slight wave of the revolver.

"I-is he dead?" the younger woman asked, voice stuck in her throat.

"Ehh…" Crescent lifted her arm to aim the revolver at the man. She didn't even look away from the woman as she pressed the hammer down, summoned some electricity, and squeezed the trigger.

For the second time, the sound of a gunshot and the crackle of electricity echoed through the empty cobbled side street, bouncing off the brick and steel buildings surrounding them. The young woman recoiled at the sound, hands covering her ears.

"Yeah, definitely dead," Crescent said, flicking out the revolver's large six-chamber cylinder and removing the two spent casings before throwing them on the body. She couldn't help but smile as they landed on the burnt, bloody patch growing on the man's waistcoat.

"He was..." the young woman choked out. "He was going to..."

"Are you hurt?" Crescent looked at the younger woman as she reloaded the empty chambers. The girl couldn't be older than eighteen. *Too young, too fucking young*, her mind screamed. She roughly clicked the cylinder back into place.

"He didn't get that far." The response was soft and timid. She brushed her hand through her now mussed-up brown curls, then looked down at her clothes.

Crescent followed her gaze. Part of the woman's skirt had been ripped away from her corseted top.

"Fucking..." Crescent hissed, kicking out, her buckled calf boots connecting solidly with the man's legs.

"He was meant to escort me home. Just walk me home."

Crescent let out a low laugh as she returned her weapon to her thigh holster. "Won't be a problem anymore."

The young woman looked down at the form before stepping out of the path of small streams of red now spreading outward through the space between the cobbles. "I didn't mean for..."

"Hey. You are not at fault. His actions were his own, and they are what caused this."

Crescent pulled her bowler hat down and began walking away, though she only got a few paces before the woman called to her.

"You're Crescent, aren't you? The vigilante everyone is talking about?"

Crescent looked down at herself. "Yes, I think I am."

"Everyone is saying you are a man because of the..." She pointed at the man's chest, where the waistcoat was still smoking. His flesh still burning.

"Ahh, yes. Well, that's a funny little story."

She started to walk away again, but the woman called out again.

"I'm Eden." Crescent turned back to look at her. "I thought you might want to know who you saved."

"I'll see you around, Eden." Crescent laughed as she allowed the fog to envelop her.

Breathing deep in the tumbler, Crescent still couldn't smell the alcohol. She huffed in frustration.

"You know, rum isn't meant to be sniffed—drink it."

She looked up at Charli, and the bartender frowned down at her. Crescent chuckled and then sipped the amber liquid, letting it burn the back of her tongue and her throat.

"See," Charli said before moving further down the bar.

Crescent took another sip, but the burning taste still didn't transfer to scent. It wasn't as though she expected it; the horrid scent of burnt flesh had all but destroyed her sense of smell.

She liked this bar. This was one of the few safe spaces she had found in the city. It was a haven for those like her, those she protected, and those she'd saved. While the outside looked run down, the inside was light and welcoming. The walls were lined with shiny brass pipes decorated with old cogs and clock parts. A long rectangular bar sat in the centre of the room, stools surrounding both sides. On either side of the bar were several tables and plush chairs, a few of which hosted a handful of women she knew. She had previously helped them out of unpleasant situations, much like she had with Eden.

Taking another sip, Crescent thought about Eden. It had been three days since she had seen the younger woman, three days since she had stopped yet another woman from becoming a statistic.

Eden had reminded Crescent of herself—the younger, more hopeful version. The one that had been beaten and buried, black and blue, beneath the stone and steel of the city.

"Hey Cres, you got a visitor." Charli again stood in front of her, nodding their head towards a figure moving nervously through the open floor of the bar. "Front sent word that she came in. Figured it would be for you."

Crescent examined the figure closer. Eden looked like a frightened animal. Her eyes were wide as she searched the room for something. Crescent smirked, before turning back to her drink. Her seat at the bar was positioned so that no matter who came, she would always see them before they saw her. She only needed to wait for Eden to spot her.

"Hello." Eden's voice was soft as she came to stand by Crescent. Looking up, she met Eden's eyes. "Hello, Eden."

"You remember me?"

"Of course, why wouldn't I? Have a seat."

"I didn't think you would," Eden said, pulling herself onto a bar stool. "You must have helped so many."

Crescent scoffed into her glass before composing herself and raised a hand to flag down Charli. "Would you like something to drink?"

"Um, sure, yes please. Thank you." Eden stumbled over her words, and Crescent was reminded of a young deer learning to walk.

"A drink for the kid, Cres?" Charli asked. "I don't think so."

"I'm not a kid. I'm eighteen."

"A kid." Charli scoffed again.

"Oh, come on, Charli, I was only a year older when I was committed to Andro. She's fine."

"Andro? Andro House?" Eden asked, but was cut off by a drink placed in front of her.

"No alcohol," Charli said as they walked away.

"Don't mind Charli. They were the first person I helped. They're a bit protective."

"You helped them?"

"Yeah, they had a bit of an issue with some men my first night out of Andro." Crescent waved her fingers, and little blue sparks of electricity danced around her fingers. "Needless to say, they're no longer a problem."

"You do have powers? How? How's that even possible? Only men have the gene?"

"Sure, they do." Crescent snarked, then flicked her fingers, sending the ball of electricity into the nearest light bulb, causing it to brighten and crackle.

"Cres, none of that," Charli yelled from the other end of the bar.

With another laugh, Crescent turned to look at Eden. She was staring, and Crescent knew what she saw in her appearance. Deep black hair cut short, almost as if it had been haphazardly chopped, then styled later as an afterthought. Shorter in the back and on the sides, with longer bits in the front that nearly reached her chin, all pushed to one side of her face. Blue eyes, which had lost any sort of brightness or light they might have once held. Purple shadows highlighted the shallow bags under those eyes.

And then there were the scars. A pair of bright pink, jagged, crescent-shaped scars graced her temple. Crescent watched Eden's brow furrow and knew her stare had reached her namesake.

"That's what happens when a stubborn woman meets electricity."

"Sorry," Eden said, looking away to stare hard at the bar top.

"It's fine. I can tell you have questions, and not all of them are about my scars."

"I do," she responded. Crescent was sure she was about to explode trying to keep it in.

"And?" The word seemed to give Eden permission to speak.

"I want to know absolutely everything. Who are you? How do you have power? Why did you save me? Why did you kill him? How do you decide? Why are you doing all of this?"

Crescent couldn't help but laugh at her quick spew of words.

"Firstly, Crescent may not be my name, but I like the moniker enough to stick with it. Second, I do this because something I went through has happened to others, countless others. Every woman knows the cruelty of men. They hate us. They don't listen to facts, figures, or truth in the words we speak, that we scream. But they'll listen to the bullet. We shouldn't have to drop their level, but I am willing to do it." Crescent didn't continue; she knew that to save others, she wouldn't just kill, she would bathe herself in blood.

"But it, but that..." She seemed to be having trouble coming to terms with the truth that had been presented. It was as if she wanted to find anything that could disagree with in Crescent's statement, to prove it wrong, or doubt it.

"How about this—you enjoy your drink, and I will tell you a story."

Eden didn't respond, but she took a sip of her drink. Crescent smiled and did the same with hers.

"Once upon a time, there was a girl and a boy. They were best friends, both from prominent families, and both with all the advantages. Their families would say they would be the perfect couple, and their children would be the city's future leaders. Their whole lives had been planned out like a business transaction. But the girl didn't mind. They were friends, after all."

She paused, taking another sip.

"Life continued, and they grew up. Then, as some boys do, he got his power and grew into himself. Suddenly, he was strong, confident, and handsome. The girl was in love and so happy. He was strong, and she was smart, they were going to be a power couple. Everything was wonderful."

She looked at Eden's face. The woman's eyes were wide as if she was being told the most riveting story. Crescent knew the next part would not go how the hopeful girl wanted.

"He saved several important people in the city, becoming well-known and even more respected. Then he changed, or maybe it was always there, but he became cocky and arrogant, demanding and selfish."

Crescent sighed before taking another sip.

"One day, he came to visit the girl. She decided to take the opportunity to try to talk to him about it. He decided that he wanted something else. She tried to fight, but he was so strong with that power of his. It may have been her body, but, so suddenly, it was his choice. She tried to tell her family, but they believed him. Everyone believed him. He even convinced her father she was crazy, that she needed to be put away and tamed until she could be a smiling little wife and mother. Andro House became her new home, and with it, came the perks of cold cells, beatings, and rounds of electroshock."

Crescent swallowed hard, before continuing.

"During one of those lovely sessions, she was injected with something. She had no idea what, but the next thing she knew, her body was on fire. Electric. A few things happened, a lot of violence, and now here we are."

Eden had finished her drink and stared at her with wide, sad eyes. Crescent watched her swallow hard before she spoke, "How long were you at Andro House?"

"Two years, but it felt longer and shorter at the same damn time."

"How could someone do that? To turn your own family against you? What type of person does that?"

Crescent forced herself to relax, to stop grinding her teeth together. She took a breath to ground herself in the moment.

"Crescent?" Eden's voice was full of concern.

"What type of person? Come with me, I'll show you," Crescent said before pushing herself away from the bar. She pulled on her long jacket and bowler hat, then headed for the door. She could hear Eden behind her, rushing to catch up.

Leading the way, Crescent walked quickly through the twists and turns of the city and passed under the elevated railway of the city's steam metro. She only began to slow as they neared the city centre. Pulling the younger woman down a detour path, Crescent eventually stopped at the entry to an alley that faced out onto the open expanse of the city centre. The makings of a large crowd gathered in the middle of the square to hear someone speak.

"Why are we here?" Eden whispered as if they were trying to hide from something.

"You wanted to see what type of person." She nodded her head to the speaker.

At the head of the crowd was a well-dressed man with blond hair and bright green eyes. He wore what appeared to be a mix of a business suit and armour. He waved to the crowd before gesturing for them to settle down. He began to speak, and Crescent heard her name. *Of course, he would talk about bringing the vigilante to justice,* she thought.

"That's Lord Tybalt Radford. The Golden Hero of the city. He's the one? . . ." Eden's voice trailed off, her eyes full of horror at the information Crescent had given her.

"You never know who someone is, and sometimes gold hides rot beneath it." She stared out at Tybalt, where he spoke to the crowd. Her words were calm and hollow, said with a cold finality.

"And that is why you do this?"

"My intention is to help. Dead men can't hurt us."

"Help," Eden paused to ponder the word. "I want to help. What can I do?"

Crescent looked at her. "You can help by doing what we do best, being empathic. Listen to people who might need help or who might need a particular type of help. If you get a name, leave it with Charli." Her gaze drifted back to Tybalt, then she turned and walked away.

The sun was creeping over the city and cold night air clung to her as she walked through the bar's back door. Another three names were marked off her list. Only she knew who was on her list, and though it made her sick to see that it kept growing, keeping it to herself had allowed her to keep to the shadows. People knew what she was searching for, word got around, and word always got back to her. If there were those uncomfortable about her actions, well, fuck them and their comfort.

Though, right now, it was about her comfort. About her need for sleep. She had waited for her last target for hours, but she couldn't exactly ask her target for an exact time when he had no idea she was watching him. When he had finally shown, her electric shot had torn through the front of his neck and exploded out the vertebrae of his spine, leaving a gaping hole that matched his expression. The electricity had crackled up his face and down through the gruesome wound, charging the flesh and bone as blood poured down the front of him. Leaving only the sound of whistling and gurgling as the blood filled his trachea and choked him.

While Crescent didn't feel bad about his death, given how he had lived, she did feel a slight twinge that having made such a shot filled her with glee.

Maybe I am a little crazy, she thought as she climbed the stairs to the small loft Charli allowed her to use as a humble abode.

When she reached the top of the stairs, she heard Charli's voice calling her name from the bar floor. She let a soft whimper of a moan escape her.

"Crescent, have you heard what happened to Eden?"

The question had her entire body tensing up as she turned to face Charli. Eden had become a regular in the bar for the past few weeks and had proven surprisingly good at collecting information. Crescent chalked it up to having such a sweet and hopeful nature.

"What happened to Eden?"

"She was arrested," Charli said, making air quotes when they said the word *arrested*.

"What do you mean arrested?" Crescent asked as she began to step down the stairs.

"Lord Tybalt took her in."

"What?" Her furious shout reverberated off the walls. Charli jumped back from the metal stairs as Crescent's electricity sparked with her anger. "Explain."

"I don't know the details, but apparently, she was snooping around and asking questions. Particular questions about him, and he caught her. Word is he is claiming she's a lead."

"Where did he take her?"

"That's just it. He didn't take her to the station. He took her to his mansion."

A harsh hissing sound escaped Crescent as her breath tried to get past her clenched teeth, and her nails dug into the flesh of her palms. She could feel every heartbeat pumping electricity through her, coating her tongue in the taste of metal.

"That fucker," she hissed. "That fucking fuck. No. He can't do this again." Her mind spun, running through her options to get Eden away from him. A wild idea hit her with lightning force, and her body moved toward the door automatically.

"Cres, what are you going to do?"

"I'm going to even the playing field. Keep your ears out for any news. I'll be back in a few hours."

Fuck sleep, fuck men, fuck this whole world, Crescent thought as she moved through the city. Her rage fuelled her until she was on the outskirts of Andro House. Only then did she pause, her stomach turning as the memories of her screams caused her throat to burn.

"Get in. Get it. Get out," she whispered to herself. "In and out."

Following the stone wall surrounding the property, she eventually reached a spot where a large oak tree grew. Quickly climbing up, she dropped onto the other side of the wall and ducked behind the bushes meant to give residents the idea they were in a garden, not a prison. Working toward the building was annoyingly slow as she kept herself hidden.

I had to do this during the day, she chided herself. When she was closer to the back of the building, she noticed they had hung a bit of laundry on a line to dry. She pulled one of the patient robes down and slid it over her head, winching as she noticed a red-brown stain they hadn't managed, or even bothered, to remove.

Swallowing hard, she managed to keep a handle on her body's desire to expel any contents remaining in her stomach. She removed her bowler hat, placing it under the robe on her stomach. Holding it with an arm, she shuffled through the halls. While she hadn't been in Andro in a year, she would never forget the feeling of being caged, and now that she was in the building again, it took everything to keep herself, not to mention her electricity, under control. Closing her eyes, she prayed to any divine higher power that the early hour would mean she wouldn't be caught.

When she reached her destination, she tapped one finger on the door's lock and heard the mechanism click, allowing her to push it open. Once in the office, she shut the door, then took a moment to rest her head on it. After several deep breaths, she yanked off the robe, replaced her hat, and moved further into the room.

The room felt bigger than it had before, but now she wasn't strapped to the chair in the centre. She wasn't being beaten, tortured, drugged, or electrocuted. No, now she was standing on her own two feet, revolver strapped to her thigh, and in complete control of the electricity in her veins.

With a rough sigh, Crescent moved toward the opposite wall and fiddled with a cabinet. With its wooden base and gear-locked doors, she had always thought the wardrobe was out of place in this room, but when she had seen inside, it all made sense. She had only ever seen it being opened once but would never forget that day or the order of the gears she needed to twist. As she turned the last gear, several others followed, slowly unlocking the door. Pulling it open, she was met with a wave of cool air. The wardrobe had been retrofitted to be an ice box, the gears on the outside being a puzzle to confuse anyone who didn't know what it really was.

In the dim light, she could see dozens upon dozens of vials half-filled with liquid that glowed a pale orange. The sight made her mouth fill with saliva and her heart race. She didn't know what it was called but didn't need to. It was what they had injected her with that resulted in her abilities.

Crescent was sure it was the same stuff that gave the men their powers. Though she figured they hadn't been strapped down.

Shaking the thoughts from her head, Crescent looked around for some way to carry the vials out, but the sound of a key in the door behind her made her pause. Quickly, she moved to hide behind the opening door.

"What?" the person entering said as they noticed the open wardrobe. Crescent instantly recognised the harsh voice of Doctor Marshall. His voice was one of the dozen that haunted her nightmares.

He took a step into the room, and Crescent pulled her revolver, before slamming the door shut.

"Hi, Doc."

Dropping his medical bag, Doctor Marshall spun to face her, throwing his hands in the air. "You! What are..."

"Shh..." Crescent said, levelling the weapon at him. "It's been a while since our last session. How about you have a seat?" She used her gun to gesture to the chair.

Keeping his hands up, he followed her instructions and sat. "What are you doing here?"

"Taking the vials," Crescent said, stepping forward.

"What? Why?"

"I'm making soup," she said with a smile before laughing at the wild look on the doctor's face. "Have to fuel up to start a war."

Doctor Marshall opened his mouth to speak, but Crescent pushed the revolver into it. "Shh, Doc. I'm running today's session."

Keeping the gun pressed to him, she ignored his whimpering and used her free hand to tighten the chair's restraint straps across his wrist, chest, and legs. Once she was sure he would be unable to move, she holstered her revolver, then leaned on the chair to stare into his eyes.

"You know, Doc, I am in a bit of a rush, but I think I can make a little time for you."

"I don't know what you think you are doing, but the moment I get out—" He was silenced as Crescent grabbed his face with one hand, her nails digging into his cheek.

"Who said you're getting out? Maybe, if you're good, give us a smile, and take it." She hissed, using the words that haunted her from this room. Words that had passed his lips as he had burned her flesh with electric rods pressed to her temples.

Crescent gave him her widest smile and called her electricity to the surface.

###

The balcony was not the closest to the square, but it still offered her the perfect view. After dropping off the Doctor's medical bag with Charli, and instructing them to rally the troops, Crescent managed to have a courier send a message to Tybalt. It consisted of only one sentence.

Me for the girl this evening in the square, with a crescent moon scrawled on the bottom.

She couldn't be a hundred percent sure he knew she was the vigilante, but she was hoping she would have the element of surprise. A look around the square gave her courage, as several of those she knew were stationed throughout. Like her, they were waiting for the main event. They were waiting for a fight. Like her, they were ready to use their blood, sweat, and tears as war paint.

And the battle was finally approaching.

Crescent leaned forward, watching a large group move into the centre of the square. They were creating a crowd while at the same time as setting a perimeter. After they had positioned themselves in a rough semicircle around the statue of the city's heroes, Tybalt emerged.

As he walked into the open to stand under the statues, he led Eden with him. Making her stand a few steps away, he turned to address the crowd.

"Good people, I come bearing grand tidings. I'm here today to end the reign of terror the vigilante has brought to this great city. Here to lift the fear cloaking our people like the mist before the sunrise. This young lady"—he gestured to Eden—"has been used as a pawn by the vile Crescent. Many times I have saved the people of this city, and today, I will do it again."

Crescent rolled her eyes as he continued to ramble poetically. She climbed down from the balcony onto the street as he began to spin a story of an enemy of the city who used the weak-willed and killed without mercy. She ignored his words as she moved through the crowd.

Her footsteps toward him felt as if they were loud enough to echo through the square, but no one gave her any mind. His tale captivated them, even though he never identified anyone as this horrible villain. Crescent knew what he was doing, keeping attention on him, waiting for someone to get angry enough to challenge him and expose themselves.

But she wasn't fuelled by something as small as anger.

Pausing at the crowd's edge, she looked around, and her people had copied her movement. Dozens of people she knew had slowly moved to position themselves throughout the crowd.

Taking and releasing a deep breath, she moved forward calmly, walking toward Eden.

"For someone who claims to be a shining beacon of this city, you have a terrible track record with your actions against women," Crescent thundered toward Tybalt. Her eyes drifted to Eden.

"Kasia?" Tybalt said in a way that sounded more like a gasp.

"Don't often go by that name nowadays," she replied. Having reached Eden, she reached out for the handcuffs, allowing a tiny bit of electricity to pop the lock.

The cuffs clattered to the ground, and Crescent jerked her head for Eden to get out of the way of danger.

"You're Crescent?" Tybalt's voice was full of angry disbelief. "You're the vigilante? The murderer?"

"Isn't it obvious?" Crescent responded, gesturing to the scars on her temple. "I figured it was an appropriate name after all."

"No. That would mean you have an ability, and that's not possible. Women can't have them. They aren't strong enough."

Crescent continued to walk, slowly circling the man in front of her. "Really? Well, Tybalt, we all know how you like to put on a show, so..." Lifting her left hand, she summoned a ball of electricity to her palm, then began to weave it between and over her fingers.

There were gasps among the crowd, and Tybalt's eyes were wide as he stared at the power in her fingers. She pulled her revolver out with her other hand and slowly brought the crackling lighting in her hand to meet it. It obeyed her will, dancing into the cylinder and clinging to one of the bullets.

"Surprise," Crescent said before levelling the gun toward his feet and firing.

There were screams of surprise as the crowd tried to move back. Tybalt jumped away as the bullet hit the stone, and electricity flew from the impact. He glared back up at Crescent.

The sound of her laughter was the only sound in the square. "The look on your face. Did you honestly think you men were special?" She gestured at him with the revolver. "The drug you used to gain your precious abilities doesn't only work on men. They just don't want the people to know." Crescent held up the revolver near her mouth as if she was sharing a secret.

"Don't..." Tybalt's voice was full of warning.

"The powers are not natural," Crescent yelled out to the crowd. "They give a select few a drug to grant abilities and herald them as heroes. While at the same time, they test the different versions on women, then kill them if abilities develop. Somehow I pissed them off enough that they injected me before remembering they weren't allowed to kill me."

"You fucking bitch."

"I may be a bitch, but you're an asshole who takes fucking pleasure in ruining lives."

Tybalt shook his head, puffing up his chest. "I don't ruin lives. I am a hero."

A harsh laugh escaped from the back of Crescent's throat. "You could have fooled me. I've experienced it."

"You're saying I ruined your life? I didn't do anything to you that you didn't want. We both know that."

"Really? I thought the word *no* would have told you how I felt—or maybe the word stop? Or maybe when I said don't? Or all the screaming?"

"You screamed because you liked it."

Crescent paused to look directly at him, her fingers aching to raise the gun. "I screamed because you held me down. And if what I said didn't make you realise it, your actions afterward prove you knew exactly what you did."

"I didn't..."

"You convinced my father his only child was losing her mind and making false accusations. Convinced him that sending me to that place"—she spat the word—"would calm me down. It did quite the opposite, didn't it?"

"What the fuck happened to you?"

"Well, between the cold cell, the beatings, and rounds of electroshock, I realised that men have no idea what rage truly is. All you know are the simmering emotions of embarrassment and fear. Those little explosions of anger, those little bits of red haze, they aren't rage. Not true rage. True rage is cold; it's calm and calculating. It's the icy bit of starlight that floods the veins. And women, we have generations of rage etched into our DNA. So when they stuck that needle full of drugs into my skin, it reacted...violently."

"You fucking whore."

"Such harsh words for the city's golden boy," Crescent said, levelling the gun back at Tybalt. "And they all hear you." She gestured to the crowd that was still present, staring at the pair.

"You fucking planned this."

"A little bit. When you took my friend over there," she said with a small gesture toward Eden who had moved to stand with the crowd, "I decided your time was up. I actually decided that a lot of people's time was up."

"The fuck you mean?"

"Did you know Doctor Marshall likes to talk when his life's on the line? He had so much to say this morning."

"What did you do?"

"I got answers. You see, he had a theory. Women are intrinsically connected to life, and as such, even our rage can create. While you get strength or the ability to fly when you are given the drugs, when we get them, we can create and manipulate the very aspect of nature."

Tybalt had enough sense to look stunned and almost scared.

"Crescent, what have you done?"

"I shared. You're not the first man to hurt a woman, and certainly not the last. There have been thousands before you and thousands before them. Our collective rage is infinite and ethereal...and now it's free."

Crescent spread her arms, and several women who had made their way to the front of their crowd held out their hands and summoned their power. Fire sprang from one woman's fingers while a ball of water materialised above another's palm.

Fear spread throughout the crowd as woman after woman showed their power. Several men pushed out of the crowd, some deep instinct telling them to try and save themselves.

"Your actions started this, Tybalt," Crescent called above the chaos. "Shall we finish it?"

"You fucking..." He bellowed as he began to sprint towards her.

Crescent didn't react, allowing the world to slow around her. Tybalt was so focused on his anger that not even a splash of water from another woman slowed him down. Crescent raised the revolver in front of her face and watched as she pushed electricity into another bullet.

Tybalt still didn't slow as she levelled the pistol at him. With a deep breath in, and a long, slow breath out, Crescent smirked as she squeezed the trigger. The bullet, with all its electricity, hit Tybalt square in the chest. There were no words, not even a scream, as his body tensed, muscles convulsed, and his heart stopped. The sound of his death was limited to his body hitting the cobblestone.

"Infinite ethereal rage," Crescent whispered, looking down at him before she turned to address the crowd.

"We have muzzled ourselves for too long for them. We've dressed up our claws with pretty varnish and done it so well that they have forgotten what we are capable of," she shouted. "It is time to remind them that women are like the wilds of nature or a loaded weapon. Intricate, detailed, fragile, and deadly. Let our rage be heard."

A roar of agreement sounded as the women of the crowd began to march together into the city, ready to share their rage.

Suddenly, Eden was at Crescent's side. "Are you okay?"

"Me? You, Eden—are you okay?" Crescent retorted, grabbing the other girl to check for injuries, her eyes catching on several bruises on her face. "Did he hurt you?"

Eden looked over at the pathetic body that lay on the cobbled stone. "I'm okay. He can't hurt anyone now."

"You are unbelievable, Eden."

"What do you mean?"

"There are so many of us whose rage will speak in violence. Who will be the flames that consume and burn a forest to the ground until nothing remains but ashes. The world is not meant to be like that. The world is meant for people like you, Eden. People whose rage becomes hope. People who can help the good grow from those ashes into a lush new life."

"Doesn't seem as powerful?" Eden asked while rubbing the lingering cuff marks on her wrist.

Crescent reached up and let her fingers graze the scars marking her temples.

"Infinite ethereal rage is nothing compared to the power of infinite ethereal hope."

The Sins of the Flame

Ryen Santana

CW: graphic depictions of burning at the stake, torture, death, murder, reincarnation, memory manipulation

Author's Note: This is a fiercely angry and violent story of a woman rising against men who have wronged her, fueled by centuries of rage and injustice. It features graphic depictions of burning at the stake, hanging, stoning, torture, and suffering, with a vengeful witch exacting brutal retribution on the souls of her male executioners. Themes of death, reincarnation, and memory manipulation drive the narrative, forcing these men to confront their past sins and endure the torment they inflicted. Centered on historical religious persecution and the oppression of women, the story delves deeply into betrayal, misogyny, and gendered violence, unapologetically condemning patriarchal cruelty.

Chapter 1: Liora the Scorned

Salem, 1692

Liora's cottage door exploded inward with a splintering crash, the icy night air slicing through the warmth of her hearth. She barely had time to rise from her chair before rough hands seized her, dragging her forward. The bowl of stew she had been eating toppled to the floor, spilling across the stones in a steaming mess.

"Witch," the constable spat, his voice trembling with a mix of fear and righteous anger. "Your sins have come due."

Liora clawed at his hands, her breath coming in quick gasps. "Let go of me! What are you doing?" Her voice was steady despite the pounding of her heart, but she knew. Deep down, she knew.

They had been whispering for weeks—her neighbors, the preacher, even the wives who once came to her for herbs and healing. Crops had failed. A child had died of fever. A baby born still. And now, they needed someone to blame. It wasn't enough with the stoning and drowning of other women. They needed fire to cleanse.

She fought against their grip, but the constable yanked her arms behind her back, his fingers digging into her skin. Another man stepped forward, grabbing a fistful of her dark hair and jerking her head back so she was forced to look up.

"You and your kin have cursed this village, Liora," the preacher said, his face a mask of cold determination. "The Lord's light will purify your evil."

"You fools," she hissed, her voice laced with defiance even as her body trembled. "It is not curses that brought you misfortune—it is your own cruelty, your greed, your neglect. You destroy yourselves, not I."

The preacher's lips twisted into a snarl. "Take her," he barked. "The stakes are ready."

They dragged her through the village, the icy ground cutting into her bare feet. Her neighbors gathered outside their homes, their faces pale and solemn in the glow of torchlight. She saw a woman peering through a cracked shutter, her eyes wide with guilt. Then Thomas, the blacksmith, stood at his forge with his arms crossed, and his mouth pressed into a thin line as he avoided her gaze. He said he loved her just three nights ago, as they lay in each other's arms, forgetting the world around them. No one moved to stop them. *No one.*

They brought her to the square where the stake had already been erected, its dark wood rising against the night sky like a grim monument to their fear. A pile of dry kindling waited at its base, the scent of tar thick in the air. But it wasn't just one stake, it was three.

Her heart lurched at the sight of her closest friend, bound to the stake beside hers. Sarah's face was streaked with tears, her blond hair tangled and matted with dirt. "Liora," she whispered, her voice barely audible over the murmurs of the crowd. Beside her was Abigail, the schoolteacher who dared teach girls to read.

Liora struggled against her captors, her voice breaking as she cried. "No, no! You can't—she's innocent! And Abigail is just a teacher. They're innocent."

The preacher's voice rose above her protests. "They aided you in your devilry, and they will burn as you will. The Lord's judgment is final."

"You cowards!" Liora screamed, her voice raw with fury. "You call this justice? You call yourselves men of God? You will pay for this—*you will all pay.*"

They tied her to the stake with ropes that bit into her wrists and ankles. The wood was rough against her skin. Sarah's sobs filled the air, mingling with the rustling of the crowd.

"Don't be afraid," Liora said, turning her head as much as she could to look at Sarah. Her voice softened, though her body shook with rage. "This is not the end."

The preacher raised his arms, his Bible held high. "Let the flames cleanse their souls!" he bellowed.

The torchbearer stepped forward, his smirk clear as he lowered the flame to the kindling. The fire caught quickly, the dry wood crackling and snapping as the flames climbed higher. Smoke filled Liora's lungs, burning her throat and making her cough, but she forced her voice to rise above it.

"With my dying breath, I curse you all," she screamed. Her eyes locked on the preacher, the governor, the constable, then the town doctor who had lied to condemn her. "You will live again and again, forever bound to your sins. And I will rise in every life to remind you of what you've done. I will make you burn as I have burned. Feel as I have felt! There will be no mercy, no peace—only agony."

Her words echoed in the air, etched into the souls of the men who damned her. Their faces paled and their eyes widened with something between terror and disbelief. Beside her Abigail screamed, "Let this world burn if it fears our words!"

As flames reached her legs, then her torso, their heat became unbearable. She clenched her teeth to keep from screaming, the agony unlike anything she had ever known. She turned her head one last time to look at Sarah, whose tear-streaked face was illuminated by the firelight.

"I love you, Sarah," she said, though she knew Sarah could hear her over the roar of the flames. "I love you."

And then the fire consumed her.

Chapter 2: Daniel The Righteous

Boston, 1794

The first breath Liora drew after awakening was filled with smoke, though no fire burned around her. It was the memory of fire, the echo of it still lingering in her soul. She sat up slowly, her hands pressing into the cold, damp earth, frost biting at her skin. The world around her was quiet, the stillness broken only by the whisper of wind through skeletal trees.

She shouldn't be here. She should be ash, scattered and forgotten, her voice silenced forever.

But her curse had worked.

The men who condemned her had not escaped. Their sins tethered them to her, binding their souls to hers across lifetimes. The curse had ensured she would rise whenever they did, brought back to life by the weight of their crimes. She wasn't reborn as they were. No, her existence was something else entirely—fragmented, a shadow tied to their darkness, her purpose singular and absolute. To make them pay.

The tether was like a pulse in her chest, faint but unyielding, pulling her east. She didn't know how long she'd lain dormant, her soul suspended between death and the living, but she knew why she was awake now.

Daniel. The memory of him was sharper than the frost on her skin. In life, he had been the preacher of her village, a man who hid his hatred behind the guise of righteousness. He condemned her with a fervor that went beyond duty, his sermons dripping with venom as he denounced her healing, her knowledge, her very existence.

"She is a servant of the devil," he had thundered, his voice rising above the murmurs of the crowd. *"Her very presence corrupts this village. The flames of hell await her—and we must send her there."*

Daniel had led the charge to drag her from her cottage, his hands gripping her arms as he spat scripture in her ear. She could still feel the roughness of the rope that bound her, still hear the crackle of the flames as they climbed the pyre.

Now, in 1794, he had been reborn into the bustling city of Boston. The tether drew her there, guiding her through cobblestone streets and alleys crowded with merchants and dockworkers. Liora moved through the crowd unnoticed, her dark cloak blending with the muted colors of the bustling docks. She found him easily, his voice cutting through the din like a knife.

Daniel stood at the base of a wooden platform, his arms raised as he addressed a small gathering of men. He was older in this life than he was in hers, his hair streaked with gray, but his voice carried the same self-righteous fury she remembered.

"Men of Boston," he called, his voice carrying through the crowd. "This city is a den of sin. Its streets are filled with harlots and liars, thieves and drunkards. If we are to save ourselves, we must root out the wickedness among us." Liora's hands curled into fists beneath her cloak. He hadn't changed. Even in this new life, he wielded his voice like a weapon, his hatred burning as brightly as it had centuries ago.

She watched him for hours, biding her time. As the sun dipped below the horizon, the crowd dispersed, and Daniel retreated to a modest home near the harbor. Liora followed, her footsteps silent as the shadows that stretched across the cobblestones. The house was small and sparsely furnished, its walls lined with shelves of books and religious trinkets. A single oil lamp burned on the desk where Daniel now sat, his head bowed over a worn Bible.

"You've spent your whole life fearing hell," Liora said, stepping into the room. Daniel looked up sharply, his hand reaching instinctively for the letter opener on the desk. "Who are you?" he demanded.

"I heard your sermon," she said, her voice calm. "I was passing by and thought I'd introduce myself."

He frowned, his grip tightening on the letter opener. "I don't take kindly to strangers entering my home uninvited."

"Then consider me an exception," Liora said, her lips curving into a faint smile.

"What do you want?" he snapped, rising to his feet.

"To talk," she said simply.

He took a step toward her, his eyes narrowing. "About what?"

"Your past," she replied, her tone sharp now.

His frown deepened. "I've no idea what you're talking about."

"Oh, but you do," Liora said, her dark eyes locking onto his. "You just don't remember yet." She raised her hand, the air in the room rippling. Daniel staggered back, clutching his chest as the memories surged into his mind. She made sure he saw himself standing in the village square, and heard his voice booming as he condemned her to burn. That he felt the heat of the flames as they consumed her, heard her scream her curse: *"You will live again and again, bound to your sins, and I will rise to remind you of them"*

"No," he gasped, his face paling. "No, this isn't real."

"It is," Liora said, stepping closer. "You took everything from me, Daniel. My life, my work, my future. And for what? To satisfy your hatred? Your fear?"

"I was saving the village," he choked out, his voice trembling. "You—you were a threat—"

"I was your *scapegoat*," she interrupted, her voice cold as the grave. "And now, you'll face the fire you were so eager to send me to."

The surrounding room dissolved, replaced by darkness. Daniel gasped as flames erupted from the floor, surrounding him in a circle of hellish light. The heat was suffocating, the air thick with smoke that burned his lungs.

"Please," he begged, falling to his knees. "Please, I'm sorry—"

"It's too late for apologies," Liora said, her voice rising above the roar of the fire. "Feel what I felt, Daniel. *Burn as I burned.*" The flames surged, consuming him. His screams echoed through the void, his body writhing as the fire devoured him. Liora watched, her expression unflinching, until there was nothing left but ash.

When the fire died, the room reappeared around her, its air heavy with the faint scent of smoke. Daniel's lifeless body lay crumpled on the floor, his face frozen in a mask of terror.

Liora stepped over him, her chest rising and falling with the weight of her fury. The pull of her curse tugged at her again, leading her onward.

"For every woman silenced," she whispered, her voice steady. "For every life stolen, I will rise."

Chapter 3: James the Merciless

New Orleans, 1864

The humid air clung to the city like a damp sheet, thick with the scents of jasmine, sewage, and the lingering tang of blood. New Orleans, alive with the echoes of the Civil War, seemed to pulse with tension, its streets a chaotic blend of desperation and decadence. Gas lamps flickered along the French Quarter's winding cobblestone streets, their faint light casting long shadows over the ornate wrought-iron balconies above.

The pull of Liora's curse had led her to a modest home on the outskirts of the city, its shutters drawn tight and its garden wild with neglect. The man inside had no idea she was coming for him. She watched from the shadows of his front window as he raised his voice again. James was yelling, his words sharp and cruel, cutting through the thick summer air. He stood in the dimly lit parlor, a tall figure with broad shoulders and a face hardened by years of self-importance. His wife, a slender woman with dark hair and a bruise blooming across her cheek, flinched as he stepped toward her.

"I won't hear another word about it, Eleanor." James bellowed, his hand raised as though to strike. "You are my wife, and you'll stay in this house where you belong."

"Please, James," Eleanor begged, her voice trembling. "I can't live like this anymore. I—I want to leave, to be free."

"Free?" he sneered, his face twisting into something monstrous. "You think you can survive without me? You're *nothing* without me!"

Liora's fingers tightened into fists as she stood outside their door. She had been watching James for days, learning his routines, his habits, the sharp edge of his temper. She had seen the bruises on Eleanor's arms, the way she cowered when he raised his voice. It was all too familiar.

Liora stepped through the threshold of the door, her presence silent but deliberate. "I couldn't help but overhear," she said, her voice smooth as silk.

James spun around, his eyes narrowing as they landed on her. "Who the hell are you?"

"A friend," Liora said, smiling . She held out her hands, palms up, as if to show she meant no harm. "I was passing by and heard shouting. Is everything all right?"

Eleanor's wide eyes darted to Liora, her lips parting as if to speak, but James cut her off. "This is none of your concern," he snapped. "Get out of my house."

Liora ignored him, stepping closer, her gaze steady. "Your wife seems frightened."

Eleanor's hands trembled as she clasped them together. "Please help me," she whispered.

"Enough!" James roared, slamming his fist against the table. The force rattled the room, but Liora didn't flinch.

Instead, she turned her dark eyes on him, her expression calm but unyielding. "You don't recognize me," she hissed. "But I know you."

James blinked, momentarily thrown off by the weight of her words. "I don't care who you are," he said, though his voice faltered. "You have no right to be here."

Liora tilted her head, studying him. "No right?" she murmured, her voice laced with quiet fury. "You speak of rights, yet you trample over hers as though they don't exist."

"Leave," James snarled, stepping toward her.

"Not until you understand," she said sharply. "Not until you remember."

She raised her hand, and Eleanor gasped, clutching at her chest as James staggered back. His eyes widening as the parlor dissolved, replaced by the crackling firelight of another time.

They stood now in the village square, the smell of smoke thick in the air. The memory of Liora bound to the stake, her hair tangled around her face, her eyes blazing with defiance. The preacher's voice rising above the crowd, condemning her as a witch. The flames of the memory roared around them, their orange tongues lashing out and devouring everything in their path. But above the deafening noise, Liora's voice cut through like a sharp knife as she stepped from the pyre. Her words were filled with anger and pain, directed at the person in front of her. "You stood by," she accused, her eyes blazing with fury. "You let them kill me. You let them kill so many of us." The air was heavy with the smell of burning wood and flesh, but Liora's words were even more scorching. "And for what?" she continued, her voice rising to a crescendo. "To protect your pride? To maintain your power over others?" She paused, her eyes narrowing as she remembered a specific healer from their village. "Do you remember Hannah?" Liora's voice shook with emotion. "She had children...they starved to death because of you. You were afraid of a woman being better than you," she spat out. "You condemned us for being healers, kind and compassionate souls. Killed us with your words, and the actions of another." She said, stepping closer to him. "She was stoned, crushed to death," Liora declared, her words dripping with malice.

James stumbled back, clutching his head. "No," he gasped. "No, this isn't real!"

"Oh, it's real," Liora said, stepping towards him. Her voice was low and deadly now, heavy with centuries of wrath. "And you will pay for it."

The scene shifted again, and they stood in a clearing surrounded by jagged rocks. The air was heavy with tension, the earth beneath them damp and soft. James looked around frantically, his breath coming in short, panicked gasps.

"Do you know how many of us they stoned, James?" Liora asked, her voice cold. "Do you know how many women they buried beneath the weight of their hatred?"

He shook his head, his hands trembling. "Please," he whispered. "Please, I'm sorry. I'll change, I—"

"You won't," she said simply.

The first jagged stone struck him in the chest, knocking the wind from his lungs. He swayed, clutching at the spot, but the next stone came faster, hitting him in the side. And then another, and another.

James fell to his knees, his body crumpling under the onslaught. The stones came from nowhere and everywhere, each one landing with a sickening thud. His screams filled the air, mingling with the memory of the women who had died this way.

Liora watched, her expression unwavering. She thought of Eleanor, of the bruises on her arms and the fear in her eyes. She thought of herself, bound and burning, her voice drowned out by the roar of the flames. She thought of Hannah screaming for her daughters as her ribs cracked beneath the weight of the rocks.

When it was over, James lay still, his lifeless body broken beneath the stones. The clearing dissolved, replaced by the dim parlor.

Eleanor stood frozen, her hand pressed to her mouth. "What—what happened?" she whispered.

Liora turned to her, her voice softening. "You're free now, he's dead, and his soul isn't coming back. He's too weak to rise again." Eleanor's eyes filled with tears, but she nodded, her shoulders trembling with relief. Liora stepped into the night, the pull of her curse guiding her onward. The rain began to fall, washing away the remnants of James's cruelty, but the weight of her purpose remained.

Chapter 4: Edward the Chauvinist

Chicago, 1922

The hospital smelled of carbolic acid and despair. White tiles lined the walls, immaculate but cold, their sterility unable to mask the undertone of blood and sickness. The city outside pulsed with life—roaring automobiles, streetcar bells, and the distant sound of jazz spilling from underground speakeasies. But inside these walls, time felt slower, weighed down by the suffering it contained.

Liora sat in a stiff-backed chair in the administrative office, her hands folded neatly in her lap. She wore a modest gray dress, her dark hair pulled into a low bun, and a worn leather bag rested at her feet. She looked the part of a nurse, but her dark eyes burned with something far deeper, far older.

The man behind the desk, Edward, flipped through her application with exaggerated slowness. He was tall, with thinning hair and spectacles perched on the bridge of his nose. His face was pale and drawn, the same face she had last seen in the village square. He had stood beside the preacher at the base of her pyre, a medical text in hand, his voice booming as he condemned her to burn. Parroting the hatred of the pious. He was the healer in the town that the men would seek. His remedies wouldn't work, so their wives would go to Liora.

Now, in this life, Edward was the hospital's chief physician. He wore his authority like armor, his every gesture heavy with self-importance.

"You've had no formal training," he said, not looking up from her file.

"I've learned on the job," Liora replied, her voice calm.

"Hmm." He made a noise of disapproval, tapping the file with his pen. "That's not the experience we value here."

Her lips curved into a slight smile. "What experience do you value, Dr. Morgan?"

He glanced at her, his gaze sharp. "Discipline. Obedience. A willingness to follow orders without question." He leaned back in his chair, folding his hands over his stomach. "And, frankly, we prefer men for positions of responsibility. Women are fine for bedpans and bandages, but anything more complicated..." He trailed off, his condescending smirk finishing the thought.

Liora's hands tightened in her lap, her nails pressing into her palms. She forced herself to remain still, her expression neutral. "I've been told I'm a quick learner."

Edward chuckled, the sound low and unpleasant. "I'm sure you have. But let's be honest—nursing isn't a profession for women with ambition. It's for women who know their place."

Liora tilted her head, studying him. The years had etched new lines into his face, but his soul was unchanged. He was the same man who had stood in judgment over her, who had twisted texts to suit his fears, who had sent her to her death with a righteous sneer.

"You've spent your whole life judging women," she said, quiet but cutting.

Edward frowned, his smirk fading. "What did you say?"

Liora leaned forward slightly, her dark eyes locking onto his. "You look at us and see only weakness, only sin. You've made a career of it, haven't you, Dr. Morgan? Passing judgment, deciding who is worthy of saving and who isn't. But tell me, who gave you that right?"

He straightened in his chair, his brows drawing together. "I don't appreciate your tone, Miss—"

"You don't remember me," she interrupted, her voice cold now, heavy with the weight of centuries. "But I remember you."

The air in the room shifted, growing thick and heavy. Edward's breath hitched, his fingers gripping the edge of the desk. "What are you talking about?"

Liora stood, her presence towering even though he remained seated. "Do you remember the village square? The pyre? The sound of the crowd as they cheered for my death?"

Edward's eyes widened, his face paling. "This is madness—"

"You called me a witch," Liora said, her voice rising. "You called me evil, and told them I deserved to burn. And you watched as the flames consumed me."

The walls faded into darkness. When the light returned, they stood in the village square. Edward gasped, clutching his chest as the memories Liora unleashed flooded his mind. She ensured he saw her bound to the stake, her face streaked with soot and tears. Liora's voice filled the room, raw and furious, as she screamed her curse: *"You will live again, and again, and again, bound to your sins. And I will rise to remind you of them."*

"No," Edward whispered, stumbling backward.

"You stole my life, my work, my dignity. You destroyed me because you were afraid of my power to heal. Because you couldn't stand the thought of a woman being *better* than you." Liora said, stepping toward him.

Edward fell to his knees, his hands trembling. "I thought I was doing the right thing," he said weakly. "I thought—"

"You thought wrong," Liora said sharply.

The scene shifted again, and they stood beneath a great oak tree. Its gnarled branches stretched out like twisted fingers, and a thick rope hung from the lowest limb. Edward stared at the noose, his breath coming in short, panicked gasps.

"No," he said, shaking his head. "Please, not this."

"This is how they killed Margaret," Liora said, her voice cold and unyielding. "She was a midwife, a healer, accused of crimes she didn't commit. They hanged her while the crowd cheered, and you said nothing. You didn't lift a finger to stop it. You endorsed her end, like you did mine."

The rope rose of its own accord, looping itself around Edward's neck. He clawed at it, his movements frantic. "Please," he gasped. "I'll repent. I'll—"

"Repentance won't save you," Liora said. "Feel what she felt." The noose tightened, lifting Edward off the ground. He kicked and struggled, his hands clawing at the rope as it choked the life from him. His face turned red, then purple, his eyes bulging with terror.

Liora watched in silence, her expression unflinching. She thought of Margaret, of the way she had gasped for air as the rope tightened around her throat. She thought of the countless women who had died for nothing but the crime of *existing*.

When Edward's body finally went limp, the oak tree faded, replaced once more by the sterile office. His lifeless form slumped in the chair, the soft bruising of a noose still visible around his neck.

Liora stepped towards him, her footsteps soft against the tile floor, and spat on his lifeless form.

Chapter 5: Richard the Damned

Washington D.C., 2020

The Capitol loomed in the distance, its dome glowing faintly under the cold November sky. Liora stood at the edge of the National Mall, her dark coat blending into the shadows as she stared at the gleaming symbol of power. The air carried the faint hum of generators and the distant chants of protesters, women who had gathered to rally against a man who had made himself their enemy.

Senator Richard Harper. The last reincarnation.

Liora closed her eyes, letting the tether between their souls guide her. It pulsed in her chest like a heartbeat, faint but insistent, pulling her toward him. She had felt it so many times before—through centuries, across oceans, in lives where his name changed, but his cruelty remained. Harper was not just a man; he was the embodiment of the hatred that had destroyed her. And he reveled in it.

Liora remembered each time she had ended him. The other men she'd meet once and never again. Their souls would give in and disappear. But Richard—Richard, was something else.

In 1813, he had been a plantation owner in the South, ruling over his domain with a whip and a sneer. She had found him among the fields he had stolen, the lives he had destroyed.

"Still chasing me, witch?" he had drawled, leaning on the railing of his veranda. "I hope this time you make it quick. I've grown bored of this life anyway."

She had burned him alive in his own home; the fire consuming the symbols of his greed. But even as flames devoured him, he laughed. "Until next time," he had called through the crackle of fire.

In 1936, he had been a judge in Berlin, sentencing women to death for daring to defy the Nazi regime. She had walked into his chambers dressed in mourning black, her eyes blazing with fury.

"You're predictable, you know," he had said, pouring himself a glass of whiskey. "You always come back."

"And you always destroy," she had replied.

When she summoned the shadows to claim him, his last words were a mocking challenge. "See you soon, my dear."

And now, in 2020, he was Senator Richard Harper, a man who had built his career on hatred. His policies stripped women of their autonomy, his speeches dripped with disdain for their rights, and his influence reached into the highest offices of power. He had made himself the champion of oppression, wielding his authority like a weapon.

The mansion was silent when Liora entered, the grand hallway echoing her footsteps. Ornate chandeliers hung like jewels from the high ceilings, casting soft, golden light over marble floors. The wealth and power on display here was a testament to Richard Harper's life: opulent, cruel, and devoid of humanity.

She didn't knock. She didn't announce herself. The tether that had drawn her here burned in her chest. She followed the pull to his study, the door slightly ajar.

He was waiting for her.

Richard Harper sat in a high-backed leather chair, his face illuminated by the flickering flames of the fireplace. A glass of whiskey rested on the desk in front of him, untouched. He didn't look surprised to see her. If anything, he looked amused.

"You've come at last," he said, his voice smooth and mocking. He leaned back in his chair, the faintest smirk curling at his lips. "I was beginning to think you'd forgotten about me."

"Never," Liora said, stepping into the room. Her voice was calm, but her rage simmered beneath the surface, threatening to boil over.

He gestured to the empty chair across from him. "Sit. Let's talk, shall we? It's been too long."

"I didn't come here to talk," Liora said, her eyes narrowing.

"Oh, but I insist," Harper said, his tone light, almost playful. "We've been doing this same ritual for centuries, haven't we? It's tradition at this point."

She didn't move, her hands curling into fists at her sides. "You're the last," she said. "The last of the cursed."

His smirk widened. "And what an honor it is. I've been looking forward to this. Plus, being your last living plaything is getting to be quite lonely. I know the other men's souls gave up after you killed them the first time. *Pathetic.*"

Harper stood and walked to the fireplace, his silhouette cast in shadows. "You've killed me so many times, Liora. In Salem, London, Berlin, Charleston. Each time, you came at me with such fury. Such righteousness. And each time, I rose again. Did you ever stop to wonder why?"

"Because you're evil," Liora said, her voice cold.

"Because I embrace it," Harper corrected, turning to face her. His eyes gleamed with malice. "You think your curse is some punishment, some divine justice. But it's a gift. You gave me the power to come back stronger, smarter, more dangerous. You think you've won every time you've killed me? No, my dear. I've won."

Liora's chest tightened as he stepped closer, his presence suffocating.

"This life," he continued, gesturing around him, "has been one of my best. A senator, a kingmaker, a man with the power to shape a nation. And I've used it well, haven't I? Stripping away your kind's rights, piece by piece. Watching as women begged, marched, and screamed, only for me to take more." His voice dropped, venom dripping from every word. "Because they deserve it. Because *you* deserved it."

Liora's voice trembled with anger. "You haven't changed," she said. "Not in all these years. You're still the same coward who condemned me to burn."

"Coward?" Harper laughed, a deep, bitter sound. "I was righteous. You were dangerous, Liora. All of you were. That's why I had to do it. That's why I still do it."

He took another step closer, his eyes boring into hers. "Do you remember their names? The women I sent to die alongside you? I do. Hannah, the healer. Margaret, the midwife. Abigail, the teacher. And Sarah, your friend, and so, so many more." His lips twisted into a cruel smile. "Do you know what they said before they died? They screamed for mercy, just like you."

Liora's breath hitched, her vision blurring with tears she hadn't shed in centuries.

"And the others, the ones you've met through the years?" Harper continued, his voice rising. "I remember them all, too. I ruined them, Liora. I destroyed their lives, just as I destroyed yours."

Her power surged within her, the room trembling as her fury consumed her. "You've spent lifetimes destroying women, Harper," she said. "And you've enjoyed it?"

He grinned, stepping into the firelight. "I've *relished* it." The room exploded with light as Liora unleashed her power. The fire in the hearth roared, its flames turning a vivid blue as shadows stretched and twisted across the walls. The air grew thick with heat and electricity, the sound of cracking wood filling the space.

Harper staggered, but quickly regained his composure. "Do it, then!" he shouted, his voice filled with defiance. "Kill me! I'll rise again, just like I always do."

Liora stepped forward, her dark eyes blazing. "Not this time," she said, her voice steady now, cold and resolute. "You've taken your last life, Harper. There will be no more rebirths. No more second chances. Tonight, your soul ends."

The fire surged, engulfing Harper in a torrent of searing light. He screamed, his body writhing as the flames consumed him. But Liora didn't stop. She reached deeper, tearing at the tether that bound their souls. She felt it resist, then snap, the connection unraveling as Harper's essence was dragged into the void.

"No." he screamed, his voice breaking. "You can't—"

"I can," Liora said, her voice rising above the roar of the fire. "For every woman silenced. For every life stolen. I will *finally* end you."

The flames exploded, filling the room with blinding light. When the fire died, Harper was gone. Not a trace of him remained—no body, no ash, no soul. He was erased, his existence wiped from the fabric of the universe. Liora stood in the silent room, her chest rising and falling as the weight of centuries lifted from her shoulders. The tether was gone. The curse was broken. She stepped out into the cold night, the stars above shining brighter than ever.

Chapter 6: Liora the Vengeful

Washington, D.C., 2020

Liora sat on a bench in the empty park, her head bowed as the frigid night bit into her. The curse was over; the tether was gone. Richard Harper, the last of the men who had condemned her, had been obliterated. His soul had been torn apart and cast into nothingness, never to rise again.

But the world hadn't changed the way she hoped it might. Liora stared at her hands, once capable of summoning infernos, now limp in her lap. Harper was gone, but there would always be others—men like him, filled with hatred, ambition, and cruelty. Men who saw power as a tool to break and silence women. She could feel their presence even now, faint echoes in the surrounding air, reminders of a world she had spent centuries fighting against.

The weight of that realization pressed down on her, heavy as the memories of every woman who had come before her. She saw their faces in her mind as if they stood before her.

Hannah, the healer, who had been dragged from her garden at dawn. They accused her of poisoning the crops, of cursing their children, but Liora knew it was because her cures worked better than the doctor's, like her own.

Margaret, the midwife, accused of bringing death into the world simply because a child had been born still. Liora had tried to protect her, but it wasn't enough. She remembered the snap of the rope, the way Margaret's body hung limp in the square as the townspeople prayed and cheered.

Abigail, the teacher, whose only crime was teaching young girls how to read. They tied her to the pyre, her voice steady even as the flames reached her. They had all been so brave. Braver than Liora had ever felt. And yet they were gone, their names erased from history, their stories rewritten by the men who had destroyed them.

There were others, too many to count. Some were known to her, their names etched into her memory, their cries echoing in her ears. Others were strangers, women from distant lifetimes who had carried the same burdens, endured the same pain, and fought the same battles.

She had risen for them. She had hunted their tormentors across centuries, her rage burning as brightly as the flames that once consumed her. But now she was tired. She had fought for so long, and while she had shattered the tether to the men who had destroyed her, the world was still filled with their kind.

"What was the point?" she whispered into the cold, empty night. "If they'll never stop, what was the point of it all?"

"You were the point," a voice whispered. Liora froze, her breath hitching. Slowly, she lifted her head. Standing before her, bathed in the pale glow of the moon, was Sarah. Her hair shone like golden threads, her face untouched by time. She wore the same kind smile she had on the day they were condemned, the warmth of it cutting through the freezing air.

"Sarah," Liora whispered, her voice breaking.

Sarah stepped closer, kneeling before her. "I've missed you," she said, taking Liora's trembling hands in her own.

Tears streamed down Liora's face. "You shouldn't be here," she said, her voice cracking. "You should be at peace, and free."

"So should you," Sarah said gently.

"I can't," Liora said, shaking her head. "There's still so much to fight for. So many men left to destroy. They'll keep coming, Sarah. They'll keep hurting, keep killing."

Sarah's smile softened, her eyes brimming with something unspoken. "Do you know who you are?" she asked.

Liora frowned. "I'm the one who—"

"You're Liora the Vengeful," Sarah interrupted, her voice steady. "Do you know how many women know your name? How many women whisper your story to one another, not in fear, but in reverence? They tell their daughters about you. They write about you. You're in their history books, their folklore. You've become something more than yourself. You've become a symbol."

Liora's breath caught, her tears slowing. "Liora, you showed them," Sarah continued, her voice rising with quiet strength. "You showed them that silence isn't the only answer. *You* made them see that it's okay to rage, to fight, to demand justice, and paved the way for them to rise."

"But there are still so many," Liora whispered, her voice trembling. "I can't stop now."

"You don't have to fight anymore," Sarah breathed. "Because *they're* fighting now. They've seen what you've done, and they're not waiting for permission to act. The women of this world are not the women of our time, Liora. They're stronger because of you. They're *freer* because of you. You've carried the burden so they wouldn't have to carry it alone."

Liora shook her head, her body trembling. "What if it's not enough? What if they lose?"

"They won't," Sarah said firmly. She squeezed Liora's hands, her eyes bright with conviction. "You've given them something no one can take away: hope. And they will carry it forward. You don't have to bear this alone anymore."

The park was silent around them, the cold air biting at Liora's skin. She thought of the women who died, the women she had fought for, the women that would come after her. She thought of the fire that consumed her and the fire she had carried ever since. Could she let it go? Could she trust the world would keep burning with her strength even after she was gone?

"I'm scared," Liora admitted, her voice barely above a whisper.

Sarah leaned forward, her forehead pressing gently against Liora's. "I know," she whispered. "But you've never been alone. Not then, not now. And you won't be when you rest."

Liora closed her eyes, her tears falling freely. The memories of centuries pressed against her, but for the first time, she felt them ease.

"For every woman silenced," she whispered, her voice trembling, "for every life stolen, I rose." She opened her eyes, meeting Sarah's steady gaze. "But now... now I rest."

When Liora stood again, the park was gone. She was in a vast field bathed in golden light, the air warm and sweet. Around her were the faces she had carried in her heart for centuries—Hannah, Margaret, Abigail, and so many others. They stood together, radiant and unbroken, their voices soft and steady as they welcomed her.

Sarah stood beside her, her hand in Liora's. In the distance, the whispers of the living echoed faintly: women's voices rising, stronger than before, no longer silenced. Liora smiled, her heart finally light. She had done her part. It was their world now.

"For every woman silenced," she said one last time, her voice steady. "For every life stolen, I rose."

And she let herself be free.

This Foul Heart

Sabrina Voerman

CW: subservience, gaslighting, manipulation, captivity, murder, body horror, abuse

You split me apart with your rugged hands and your sharpened blades. Warm fingers tear apart the flesh on my bones, peeling away the decay, leaving only that which isn't rotten. How foolish of me to think any part of me isn't spoiled, not meat full of maggots and worms, but soured from the inside.

How foolish of you to believe I can be anything but decay.

You prise my chest apart with a rib-spreader, one snapping in the cranking process. You ponder fixing it, adhering it with your concoction of collagen and sinew. But no, you think, this was how it was meant to be. For me to have less than you. You will always ensure I have less than you, and it starts at my origins. Humble beginnings, you will later tell me. Rib cage spread, your hand plunges into my cold carcass. Not yet a body, no. A body belongs to a *person*, a thing I am not.

A person has body *autonomy*. A person has a voice, *a name*.

Hand on my heart, you tear it out without ceremony, without care and consideration. My pain is nothing to you; if you cannot feel it, it doesn't exist. It is not tangible. It cannot be measured or perceived by you. I am just a cadaver, not worth respect. Perhaps when these graying lungs draw breath, you will begin to see me as . . .

She.

Putrid fluid tries to pulse through the arteries that connect to no organ. The heart you hold in your hands is brown and turning black; too long without oxygen; it is too far gone. The other organs inside of me fare better. You decide they can remain where they are. But this foul heart you hold cannot remain.

What once pulsed lifeblood is now discarded in an emesis basin.

In another body you kept my new heart alive for as long as you needed before you carefully cut it out of her and attached it to your catalyst: electricity. The pulse mimics the beating like you want me to mimic the living. This is the difficult part, time is short, you must move quickly. Prongs in either end of the crimson organ, you lift it, ensuring your rubber gloves are secure so no shock is felt. With a surgeon's delicate hands, you mould her into me, stitches done with the care of a mother tending to a child.

Out comes the crank, my spread ribs move back to their rightful place. Needle through flesh, thick black thread ties me up. I am a doll with new stuffing, sewn together with your precision. You have made me whole, a completed work, and all you must do now is flip the lever.

You have done this before, and this time, you know it will be done right. For you have taken the subservient sex and put me in my rightful place. Pieced together by all the ones you loved the most, but never gave you *everything*.

You hold the power to give me life entirely within your palm. You are in control. You are my creator.

And so, Man creates woman—to feel like a god. Because he has discovered that God is a lie, and so he must take the mantle.

She enters this world screaming.

Agony is the only thing she knows. This *torment* floods her with each pulse of blood pumping through her veins to atrophied muscles. To be filled with the suffering of the lives before her, their collective pain being eked out of their combined parts, seeping into the whole he has made.

Endure, he tells her, Endure it for me.

His whisper is a lover's soft serenade. Misery is replaced with affection. She responds to this, and he knows he has said the right thing, used the correct tone. Eyes flutter open, revealing their mismatched stare; one green, one hazel. Her pallid lips part and draw in breath, filling those gray lungs, her chest rising.

Tubes infiltrate her skin, pumping the blood through her until she regulates. A puppet attached to his strings; removal of one of these will mean her death. This is the power he has over her. Control over her heart is control over her body.

She turns her head and closes her eyes; eyes that know what they have seen before. Her heart beats quicker at the sight of him—it has ached for him before. Tears slip from her eyes. They are hers and hers alone. These tears are not for him. She hides them, for her grief is hers, and all the women she is made up of.

Her first insurgence.

Using a pipette, he permits her to drink small droplets of water. Her tongue reaches for more, pulsing under the sweet nectar that slowly drops into her wanting mouth. When he draws back the offering, she moans. Her mismatched eyes catch the way his lips pull into a distant smile. He wants her to be hungry for more.

Not so fast, he says, You are new to this world and must not rush.

Dry lips part to speak, vocal chords strain against the air forced through them. Alas, it is no use, they are not ready. Or, perhaps, they were never put in to function.

Don't try to speak, he says, It will cause too much pain.

His brows knit. Drawing away from her after a moment's reflection, he gently places the pipette upon the table. Water sloshes in a basin. A warm cloth under his careful touch against her skin. She responds, pulling against her restraints desperate to get closer to this feeling of comfort. Each stitch is gently cleansed by his hand, dried blood crusted between the thick, black thread dissipates.

This care ignites her body with rapture; it spreads through the slow-moving blood within her, reminding the nerves they have come back to life and must respond. They flare at every synapse and spark to the tips of her fingers and the follicles upon her scalp, where long black hair cascades. It, too, needs washing. Each stroke of his hand, brush of the cloth, and trail of soapy water sliding down her skin brings life into this reanimated form.

She will do *anything* for this feeling.

With the softness and care of a surgeon, the unspoken promise of *do no harm*, he unwraps the bandages covering her stitches. A circle of gore around each wrist. With metal tongs, he drops the bloodied, foul-smelling gauze into a metal bin at his feet. He grabs a bottle and douses a cloth with the substance, then dabs gently at her healing wounds. The crust made of platelets, fibrin, and blood cells falls off from the motion, sprinkling over her surgical gown like red dust. In his hand, he replaces the cloth with tweezers, slipping the black thread out of her healing flesh.

His concentration as he tends to her allows her a moment to study his features. Steady breathing, eyes narrowed for focus, and, every few moments, his tongue dampens his pale lips. When she is free of the threads that bind her parts together, he holds her hands in his—the pads of his fingers press into the hollow of her palms.

He repeats this process on her throat, then the spot on her chest where he tore it apart to replace her heart. He dabs at the tears and pus that leak involuntarily from her eyes. The hours slip away from dusk until dawn, when he must go away again.

I have brought you something, he says.

She looks up at him, wanting to feel hope, but her heart will not allow it.

He opens a trunk behind him and takes out a gown. Ebony with rich green trim over the bust and a shimmer over the skirt in the right lighting. Whale boning keeps the bust in perfect form. It is a gown she has seen before, but she cannot remember where. Someone she once knew wore it. It is not a gift, but she must act as though it is.

Her lips twitch into a smile. She lifts her battered arms and reaches for it. Allowing her to touch it, he smiles as the fabric weaves through her fingers.

This is the finest satin, he says. I knew you would like it.

She nods her agreement. The healing suture wounds throb.

He takes the dress back and stores it in the trunk.

It will be for when you are healed, he says.

When she is ready to be taken off her pumps and tubes, the needles removed from her veins, he guides her to a seated position. The cold gurney that has been her bed for a fortnight is a comfort not in feeling, but in location. If she takes a step her legs may not work, she will fall, fail, disappoint. She cannot disappoint him.

Come, he says, I'll support you.

She looks at him, the trust within her eyes childlike. With her bruised hand in his smooth, uncalloused one, she reaches her feet to the floor, one at a time. A chill tears through her, and she withdraws.

Don't be afraid, he says. I've got you, trust me.

These words drip with false promise—an apple with scales for skin.

Holding his hand tighter this time, she commits to the drop, hoping her legs support her. Not her legs, they were once someone else's. Taken from one, given to another. They shake as they attempt to hold her weight. Drawn to his warmth and his strength, she leans into him. A faint chuckle comes from him; patronizing.

Well done, he tells her.

Pads of feet against cold, tile floors. Floors that have seen blood and gore, minds lost, and bodies destroyed. Senses within her come to life at the movement. Though he guides her, holds her, coaches her, it is her determination, her *need* for affirmation that encourages her to take each step. They round the room in lazy circles until she no longer needs his support. He remains close, never more than an arm's length away.

When she stumbles, he catches her.

As her eyes catch the darkness of the far corner of the room, she sees something that intrigues her. Turning her head, she locks eyes with him and then gestures towards the dark. He shakes his head.

No, he says, Those are not for you.

She blinks. Why should there be things for him and not for her, she wonders. Without a voice to question, there will be no answer. More rounds are made, until he shows her to a bed. Soft with down pillows and a duvet, she drowns in this warmth. He gives her this, and she cherishes him for allowing her such niceties. He does not get in with her; the swell of comfort grows, and yet, a hollowness blooms inside her chest, just beneath the breastbone. A tightness that makes her ache.

She wakes to a vase with flora beside her. Dark green stems at the base, bursting with crimson petals at the top. Rising, she swings her legs over, knowing that she can trust them now. With eagerness, she reaches for the flowers and plucks one from the vase. The sharp thorn pricks her finger and blood beads to the surface, the same colour as the flower, as though they were grown in carnage, like she was.

Studying this wound, she does not know what to do, but then he is there and he is soothing her, comforting her with his words. *It'll be okay*, and *You must be more careful*. Surgical pads press to the wound, a splash of something that smells so strongly that her nose wrinkles. He takes his time as he wraps the gauze around her finger, then brings it to his mouth and kisses it.

I cannot bear the thought of you hurting, he tells her. You must be more careful.

Moments drift between them, their breath hovering in the air. She cannot stand it any longer, and looks towards the flowers, then back to him. Dark brows knit in frustration; he brought them to her. She cannot speak her frustration with him, without a voice her tongue cannot be sharp, but her glare can pierce.

His gaze matches hers, a fleeting look of something monstrous lingers just beneath the surface. Then he rises, releasing her hands, and grabs the vase. With more rage and strength than she thought possible, he hurls it across the room. The shattering glass is deafening, but not as much as the fear that runs cold through her veins.

I'm sorry, you look so much like—he stops, sighs. His hand goes to her cheek to cup.

She recoils, and he catches the side of her neck. She freezes, eyes wide and looking into his soft brown ones. Under his menacing stare she is forced to look away, incapable of holding it, submissive to her core. After all, he plucked these eyes from his most obedient love.

Forced to lean in when he pulls her into his frame, she allows him to kiss her forehead; she has no other choice. Warmth spreads from where his lips touch her, dulling the trepidation accosting her. Rigidity seeps from her frame, her posture like a crumbling statue, dissipating along with all her feelings of doubt that she cannot express.

There is nothing she has experienced like his touch save for the rose. An elegant thing adorned with pain.

Alone each day for hours, she has learned to read the clock that ticks. Her stitched wounds have healed and her flesh, though tender and swollen, adhered together. No longer a mere collection of parts, but a whole.

He is gone, she knows what length of time he is away, and so she finds herself alone in the dark corner he warned her against. A place of knowledge, this forbidden thing, something not for creatures like her.

Medical texts containing things similar to her are the first to draw her in; bodies sliced open, their organs displayed. Pictures she understands. Solemn faces that scream for her with lips sewn shut. They, too, do not have names.

Though she does not tire of these, she aches too deeply. Her fragile heart is not made for these horrors. The weight of their undying sorrow becomes too heavy for her hands. The books she plucks from the shelves are difficult to understand, so she persists with the desperation of all these amalgamations she is. Their names, too, a mystery, though she is all of them.

She falls asleep teaching herself the art of written word, and when she wakes, her head upon her extended arm, eyes parallel with the floor, she spots the black book just underneath the bookcase. Blinking to clear away the residue and liquids her body produces, she extends a hand to grab it.

Suddenly she is yanked back from the bookcase, her whole body ripped away from absolution. He forces her onto the chilled leather couch, gripping her chin within his uncalloused hands.

I told you those are not for you, he says. Do you understand?

Every part she is made of wants her to shake her head. They do not want her to agree, they do not want her to submit to his rage. They fight against her, and who is she to deny them? But she knows in the marrow of her bones that if she defies him here, soon he will see the parts of them that he did not like, soon he will see she is nothing more than their collective disappointments.

And so, she nods her free will away.

I'm sorry I overreacted, he says. Then he kisses her forehead.

The fear he instilled in her a moment ago shrinks into naught more than a seed. Replaced by the blooming of pleasure. Beginning to hate the feeling of gratification, she allows him this façade. It will be months before this seed grows into brambles, sharp with thousands of thorns, protecting her delicate heart as it learns to beat not for him, but for her.

You're growing bored of it here, he says to her. Then he rises from where he was crouched before her. He tucks her hair behind her ear, hand resting against her cheek the way a lover might. This is what he wishes to be, in time, her lover.

Come, he says, I shall show you the Garden of Eden.

Taking her hand, he forces her to her feet, a tenderness in his touch that wasn't there moments before. This shift in him makes her body feel tight, as though every muscle is prepared to flee the moment a door is left unlocked or a window cracked. But he is not negligent; a man of his designation would never subscribe to such carelessness.

With brass keys that hang from his belt, he slips them into the heavy metal locks. The crack of the mechanism is, to her, the sound of freedom. She'll finally see what lies beyond the brick and mortar, the gurneys and medical equipment.

Sounds she has heard before, the woman who owned these synapses before her, brings her a fleeting moment of joy. The soft twittering of birds, they are not caged like her. She wants to hate them, but settles with envy instead. That is reserved for him and him alone. Yet it, too, fades as he holds her hand in his. The shocking green colour of the trees, the grass, and the hedges that line the extensive yard match her left eye.

But it is the air here she tastes and feels; it's not like anything she has experienced in this lifetime. It caresses her skin in ways he cannot, for it does so without expectation. It does not care if she were to leave or what she would say if she was given the ability to speak. The wind has no desire but to tangle her hair, make her skin alight with chills, and kiss her cheeks until they are tinged with red.

She withdraws her hand from his and reaches to the grass, touching it against her skin. Each blade is a dream, a thought, fleeting yet lasting. Rain falls, landing on the backs of her scarred hands and wrists. Only it is warm, and she realizes these raindrops are her tears.

This is too much for you, he says, I can see that I have overwhelmed you.

Her visitation to the world outside only suffocates her further. She has had a taste and she is deprived of the nourishment it offered her.

When he returns from his hours away, she is seated by the window, boarded from the outside, eyes shut imagining what it looks like, feels like. The plethora of smells: fresh rain, damp soil, growing grass, and flora and fauna.

He returns to see her there daily, and one day, fed up he says, You ask too much of me.

Taking her hand, they walk side by side toward the corner with her bed. Beside it a table that once held flowers in a glass vase, now holds nothing but the dead skin that has flaked from her body, turned into finite dust particles. Assisting her to sit down, he pulls a metal chain from under the bed.

I didn't want to use these, he says. His eyes are seeping with melancholy as he attaches the chain from the foot of the bed to her ankle. He tells her, I can take better care of you this way.

So, she locks this dream of outside away, as she is locked away. To pass the time, she must find something else. He is here more, presence haunting, delirium creeping in as his distrust of her blooms into something that overtakes the garden. Yet he still imparts upon her moments of relief, when he is forced to leave; academia does not wait for him, and he will be left behind. This is why he must leave, he tells her.

Freedom of the outdoors is but a fragment now, a memory that could have been naught more than a dream. What's left in its wake is the agony of knowing, and the despair of forcing herself to forget. So she seeks solace in what little she can glean elsewhere.

The floor is cold underneath her palms and knees. Wearing no more than a shift, thin and loose, she crawls over to forbiddance. Out of reach, she cannot even press the pads of her fingers to the spines. Her tether will not get the best of her, she decides, and she crawls back to her bed. The bars on the metal headboard rattle, they are loose. She wrangles one of the bars off the frame. The force of the release causes her to jerk back and the metal slices her thigh, an inch above her knee. With the blood bubbling to the surface, she watches with mild fascination. The scent of it is nauseating, like old fruit, festering with flies; she is dying here.

Had she a voice, she would curse him from bringing her back from the dead; how many women died for her to live? Only for her body to start failing; she is his failure. Man was never supposed to create life.

A strip from her bed linens tied tight around her thigh; a tourniquet to stop the hurt. With the bar in hand, she crawls back towards the books. The bar makes a tinny, hollow noise against the floor, followed by the metallic scrape of the chain around her ankles dragging behind her.

Thunk.
Scrape.
Thunk.
Scrape.

She beckons now to that which called to her all these months locked away. Using the bar, she swipes under the shelf. The black book underneath that beckoned to her shifts, moving further away. She inhales sharply, this time steadying her grip on the bar, ensuring it tucks behind the book, pulling it toward her as she bends her battered wrists.

Elation, an emotion she has not yet felt, fills her from the belly and spreads along her toes and fingers to the very scalp under her black hair. Scurrying back to her bed, she is desperate to read these pages. The bar goes under the mattress, where it won't be found. He has not changed the sheets since her external wounds healed. With her legs tucked underneath her, she flips the journal to the first page.

A collection of names in four delicate hands; Evelyn, Diana, Elizabeth, Nadine.

We are his dolls. Played with at his command, discarded when he tires of us. A collection of things he loves in this world, submission, servitude, beauty, <u>fear</u>. We are caged, and we fear that he will grow tired of us soon. Passion turns so quickly to rage; a wrong word, a glance not to his liking. Fear is what has filled this room now. We do not sleep, save for brief moments where we hold each other.

Tonight, I will take the hurt.

Tomorrow it will be Diana.

She reads with fervour; horror seeping through her. What he will do to her when she has healed. But she is putrefying here and will certainly decay before then. He will see it soon, he will notice her scent. Not sweet like roses, but sweet like rot.

Elizabeth has returned to us, scars on her throat, just beneath her chin. She will never speak again.

So, I am Elizabeth, forced into silence, she thinks.

He threw Diana into our cage with scars on his face, blood had dried upon his pallid complexion.

She has no hands.

Her hands tremble.

Nadine did not return tonight.

The pieces of her that are whole are Nadine.

The elegance of the writing changes into chaos. Words overlap.

He has taken my eyes.

For the one who finds this, heed our warning; he will grow tired of your parts. For they are made of the women who could never love him.

I know he will take this foul heart of mine next.

Up above, in the world she is not a part of, the sounds of her prison rattle. Key in lock. Her keeper has returned to his home, her cage. She has moments to act. Slipping the journal under her flat pillow, she grabs the metal bar from beneath the mattress. Gripping its slender girth in Diana's hands, she rises to Nadine's feet, sturdy legs that will support her. With Evelyn's eyes narrowed, she waits for him to descend the stairs. Each thud of his shoes against the wood causing Elizabeth's mind to stir, Evelyn's heart to pound.

He turns to where she is standing, hands behind her back, waiting like the obedient dog she's made him believe she is. A smile forms on his lips; genuine—it reaches his eyes. Crossing the room, he hurries to her as though they are man and wife. Only she is shackled by different chains. When he is close enough, she plunges the bar into his guts. Blood leaks from the wound, and she pulls it out. A chunk of viscera falls out of the hollow bar.

She stabs him again.

Evelyn does.

Diana does.

Elizabeth does.

Nadine does.

He falls to the blood-covered floor. She falls with him, discarding the weapon. Her hands push him away as he weakly bats at her. Straddling his frame now, she grips the side of his head and pushes it hard against the stone floor. There is a satisfying crack and a groan.

Please, he begs while her thumbs prod against his sockets, locating the softness of his eyes. They slip so easily into the holes, like they were made for her. Her weight is insurmountable for she is made up of the rage of all the other women.

Have mercy, he pleads.

But she is not made of mercy.

Only when his body is cold and rigid under her does she rise to her feet. Though she knows she has little time left in this world, she peels the bloodstained shift from her cobbled-together body. Staggering to the trunk, she withdraws the black and green gown. It fits her well; it must have been Nadine's, she surmises. Taking the brass keys from his cadaver, the black book from the bed, she leaves behind this cage and enters Eden.

Vanessa

Julia Greenshaw

CW: mentions of sexual assault, violence, blood, murder

I once lived in a castle with one hundred and twenty-two doors. One hundred and twenty-one of them were unlocked, one hundred and twenty-one thresholds I crossed. It was through the exploration of my husband's halls that I came to learn they were haunted, but by what nature of daemon I knew not. I was earnest and callow when I first arrived, and all was well, for a time. As well as could be expected for a young woman from a middling family in a small, isolated village. Despite being married to a man twice my age who had had several wives before me, I knew I should be glad of this match. He would provide for me, and I would be safe. Cared for. In an existence where those were temporal possessions granted to me, not things I could acquire myself, I feared what my life would be like if I did not have them.

Mostly I spent my days reading, strolling miles of splendid gardens, and planning elaborate parties like the one my own family had been invited to. I had never been to a ball like that before, with food enough to feed my entire village and extraordinary performers of all kinds. I didn't know it then, but that night would change everything. It led me to the one hundred and twenty-second door. I might've been frightened or bitter about everything that followed, but instead I decided I would wield my anger. Vanessa taught me that.

Oh, but I am getting ahead of myself.

I grew up not far from the Count's country seat, in a little hamlet called Alburgh. Like all girls in my village, and all the women of my family who had come before me, I was prepared, from how I sat to how I ate to the limits of my education, to be attractive for marriage. It seemed like everything I was taught in some way came back to preparing me to be likeable and docile, to be chosen. Curiously, the day I met my soon-to-be husband, I hadn't been thinking of marriage at all. I cared only about following my elder sister around like a lost kitten.

"Why do I need to go to the ball if you're going?" I yelled over my shoulder. My sister, Lydia, giggled as she chased me through the switchgrass and asphodels. The sun was bright against a cloudless summer sky, setting the strands of red in our dark brown hair all aflame.

"Maybe mother thinks you will find a match too," she said, gasping for breath as she caught up to me. "With one of the Count's hogs!" She flicked my nose and took off running again.

"And dare to outshine your chance at true love?" I called after her. "I wouldn't dream of it!"

And it was true. I was content to spend my days helping out at our parent's apothecary and traipsing through the wilds by sunset. I could've lived my whole life that way. I loved learning the medicinal properties of herbs and mushrooms from my mother and going on expeditions to find them with my father. Looking back, perhaps I cursed myself saying that to her.

The Count's estate was grand yet lonely and sat atop a rugged hillside on a rocky crag overlooking the valley that cradled the Bloodroot River and Alburgh, at a considerable distance, on its banks. As we made our way up the long, winding drive in our carriage, I gazed at the imposing towers on either side of the portcullis. I imagined knights storming the keep in an earlier age, clashing with guards in the gatehouse.

"Come on," my sister chided, ushering me out of the carriage toward a set of impressive doors, open like a great maw embedded in the castle walls. Footmen led us to the parlor, where drinks were served and guests mingled. I set my eye on a plate of cream-filled pastries, eating three before my mother and father pulled me away.

As soon as we walked into the dining hall, a sense of gloom pervaded me. Torches adorning the walls burned low, casting deep shadows about the corners of the room. At the head of the table sat the Count. I noticed his protruding, glassy eyes first, for they followed me about the room. Thick brows that gave him a permanent air of displeasure, while his long, sloping nose and thin lips wreathed by a full beard reminded me of the holy men who sometimes passed through our village giving alms. He frightened me, but then he stood and so graciously thanked us all for coming. His voice was warm and gentle, and when he smiled, the harsh lines of his face seemed to soften into something more amiable.

The feasting and merriment began, and he told many light-hearted jokes and enthralling stories. The more he spoke, the more I thought my first impression of him had been all wrong. He was generous with his attention and his wine, and he even prepared marvelous gifts for all in attendance. My mother received a charming alabaster box engraved with flowers, my father tobacco and a snuffbox. My sister and I received bouquets, candied nuts, and exotic fruits. I remember I had never had a pomegranate before.

I'd prefer not to write about what happened next in great detail. I still regret how I hurt Lydia, though I hadn't meant to. It wasn't my decision.

The party continued late into the night and, after our shoes were worn out from dancing, many of the Count's guests ended up staying the night. Lydia and I were so excited about our whirlwind evening, we spoke in excited whispers underneath the covers until we could no longer keep our eyes open. What we didn't know, while we slept soundly from hours of dancing and imbibing, is that my father came to an agreement with the Count that I would be his bride. The Count wanted me, and not Lydia, even though I was younger and she was ready for marriage. Lydia never forgave me for that. Now I know that the count wanted me *because* I was younger. Because I would have no idea what to expect from a husband. And he was right. No matter how much I thought I knew, he was right.

We were married that winter.

The beginning of our marriage was, despite my newly lavish surroundings, a harsh and comfortless time in my life. During the day I wandered, bored out of my mind, past endless trophies of my husband's life, the whole castle a gallery and I a living statue. At night I cocooned myself under mounds of furs and blankets, letting their warmth carry me off to sleep beneath solemn, looming walls that were the only witnesses to the Count's use of my body every evening. As I lay there I begged someone to save me, but time marched on, uncaring.

I had many strange experiences during those days, even on our wedding night—books falling from shelves without any force applied to make them fall, whispering voices in the hedges, hearing footsteps only to run out into the hall and find no one—but one occurrence scared me more than all the others.

It was late into the evening, in my first few months at the castle. I was laid up reading by dim candlelight. A book of love poems, I think. I'm sure I had a stack of romance novels beside the bed too. I devoured anything like that in those days, I think because I was searching for something. Something I didn't understand about love.

The Count was staying late in his study, and those rare nights were my favorite because it meant I wouldn't have to share his bed. I had just begun to doze off when the weighty silence of the night was broken by an unearthly sound, like a cry from the heavens. I don't know why it drew me from my bed—I remember shaking with fear—but it beckoned to me and, before I knew it, I was standing in the doorway.

I wandered the darkened corridors in search of its source, but I never heard it again. It was on my return to the bedroom that I encountered a strange door near the cellar stairs, reddish in color—cherrywood, perhaps—that came to a point at the keystone. It had an intricate, unwelcoming iron doorknob and, oddly, no keyhole. Instead it was latched with a padlock. I thought I'd been everywhere in the castle by that point, so I stared at it for a long moment and examined the lock.

"You are welcome anywhere in my home," the Count had said, and up to that point, I had felt that I was. I wondered why he hadn't mentioned anything about this room but reasoned that there must be some rational explanation I was too tired to think of. I resolved to ask him about it at breakfast and turned to head back upstairs.

I had just passed by the library when I saw what I thought was moonlight streaming in through the window of one of the sitting rooms.

Only moonlight doesn't move.

I turned back and peered around the doorframe, eyes wide and disbelieving. I was worried I might be noticed and fought the urge to step backward into the shadows, but the sight before me had me transfixed. The figure I'd seen was pale blue, almost silver, and transparent. I realized then that it was a woman, hunched over by the cold hearth. Everything about her seemed to sag toward the ground—her long, straight hair, the robe that hung on her frame. Behind her, spectral chains dragged along the floor. She looked to be focusing intently on something, and I saw that she was gathering up pieces of a broken teacup. I tried to make sense of what I was seeing, but my thoughts were far away. The woman's shoulders heaved as she took in deep, racking breaths, and I realized she was sobbing. Then she began to wail, and I stepped backward, my foot catching the edge of the runner in the hall. I stumbled and the apparition turned, looking me straight in my eyes from where she knelt, and I ran.

I ran all the way back to the bedroom, slamming the door behind me. To my horror, I realized there was no way for me to keep the daemon out, for I had no key to lock the door. I stayed awake for some time watching the sliver of light under the door, then slept in fitful spells. In the deepest part of the night, distressing thoughts came to me. Why hadn't the Count come to check on me when that scream rang out? What if I had been hurt? Perhaps he had not heard it... but his study was just downstairs, and the apparition's cries were so loud that I could hear them ringing in my ears even then. Was I going mad? Was he the cause of it? My blood ran cold. This was, after all, his home. Perhaps the Count already knew about the daemon, or who the woman was.

I worked up the courage to run down to his study, even though I was fearful of what he might say. Instead, I found the watchman of the grounds, Arturo, taking something small from one of the desk drawers.

"Is something wrong, mistress?" he asked.

"I—I heard a strange sound, and..." What was I going to say? "It frightened me. Where is the Count?"

"Oh, I'm afraid he's been called away." He smiled sympathetically. "I'm sure I didn't hear anything, but I'll check upstairs. Why don't you return to bed? Everything's all right."

Tired, and feeling silly, I acquiesced. The rest of the night passed uneventfully.

The Count was not at breakfast the next day, or the day after that, but I knew he was still at home because his favorite stallion was still in the stables.

In that intervening time, I saw apparitions on several more occasions. One, a different woman than the one I had seen that first night, returned my locket to me after I left it by the fountain in the garden. I remember I was in my bedroom, sitting in front of the mirror. I heard the sound of rattling chains first.

"Who are you?" I cried, not daring to turn from the mirror and face her.

She watched my reflection, cocking her head. "You don't have to be afraid. My name is Vanessa."

"You're not the woman I saw before."

"No, but I know her. I'm a friend." She was close now, standing at my back. She ran a spectral finger down my arm, and I jumped at the shiver of a touch.

"Stay back!"

"I told you, I'm not going to hurt you." She was calm, and seemed almost amused by me.

"What do you want?" She smiled, and let my locket drop from her transparent hand.

"I found this."

"How did you—"

She quickly turned her head, seeming to hear the footsteps on the staircase landing before they even registered to my ears.

Arturo's voice rang out. "Mistress?"

"I have to go. Don't tell him you saw me. Please, you have to trust me." She hastily placed the locket in my hands and then, to my astonishment, sank into the wall and disappeared.

I was still stunned by the time Arturo walked through the door.

"What's gotten into you?" he said. "You look like you've seen a ghost."

I couldn't help but choke out a laugh at the absurdity of the situation. "Sorry, I'm just... feeling a little bit under the weather."

"I see," he said, cocking his head. "Are you well enough to meet with the musicians for the banquet? I can tell them to return tomorrow."

"No, no," I said. "It's alright. I just need a moment."

"Of course."

Mercifully, he left me alone to collect myself.

I became less afraid of the ghost-women after that, but still I didn't understand who they were or what they wanted from me. The Count returned the following morning.

"Good morning, dear," he said, as he joined me in the parlor. He didn't look his normal self, and was unusually disheveled, his hair and beard unkempt and eyes red-rimmed. He kissed me on the cheek, a gesture that might've seemed sweet to the outside observer, but felt more like a threat.

"Where have you been?"

He looked slightly affronted, and I felt bad for starting off the conversation that way, but I couldn't help my anxiousness.

"Oh, some matters of urgent business came up," he said, taking a bite of sausage, "to do with the contract with Lord Farrin. In fact, I'll be away for the next few days on a hunting trip to finalize the terms."

"Oh? When will you be leaving?"

He pulled out his pocket watch. "In just a few hours." He took another bite and began talking while still chewing. "I heard you had quite a fright the other evening."

"Yes, I wanted to ask you about that. I heard a strange sound. A scream?"

He smiled coolly at me. "A scream? I'm sure I don't know what you mean. I was in my study and didn't hear anything of the sort."

A lie.

"But don't worry, Arturo will be here while I'm away, and I can always summon more servants to our wing of the castle, if you'd like."

"I don't think that will be necessary," I said, eyeing him.

In answer, he pulled out his ring of keys and dropped them on the table with a thump. "Now, there's something I must tell you. These two," he said, identifying two small gold keys, "will give you access to all my stores and gold, should you need or desire anything while I'm gone."

He held up another, larger key. "This is the key to our private chambers." He went on this way for another minute, explaining the uses of each one. "And this," he said, holding a small wrought iron key just inches away from my face, "unlocks the door between the kitchens and the cellar. Now, I haven't mentioned this before because I haven't needed to, but without me here, I must warn you. When I said you are welcome anywhere in my home, I meant it. But I must ask that you do not open that door. In fact, it is the only thing I will ask of you. If you do open it, rest assured I will know, and you will face my profound anger at your disregard for my rules."

The one hundred and twenty-second door. What lay behind it had tormented me for days. I knew it was some daemon, some curse, that haunted this place, but I couldn't conceive of what it might be. Beyond that, all I could think about in that moment was that I hated being talked to like a child. I decided then that I would open that one hundred and twenty-second door, and he would be none the wiser.

Later that morning I watched him ride off on horseback into the opaque fog that had swallowed up the valley, making his way down the drive until he was out of sight. My eyes focused on my reflection in the window, and I saw another apparition duck out of sight behind me. All I caught were the skirts of a floral gown whirl around the doorframe. Then it was gone. I wondered if I would be brave enough to open the door after all.

Two days passed before I worked up the nerve.

I went to the mysterious door at midmorning, for it was the time of the day when I felt the most courage. Even though a light, late spring snow dusted the castle grounds, the sun shone brightly that day and made me feel less afraid. I found the small key on the ring the Count had given me, and removed the padlock, dropping it on the floor with a dull clang.

I swung open the door, but I could see nothing at first. The room was small and had no torches lit, so I walked back to the closest room and returned with one. I held it up to the dark, windowless chamber.

An inhuman sound escaped me, something between a strangled cry and a retch, for the floorboards were stained red with blood. Breathless terror washed over me as I got a closer look at the wood of the door that had appeared red to me that first night. The red was deeper around the edges and in the grooves of the grain, because blood had seeped into it. There was blood all over the walls.

The walls. . . on the walls hung female bodies in varying states of decay—some completely skeletal, others with bits of hair and flesh still on them. I rushed to shut the door but, in my panic, I had dropped the key. I waved the torch back and forth, cowering from the horrifying scene. Torchlight flashed against the key, lying on the floor in a dried puddle of blood. I scrambled to pick it up, wiped it off on my sleeve, and put it back on the ring.

It took me several moments to secure the padlock on the door, for my hands shook uncontrollably. I must've been making quite a racket, but I could hear nothing over the sound of my own heartbeat in my ears. I made it three steps before I began to cry. I ran upstairs, threw my clothes in a heap in the back of the wardrobe, and scrubbed my skin raw in the bath, still unable to stop crying. I felt sick, torn between wanting to flee the castle altogether or bide my time until I figured out what to do. I knew I couldn't just leave with nothing and expect to make it through the night alone in the woods, so my only choice was the latter.

I acted as normally as I could while I dined, picking at my food under the watchful eye of Arturo, who seemed, in my paranoid state, suspicious of me. I must've drank a bottle of wine all to myself, and fell into a stupor. Upon waking sometime around two o'clock in the morning, I broke into a cold sweat as the memories of the day rushed back to me. I tried to convince myself that it had been some kind of nightmare, that maybe I was going mad after all. What happened next, ironically, assured me that this was all too horrifyingly real.

One by one, seven ghosts strode into the room. One I recognized by her long hair and the robe she wore, and another was wearing the same floral silk gown that I had seen the day the Count left. One of them I knew better than all the others.

"Vanessa? What is this?" I blurted, squirming back against the headboard.

She sighed. "You know now." Her voice was gentle.

It broke my heart. I don't mean that in the way people usually do. I mean that it fundamentally, irrevocably broke something in me.

"That was... you. All of you..."

She gave me a sad smile. "Yes. Let us introduce ourselves. You and I have already met, but what I haven't told you is that I was the Count's third wife."

I felt a tear roll down my cheek, but I didn't know whether it was from sadness or fear. Maybe both.

"This is Liliana," she said, gesturing to the woman to her left with hair like golden thread and a knowing look, "the Count's second wife. She tried to warn me when I first arrived. I didn't listen." She paused. "This is Isabel." She gestured to woman with the floral dress I had seen earlier.

"Roza, Celia, and Iris," she said, introducing the others. "And this is Cressida, who you saw before, the Count's first wife. He murdered her for breaking a teacup."

"He always had quite the temper," Cressida added. "I guess he found he took a liking to violence."

I was speechless. I'd like to say it was because of rage or shock, and it was partially, but it was also because a deep pit of understanding was forming in my stomach. I knew what I had seen behind the one hundred and twenty-second door. Each of his former wives, brutally murdered and locked away.

"*Why?*"

"Does it matter?" Vanessa said sadly.

"No," I whispered.

Even in Alburgh, rumors reached us about the poor count's bad luck in love. Two of his wives had gotten sick, one had disappeared. No one believed that anything so terrible had happened to them. The entire village felt bad for him, only ever talking about how tragic it all was for him. We hadn't known about the others.

"I would've escaped, if it hadn't been for Arturo," said Roza.

"Arturo knows?" I could hardly contain my shock.

"Yes," Roza scoffed. "He and the Count have... similar tastes."

I felt sick. The shadows in the room spun. "The Count said he would know if I went in the room. Please, you must help me! He can't know!"

Vanessa sat down on the bed and took my hand, holding my palm to her cheek. I was surprised to find that although she was a ghost, she was corporeal. She had no heartbeat, but I felt her cool, transparent skin. She was beautiful, with dark eyes and hair that spilled over her shoulders in waves. "We are alike, each of us. As I said before, you want what we want. You want to be free."

I nodded.

She let our hands drop and glanced down at her lap as she began playing with the ring on my finger. "Even before you knew about the murders, I'm sure your wedding night was something like all of ours. Even after the bruises fade and you wash off the feeling of his touch, well, it stays with you."

I shuddered. She knew.

"How?"

She looked into my eyes, more deeply than anyone ever had before. "I see how you're afraid of him. We all were once."

"You're not anymore?" I asked, surprised.

"No." She stood and walked to the window. "We're angry."

Anger. I rolled the thought of it around like a hard peppermint candy in my mouth. What would that be like? To acknowledge that I had been mistreated, to harness that feeling and grant myself the power that I lacked.

"You feel it," she continued. "Like a pit in your chest. Holding your tongue, smiling prettily, it wears on you."

I nodded.

"We could be so much more."

And so we devised a plan. There were seven objects around the castle that I would destroy, tying them to their lives here: a ring, a hair ribbon, a hand mirror, a vase, a portrait, a dress, and a silver spoon. I was worried that doing so would mean they would be gone from this world, but Vanessa assured me it wouldn't have to mean that. They would finally be able to go where they pleased, to be released from the endless torment of reliving their deaths.

"Will you stay with me?" I asked. I couldn't imagine going home to my village, where I would be thought of only as a disgrace, but I didn't want to be alone in the world.

"Is that what you would like?"

I nodded.

Vanessa smiled then. I so loved seeing her smile. "Then it shall be so."

The Count returned the following evening, but not before I sent the footmen, the cook, the servants, and the stablemaster away. I couldn't risk Arturo finding out about our plan, though I hadn't seen him all day.

The ritual was elaborate.

I gathered the items and brought them to the hearth in the dining room. Roza's had been the hardest to acquire. Arturo kept her ring locked in his office, but because I had the Count's keys, I managed it. Vanessa joined me first, carrying a large book in her arms.

"What is that?" I asked.

"My mother's grimoire. She gave it to me so I could protect myself, but I couldn't get to it in time. It was still tucked in the back of the shelf behind the Count's atlases, right where I left it."

"Your mother was a witch?"

"In a way," she lamented. "You might call them witches, but to our people, they are priestesses. Venerated, not shunned. I don't think my mother knew what she had lost when we came here, until it was too late."

Not knowing what to say, we fell into a comfortable silence, preparing the items to be burned. The others joined us then, and Iris, his wife before me, told me of how she had discovered where Roza's ring was kept. She'd tried to gather the items as well, but in the end she met the same fate.

"It's a shame," Vanessa said, dropping fine velvet into the flames. "I liked that ribbon."

She began reciting the spell in some language I had never heard before, and I wrote her words in blood on the slate before the fire, our gazes bound to one another. She watched me intensely, as if to say, *Promise me this will be the end.*

There was no mistaking the answer in my eyes. *I promise.*

The blood was mine, fresh, and a mixture of theirs, powdered. Isabel went back into the locked room to get it, and I don't know how she could stomach it. It was bravery unlike anything I'd ever known. With the incantation recited, we only needed one last thing. The Count's blood. I didn't dare think about what I'd do if any part of our plan went wrong, if the Count discovered what was happening before we could act. This had to be the end.

I had just finished setting the table with wine when I heard the count's heavy footfalls behind the door to the dining room. I did my best to steady my hands and my breathing as the doors opened and he strode in. Though every part of me wished to run away, I knew I needed to do this for Vanessa.

For Cressida.

For Iris.

For Roza.

For Celia.

For Liliana.

For Isabel.

For myself.

And for a woman who could have any name, who would follow if I failed.

Whatever may come, I promised myself that these castle walls would not be the last thing I saw.

"There you are," he said, grabbing me by the neck and kissing me, his eel tongue puncturing my lips. His touch had a way of turning me to stone, but my fear and disgust were overshadowed this time by something else. Vanessa's voice in my head.

We're angry.

"Ah, my keys," he said, picking them up from the table. "You're quiet today." He stopped, eyeing me as he sat down in his seat at the head of the table.

"Just feeling a bit ill," I replied.

He made a gruff sound of acknowledgement and began looking through the keys. When he got to the closet key, he looked at it for a long moment. I held my breath.

But he said nothing. He just continued checking that the other keys were there before calmly setting them down and taking a long sip of wine.

"Maybe you need more rest. Are you sleeping?"

"Yes," I said, trying to keep my voice steady. "I'm sleeping fine. I'm sure it'll pass."

He cocked his head and stared at me like he was assessing something. "I see."

"What?" My voice had turned to a shrinking whisper, betraying me.

"I'm glad to hear you've been sleeping well." He gave me a smile that made my blood run cold. "I find your story peculiar, though, because Arturo told me you have been up at all hours these past few nights. He heard voices in your room. Now you've just lied to me."

"You're having Arturo *spy* on me?"

"For good reason, it seems!" boomed the Count. "I wonder who my little wife has been meeting. Who were you with?"

All I could manage was, "I wasn't—"

"What's worse, the key I specifically told you not to use... maybe you didn't notice." His voice went cold. "It has blood on it." He held the key up. "A small red dot, just on an edge here. I might not have even noticed it if not for a trick of the firelight."

He set his raving eyes upon me.

"You went in the room."

"Don't touch me," I said quickly.

"You couldn't listen. Well, now you will join them!" he yelled.

"No!" I screamed.

I jumped from the chair, knocking over my wine glass, and pulled out a knife I had taken from the kitchen when I went to retrieve Celia's silver spoon.

He laughed, crouching low and moving around the table as if to begin chasing me. "You think that will save you? You think you can stand against me?"

I wanted to run, but instead I held firm, holding the knife out before me in my trembling hand.

"No, not just me. All of us."

I heard those eerie chains, then. Where once they made my blood run cold, now I welcomed the sound as if it were beautiful music. Our coven. The seven of them rushed in and, lunging for him, tied him down with their phantom chains.

"What is this?" yelled the Count. "What are you, you, you *devils*?"

"What you made us," Iris replied.

He must've looked at their faces then, for he cried out, "Iris? Cressida? Vanessa?"

"Now!" Vanessa roared.

I thrust the knife into his heart.

The Count bucked against the chains, his face mottled red and brows pinched in a furious expression. I found it fitting that, in the end, the temper he thought made him powerful would become his death mask. We watched Vanessa collect his blood in her hands as it poured out through his shirt, coating her fingers. She pulled his head back by his hair and leaned in.

"Do you remember what I said to you, right before you murdered me? I said you would never do this again. To anyone. You laughed in my face. I bet in that moment you thought you had won. You thought you were powerful, as I lay in defeat. But the reach of a wronged woman is long."

The Count's eyes watched her, but he could no longer speak as blood began spilling from his lips. She opened her hand and let his blood fall in rivulets through her palm, dripping on the marks I had already painted on the stone, completing the spell. We left him there. Broken spectral chains trailed us out the door and all the way down the hall.

As we ran, we grabbed torches off the walls and set everything we could—tapestries, carpets, wooden beams—in the castle alight. I had readied the horses earlier, and now the door to the yard where the stables stood lay just ahead. As we burst out into the moonless night, smoke was already billowing out from several windows and the horses seemed just as eager as us to be far away from the burning castle.

"What have you done?" roared Arturo, who came charging out of a door across the yard.

We said nothing, taking off at speed and passing under the gates as the wooden structures on the outer shell of the castle buckled and collapsed. Arturo gave chase on a horse of his own, the blazing orange fire lighting up the night behind us. We were halfway down the drive when I heard him galloping at my side. He closed in on me then, nearly grabbing my hair and pulling me out of the saddle.

I slashed backward with the knife I still held in my bloodied hand. He screamed and was lost to the unceasing darkness.

It wasn't long after that we found out we had made a bit of a name for ourselves. Rumors flew. We were branded dangerous vigilantes, terrorizing the countryside. The Count's murderous wife—a witch—and her seven phantoms. I suppose for the men we were after, that was one way of looking at it. We saw only freedom. I don't blame those in the nearby villages—my family among them, I'm sure—who could not understand why we became like villains. Sometimes, the cavalry does not come for maidens in towers. But, perhaps, the maiden is glad of it because she has found a different kind of invulnerability.

In our travels we rode through many bandit camps and down dangerous roads ruled by highwaymen, but none were as hunted as we were. Arturo hired mercenaries to help him in his pursuit, even sending hounds after us at one point. He knew that we knew what he was. Like the Count, he would never stop.

But neither would we.

It was nearly a year before we found the mercenaries' camp. In that time, Vanessa and I grew closer, into something more even than lovers. We slept by day and raided by night, surviving off the land and her holy power. We hadn't been planning to travel south that day, but Celia wanted to see the asphodels in bloom. I thought of Lydia then and wished to see them too. Their camp was nestled in some hills by the sea, on the outskirts of the village where we had last been seen. We crept in at night. Roza, Vanessa, and I were the ones who found him. He was alone. We crouched on either side of his sleeping form and watched as he took soft, gentle breaths.

Roza reached out and grabbed his chin. "Wake up, Arturo."

By the flickering light of the lantern, I saw his face, and I saw the injury I had given him. He could not see us. He could not see anything at all.

"Death," he gasped, staring desperately into the black night. "Is that you?" I think he knew we had come for him.

"No," I said softly. He opened his mouth to yell, and Roza moved then. The glint of a dagger. Arturo groaned and began sputtering. Slowly, she pulled the blade from his gut.

"But Death *is* a woman."

Acknowledgements

For all of the authors and poets who contributed a story or poem to this anthology, thank you. Thank you for lending us your rage. Thank you for being vulnerable. Thank you for all that you do. Art is a powerful tool. May your voices never be silenced. Thank you.

Thank you to those who contributed art pieces to the anthology. They are as beautiful as each and every one of you. Thank you.

A special thanks is owed to the assisting editors on this anthology, Heather, Leigh, River, and Wren. Without their eagerness and dedication to helping with this project, it wouldn't exist. They worked tirelessly and with great care and attention to detail with each piece they were given. And, in the eleventh hour, they came through when the unexpected happened. I am so grateful for them and all they contributed. It is because of them that I still maintain (most of) my sanity. Thank you, thank you, thank you, thank you.

Big thank you to Jinapher for making the beautiful cover. To Maggie for laboring over the edits and keeping us organized. Both of you made this anthology possible, and I appreciate your endorsement of my rage-filled ideas to protest the injustices in the world. Thank you.

The most special thank you to our hidden hero, Julia, who swooped in and saved us all with formatting the anthology and being the biggest supporter and helping hand. You saved us and this anthology, it wouldn't exist without you.